I0669930

NEXT DOOR NIGHTMARE

JAQUELINE SNOWE

CITY OWL
PRESS

NEXT DOOR NIGHTMARE
Shut Up and Kiss Me, Book 3

CITY OWL PRESS
www.cityowlpress.com

Cover Design by MiblArt. All stock photos licensed appropriately.

Edited by Mary Cain.

For information on subsidiary rights, please contact the publisher at info@cityowlpress.com.

Print Edition ISBN: 978-1-64898-087-9

Digital Edition ISBN: 978-1-64898-120-3

Printed in the United States of America

To Andy,
who always encourages me to do what I love
and love what I do

Praise for Jaqueline Snowe

"Brooding ex-athlete, check. Sassy yet thoughtful heroine, check. Jacqueline Snowe has written a lovely novel that ticks all the boxes for contemporary romance. the perfect read for a chilly fall night in front of the fire or cuddled under a blanket. A sweet, sexy beginning to the *Shut Up and Kiss Me* series!"
– *InD'tale*

"*Internship with the Devil* is an addictive, charming contemporary romance packed with snappy banter, tons of heart, and an immensely satisfying slow burn attraction that erupts into an inferno. The chemistry between Grace and Brock is absolutely scintillating."
— *Kat Turner, author of Hex, Love, and Rock and Roll*

"First rule for Grace's internship—don't fall for her grouchy boss, Brock. *Internship with the Devil* is a smart and sassy contemporary romance set in the world of athletic trainers for a college football team."
— *Miranda Darrow, award-winning romance author and #RevPit editor*

"Enemies to lovers, slow burn, AND sports? I am so in. If you're a fan of Mariana Zapata, then you'll love this novel. Grace is one of my favorite heroines--she's so down to earth and funny. Then there's Brock, wonderful, caring, sexy Brock. And the ending--I sighed and had the biggest smile on my face when I finished it. It's that good. Put it on your lists!"
– *Ashley R. King, author of Painting the Lines*

"This is a slow-burner that will keep you hanging on, just waiting for that first kiss!"
– *Melissa, the Archaeolibrarian*

"*Teaching with the Enemy* is a page-turning tale with colorful characters and piping hot chemistry. Jaqueline Snowe delivers a spicy, cute, and memorable read. There's much to love about this rollercoaster romance and its charming classroom backdrop."
— InD'tale

"Jaqueline Snowe is a new author to me, but this book has made me want to read all her others! *Teaching with the Enemy* has so much drama in the form of secrets, blackmail and even theft. Plus lots of lots of steam. A a fantastic read that I just couldn't put down!"
— Love Books Addict

Chapter One

THE SMELL OF FIRE AND BUG SPRAY CLOGGED MY NOSE AS I buckled in and took a deep breath. The week-long camping trip went way too damn fast, and now I was heading back to an empty apartment where I would be until I woke up and went to a job I hated. I'd hoped to leave the woods rejuvenated, but the second I got into the truck, reality set in. Back to the grind.

I scratched my jaw, enjoying the beard I had started growing a few weeks before the trip. It was full-fledged now. My sister and Grace were going to give me so much shit. Still wasn't going to shave it. The only person I worried about impressing these days was myself. One of the many benefits of not dating.

I gripped the steering wheel tighter and took a long breath, thinking about the hikes and beers, and allowing driving with the windows down and my music blasting to calm my soul. I'd proved to myself I could survive in the woods for a week. Rich kid or not, I'd always been valued practical skills. A silver spoon helped nobody.

My inheritance caused more problems than it solved. People wanted a part of it—always would—so I'd taken to hanging out with people who didn't give a shit about my money. Which was currently about four people.

My phone blared from the passenger seat, and my mother's name appeared on the screen. I tapped the screen, putting her on speakerphone. "Hey, Mom." I sighed and ran a hand through my hair. I loved my parents. I did. But they never called to just talk. They always wanted something from me.

"I'm in desperate need of your help," she said, her high-pitched voice a bit frantic.

Of course. "What's up?"

"Your father and I are in the jet, about to take off for Brussels. It'll be months until we sort this fraud debacle, but you don't need to worry about that." She cleared her throat and spoke too fast, reminding me of my sister, Gilly.

They'd trusted their advisor overseas for years until he'd retired and passed the business to his son. My parents should've vetted him instead of blindly trusting. My inheritance caused more problems than it solved, so I'd taken to hanging out with people who didn't give a shit about my money.

I waited for the ask from Mom. If I didn't love my sister so goddamn much, I would've been irritated that they always asked me for favors. Never her.

Gilly seemed to think it was because they liked me more, but I called bullshit. It was because I was the oldest. The firstborn. The son. The one who would carry on the Carter name and legacy. It didn't matter though. There was little my mom could ask that I wouldn't agree to. Maybe it was the fact she and my dad worked hard to give Gilly and me the life they *thought* we needed.

"What's the favor, Mom?"

"Steve and Julianna Atwood's daughter, our goddaughter, Leanora."

I made a face even though she couldn't see me. "Uh, is she okay?"

"You need to pick her up at the airport in...forty minutes."

Holy Mother of Junior High, I hadn't seen her in a decade. Not since Gilly and I had stopped socializing with the *elites* our parents loved to rub elbows with. Nora used to be feral when we were kids, always playing in the dirt and her hair in long braids. She'd bring snakes to dinner events and wore lime-green-and-black striped knee socks with her first communion dress. Last I'd heard, she still lived in her parents' mansion and attended all the uppity events, schmoozing with the elites. She could have a reality TV show for all I cared because that rich heiress life was *not* for me.

I could think of no worse way to spend my Sunday than retrieving Leanora Atwood from the airport. Because there was no way it would be as simple as picking her up and dropping her off at her hotel.

My temples pounded, and the words *hell no* were right at the tip of my tongue. She could take a goddamn taxi for all I cared—the last thing I wanted to do was deal with a high-maintenance socialite.

Then my old friend, guilt, clawed up my throat, and my mouth went dry. When I was fifteen, my dumbass had driven her father's 1956 Ferrari without permission and dented all thirty million dollars' worth of it. My parents had already warned me I was on thin ice. One more infraction, and I'd be packing my bags for reform school. I'd never understood why she did it, but Nora took the blame.

"Fine. I'll pick her up."

"Yes, you'll do it?" Hope rang out of her chipper voice.

"I'm heading home from camping." I eyed the beat-up truck I'd borrowed from my buddy. She made more noise than a train, but she was sturdy. My brand-new Beemer didn't have four-wheel drive or the trunk space for all my camping gear. "Let me drop the truck off—"

"Her flight gets in soon, Anthony. You can't be late. You surely remember that she's...delicate."

"What the hell does that mean?" Delicate? She wasn't made of glass.

"I promised her parents we'd take care of her." She exhaled, and my dad mumbled something in the background. "We're taking off. Look, she's staying in the unit across from yours. Just pick her up, let her into the unit. She'll be at the foundation for a few months. I'd hoped I'd be able to fill you in on this before, but I'll email you all the details once we get in the air. Love you. Tell Gilly good-bye for us, will you?"

"What about Gil's wedding plans? You bailing?"

"I'll call her." She hung up, ending the conversation, and I had to laugh.

My sister wouldn't even blink when she heard the news. Our parents were loving and provided for us, but they were always on the move, always finding ways to help others. It was hard to be upset about their constant absence when they were doing so much good, but it had been the catalyst for Gilly and I deciding we wanted to put down roots, and our promise to always be in each other's lives. My sister already had the roots part figured out. She had a job she loved and a man she wanted to be with *forever*.

Just thinking the word made me almost barf. After all the bullshit with my ex, the deception and learning she was using me for my money, I'd never be able to even consider having a forever with someone.

From here on out, all I needed was beer, a campfire, and my buds. If I could just figure out something meaningful to do with my life, I'd be set.

I turned the opposite direction to head toward the airport. Hopefully, Nora Atwood was still into dirt and grime because I smelled exactly like someone should after living outside for a week with no access to a shower.

I turned up my favorite alternative rock station and tried to picture Nora Atwood all grown up. In my mind, she definitely wore a tiara and a poufy dress covered in dirt. Long black hair, rosy cheeks. She always had that deer in the headlights look that was cute when she was ten, but as a woman? Not so sure that worked.

Tapping my fingers to the beat, I fought a smile as I remembered the time Nora brought a real ass frog to the dinner table at her parent's estate. Gilly screamed bloody murder, and it was absolute chaos. Maybe this wouldn't be too bad. It'd be a trip down memory lane. Back to the days before I realized that having a trust fund meant someone *always* wanted a piece of me.

An hour later, irritation prickled down my spine to the point I thought about leaving delicate Nora to her own devices. There were no more scheduled arrivals for the morning, and throngs of people had already left the airport and driven away. What the hell could she be doing?

I ran a hand over my face, giving myself a once-over. My jeans were filthy, my plaid shirt covered in dirt, and while I gave my sister shit for her vanity, I wasn't much better. Presentation was everything, and while I didn't expect to come straight from camping, smelling like a pinecone, looking like roadkill wasn't exactly my thing. I grabbed an old baseball hat, put it on backward to hide my unruly hair, and got out of the car and made my way into the airport. Then I waited. And waited. And waited some more. Maybe there was a line for the bathroom, or she fell, or…

There she was.

Nora Atwood had a certain air about her that screamed untouchable, and holy shit. I had to cover my mouth to not laugh. She seemed *different*. Bracelets covered both her wrists in every color imaginable. Her once-long black hair was short…the kind of short only achieved by a set of clippers, and it had hot pink tips at the end, which clashed with her dark-green oversize T-shirt that made it look like she wasn't wearing shorts. Which she had to be. My smile shifted into a frown as I approached her. She blinked large brown eyes rimmed with long lashes rapidly as she stared at the lobby with a blank look in her eyes, her arms crossed tight across her chest and a goofy backpack hanging off her shoulder. She reminded me of those goddamn influencers on social media, but my annoyance evaporated when she bit her bottom lip and had tears in her eyes.

I fought the urge to roll my eyes. She appeared worried and afraid. *Delicate*, my mom had said. I took another few steps toward her and raised a hand. "Hey."

Her gaze darted to me, and she took a step back. "I'm fine."

"Are you?" I tilted my head and tried not to take offense that she literally took two large steps away from me. Must be the smell, or the beard. "You waiting for your luggage?"

"It comes through that thing, right? Is there a person in there?" she asked, jutting her chin toward the belt with the same expression I would've had in a makeup store. Like she didn't have a damn clue what was going on.

"Yes." *Don't laugh.* "I'll help you. Just tell me when you see your bag."

"I have five."

"Right." I forced a polite smile. A few bags came through, but Nora remained quiet. The belt went all the way through, and at least five minutes went by without her saying a word. She clutched her stainless-steel water bottle with a million stickers tight and kept glancing at the exit. "See them?"

"Oh, is my ride here? Gosh, I'd love to see a familiar face. They'll have someone who can help me with all this…traveling stuff."

I coughed to cover the urge to laugh in her face. "I meant your luggage." Good god.

"Oh, no." She frowned again and got out her phone. "I'm waiting for someone. I should wait outside, right?"

"The Carters?"

The second my words hit her, relief flooded her face, and she smiled so wide, it caught me off guard. "Yes! Did they send you? Oh! Are you my ride? Thank goodness. I just…okay. I assumed they would pick me up, but this works." Her entire body relaxed, and for the life of me, I just nodded.

She didn't recognize me. Hell, I couldn't blame her. My beard had grown out, and I was caring less and less that it resembled a small beaver. I jutted my chin toward the belt, and the same lost and worried look returned.

"My bags aren't here."

"They can get lost sometimes. Rare, but it can happen. We need to go to customer service."

"Lost?"

"Yup. Someone could've put them on the wrong flight. Usually takes a few days, but they'll turn up."

"Days?" she said, her voice so high I flinched. "I can't go days. My stuff. My things. My materials! This is unacceptable. How does one mix up bags?"

"Ms. Atwood, it can happen. We'll just—"

"Absurd." She shook her head violently, and her cheeks turned a bright pink, almost the same shade as her hair. "I will not stand for this. My items are there. My gloves, my books, my notes. *No.*"

Nora stomped her foot before marching over to a small café and demanding to talk to the person in charge. It was almost comical to see her yell at the poor barista, but I had to be the better person. "Nora, that is not customer service. You need the airline counter."

She turned on her heel without missing a beat and headed in the direction I'd pointed my finger. At the airline counter, she rambled about all the things she desperately needed.

They sounded…insane. Dissolvable pots. Recycled journals. Bags of hair. *Uh, what?*

The woman behind the counter looked as freaked out as I was.

I plastered on a smile and tapped the counter with my hand, cutting off Nora midsentence. "She'll be staying in the same building as me. Here, let me write down my number. I'll come get it when it makes its way back here."

"Sounds good, sir."

"Are you searching for it now? Who is looking for my stuff? How does this work?" Nora asked, her husky voice catching me off guard. It was a great radio voice, but the brief moment of appreciation evaporated when she huffed and pouted.

A grown-ass woman pouting was not a good look.

"Let's go," I said, putting enough sugar into my voice so it didn't come across rude. Nora planted her feet down, and I gently tugged her elbow with two fingers and she moved away from the counter. "Do you have enough stuff to get through tonight?"

"Get through?"

"Yeah. Clothes, toothbrush, that stuff." I guided us out of the exit and toward the truck. She stopped about ten feet away and raised her eyebrows. "What?"

"Is *this* your vehicle?"

The judgment in her tone had me grinding my teeth to keep my reply professional. "I'm driving it for a bit."

"Hm." She twisted her lips into a scowl, and while I moved to get in on my side of the truck, she stared pointedly at the passenger-side door.

"You can open the door yourself, Atwood." I shook my head, already imaging the horror on Gilly's face when I told her about this. Nora Atwood had grown up to be a prissy, stuck-up weirdo.

Nora grimaced and opened the door. She slid into place with her nose turned up and clutched her bag against her chest like I was going to steal it from her. My god, she was not the same girl she'd been at eleven years old. *That* girl would've dived headfirst into the back of the truck with her tongue out. But this woman looked horrified.

I sneaked a glance at her, and she played with one of the million bracelets on her wrist. *SAVE THE OCEAN* popped out in big letters, and I let myself roll my eyes. Judging people on appearance was shitty, but there were so many red flags right now, I couldn't stop judging her. "Care about the ocean, huh?"

"Yes. People are so careless about the trash growing in it. Something needs to be done."

"And bracelets help?"

She slid me a look cold enough to make me almost feel bad. "Yes. All proceeds go to clean water charities."

"Okay then." I tapped my fingers to the beat of a popular rock band and found myself highly amused. I had no idea what my mom was doing or why Nora was here and going to be living across from me, and a part of me wasn't sure Nora even knew. "Why are you coming to live in this wonderful small town? The nightlife here is nothing like the city."

She scoffed and crossed one leg over the other, forcing her large T-shirt to ride up and expose skintight black shorts. Relief flooded me that she did have something on underneath, which was a weird thought to have. She was an adult. She could take care of herself.

"My parents left me no choice. I must show a 'real' commitment and be forced to *live on my own* for a few months. Then I get my inheritance to start my Good Vibes Greenhouse Plant Therapy business. Honestly, I don't understand why they are so upset that I blew through money. It was just a million dollars. *Like*...we have the money." She waved her hand in the air, causing the bracelets to move along her arm. The whole rainbow of them.

"You blew a million dollars?"

"Not *blew.* They wanted me to donate to a local school, and instead of getting them books, which they have at the library, I bought them plants. Oh, you should've seen their faces. Awe. Joy. They were thrilled, and the teachers were *speechless!*"

Yeah, no shit.

"Anyhoo, that's why I'm forced to do this. Show them I can…live on my own so they'll give me the start-up money."

I bit my cheek to prevent myself from saying I doubted she'd succeed. "Oh," I said, swallowing down the urge to laugh. "I see."

I did not see. Not at all.

"It's no worry. I have a plan."

"Yeah? What's that?"

"Anthony Carter will agree to marry me. He owes me a *huge* favor. We can make it quick, and being married will meet the requirements of my trust. It's either get hitched or wait until I'm twenty-seven," she said, her brown eyes lighting up with hope as she smiled. "Do you work for him too? I haven't seen him in a while."

That was me. I was Anthony Carter. No one called me that except for my mom and dad. To everyone else, I was just Fritz. It began as a kid when my favorite uncle started calling me it. Said he had a buddy in the army with the name and that I reminded him of his friend. It always made me feel cool, and it stuck around.

My mouth felt like it had eighteen balls of cotton in it for an array of reasons I didn't want to think too hard about because it shouldn't bother me. One thing was clear though: she didn't know who the hell I was. She thought I *worked* for the family, and holy shit…she was going to cash in on the favor with *marriage*?

Hell no.

It was dumb. I knew it was. I should've corrected her, but marriage? To her? No, no, no. No fucking way. "I work for the family. My name is Fritz."

"Fritz. That's an odd name for a chauffeur."

I pinched the bridge of my nose as regret weighted my gut down. *Correct her. Do it.*

I was about to tell her that I wasn't a chauffeur, that I wasn't who she imagined to be, but then she opened her mouth and said, "I'll need to set up an appointment with Anthony as soon as possible. Could you reserve us a spot at a restaurant in town? The town is called Champaign, so they must have one fancy location. Oh! I need to order plants. I'm assuming Preston didn't make the trip if they lost my luggage."

"Preston?"

"My sweet mint plant. I bundled him up in the suitcase, but I'm not expecting him to make it. Shall I write this down for you, Fritz? My parents' in-house help are older, so I'm used to making lists."

Jesus Christ.

She names her plants, thinks I'm a chauffeur, and wants to marry me. The day could not get any fucking weirder.

Chapter Two

THE KNOCKING WOULDN'T STOP. THIS HAD TO BE A JOKE. NO ONE stood at the door and pounded their fist against the wood for a full minute.

I rinsed off and hopped out of the shower as fast as I could when her voice came through.

"Fritz. I need you. I know you're in there."

Nora. It had been fifteen minutes since I'd showed her the temporary one-bedroom she could use—per my mom's brief and unhelpful email. I had to stop for gas, checked my phone to find out where to take Nora, and lucky me, she'd be living *across* the damn hall. Awesome.

Anthony—Leanora will be living in your building for three months. Give her the keys. Help her to the foundation tomorrow. Talk soon.

"Fritz, this is unacceptable behavior."

Jesus. I wrapped the towel around my waist and yanked the front door open just to make the damn noise stop, and she gasped. I probably looked wild with wet hair and an annoyed expression even my mountain man beard couldn't hide. "What?"

"Oh, uh, well, you're busy. I see that. When you have a spare moment, I need help." She eyed my chest for a second before leveling her gaze with me, the soft brown eyes narrowing at my silence. "Has the airport called you? Do you think my bags are here?"

"No." I held the towel tighter at my waist. Guilt, or deception, whatever this feeling was, I wanted no part of it. "I'll let you know when they do. You gave me your number when I let you in."

"When is food delivered?"

"Delivered?"

She nodded and clasped her hands together, letting them rest on her stomach as she smiled. "Yes. I never ate lunch and was hoping to find a salad prepared. How do I make a special request for the chef?"

"Not sure what my—Mrs. Carter—told you, but there is no chef. No delivery. It's called a grocery store." I laughed at the bewilderment in her expression and sighed.

"Where I find...food." She rubbed her full lips together hard, a line appearing between her eyebrows, and she shifted her weight.

Son of a bitch. My first real memory of going to a grocery store ended up with me getting lost for an hour, and my nanny screamed at me the whole way home. It was intimidating to be in a place with endless aisles if you had no idea what to do. The need to help outweighed my desire to watch baseball and psych myself up to go back to work the next day. "Give me ten minutes to get dressed, and we can make a trip to the store."

"To the store. For supplies."

"For food," I said slowly, even though I knew she understood me. Her *heiress* lifestyle had obviously prevented her from having any common knowledge. In her palace, everything was done for her. It made her a harsh mixture of pathetic and aggravating. "Ten minutes. Be outside."

I didn't wait for her to respond before shutting the door and making the way toward my bedroom. Finding a clean pair of boxers, jeans, socks, and shoes took less than three minutes. I put on deodorant and was glad to not smell like outside and threw on an old college shirt before grabbing my keys, phone, and wallet. As I was going to meet my temporary neighbor, I smirked and sent my sister a text. She was going to freak out.

Fritz: guess who TF is living across from me for three months. Guess.

Gilly: Oh, this sounds juicy. A former fling? A stripper? A drug dealer?

Fritz: what is wrong with you?

Fritz: Leanora Atwood.

Gilly: WHO LET HER LEAVE HER CASTLE

Fritz: Mom is doing her parents a favor. It is wild, Gil. Come over for drinks asap. Grace needs to be in on this too.

Gilly: in on it?

Fritz: trust me.

I snorted and pocketed my phone. The absolute cluelessness of the heiress was a lot to take in. *"When is the food delivered?"* Good lord, the woman was not going to make it. I locked my door and found her leaning against hers, her pink hair clashing with the deep-cherry wood of the doors I'd had replaced a few months ago when I'd bought the building. Four units, all restored with exposed brick and new appliances. I loved the entire process and being able to keep rent down for at least two tenants. This extra unit was leased by my parents to use as a *guest apartment.*

"You ready?"

Her gaze was glued to her phone, and she held up her pointer finger at me to *hang on.* Here I was, doing her a favor, and she was making me wait. This gesture, this entitlement was exactly the reason I hated my parents' lifestyle. The rich people, the expectations, the rudeness.

It made my blood boil, and I said, "No, we leave now, or you figure shit out on your own."

She blinked and her eyes got all watery, but I refused to feel bad. "There was a social media campaign to raise awareness in helping older animals find homes, and it required use of hashtags. I needed to contribute."

"By using a *hashtag?*"

"Yes," she said, in a what-planet-do-you-live-on tone. She held her head up high and jutted her chin toward the door. "Shall we?"

"After you," I said, eyeing her backpack and water bottle covered in stickers. Stickers. A grown-ass adult wearing stickers. This chick was *wild.* She didn't just walk either. Oh, no. The weird baggy T-shirt hid the sway of her hips as she took long strides, and I was thankful for that. Admiring her curves was out of question.

Her checkered Vans didn't have a spot of dirt on them. They had to be right out of the box.

My BMW sat three cars over from the truck, but seeing how much she hated riding in an old car, I wanted to mess with her. Plus, she thought I was a pseudobutler, and if I was owning this part, I needed to act like it. "The back of the truck should fit most of your stuff. You need clothes and food, right?"

"Clothes." She frowned, wetting her full bottom lip. Sunlight hit her earrings and drew my gaze to the four piercings in each of her ears—all different colors and shapes, all various forms of flowers. Or were they trees? She took out the water bottle and took a long drink before looking right at me.

Her stare unnerved me. Like she'd finally recognized me as Anthony, her betrothed. But then I realized I'd mistaken vulnerability for recognition. She released a short breath and nodded. "I do require clothes. I'm expected at work tomorrow and surely can't wear this."

"I imagine those at the Carter Foundation would have issue with it." I smiled, picturing my mom's assistant, who ran the whole place, eyeing this chick. Penelope would lose her mind if Nora showed up like this. Part of me wanted to let it happen just for shits and giggles.

"I want to hear all about the foundation! The causes they support, the galas, the events. Oh, it'll be so fun!" She clapped her hands and looked from right to left. "Is there a boutique nearby we can stop for clothes?"

"Oh, sweetheart," I said, unable to hide my mocking tone. "We're going to a superstore that has food, toiletries, *and* clothes all at once. It'll blow your mind."

She squirmed in her seat the entire drive there, and a light glow of sweat formed on her brow. Maybe I was an asshole for enjoying her misery. It wasn't right that she had her whole life handed to her. Her parents even got her a job at my family's foundation. Had this woman worked a day in her life? Had she ever worked hard at something? Had her heart broken? The fact she lived a sheltered, privileged life without real hurt or sacrifice pissed me off, and I shut my door a little too hard when we got to the parking lot.

She shifted her bag on her back, her jaw tensing as she studied the various people around us, and swallowed hard.

"You can do this, Nora. You got this. Your plants need you."

Was she talking...to herself?

She nodded a few times, bounced on the balls of her feet, and mumbled a few more things before marching toward the large building. She totally gave herself a pep talk. For a grocery run. This was like shit from a movie. It felt that surreal.

My lips quirked up before I could stop myself, and I used a hand to cover my mouth. She didn't need to see me laughing at her.

She waltzed into the store, and I had to pick up my pace to catch up to her, but she twirled in a circle, her eyes bright with excitement? "Fritz," she said when I approached her in the aisle between chips and stacks of beer. "This is exhilarating."

"Well, that's one word for it."

She reached over to my forearm and gripped it hard, her palms sweaty as she frantically looked from person to person as her smile widened. "There are so many people here. That woman has a dog! Oh! That one is wearing... What are those shoes? Those better be recycled material."

I followed her gaze to a middle-aged woman wearing bright-orange Crocs. I shook my head and guided her to the shopping carts. Her eyes went wide when I pushed one right at her.

"Wh— Um, well," she stuttered, her face getting red again. "This basket is for food, right?"

"Correct." I jutted my chin toward a couple walking by us. They'd filled their cart with beer, hotdogs, toothpaste, and a swimsuit. All the essentials. I wished I was heading where they were going. "Now, I have somewhere to be in an hour, so let's go."

"Other tenants to attend to?" she asked, frowning as she studied the couple and pushed the shopping cart down the way toward the pastries.

"Something like that, yeah."

She reached over to touch a loaf of bread before furrowing her brows and giving me a look that twisted my gut. She was lost. Out of her element. And yeah, I thought she was an airhead, but she could easily be taken advantage of, and that didn't sit right with me.

"You want some help with basics?"

"Basics. Yes. Basics sound perfect." She exhaled and the muscles around her shoulders relaxed.

I took the cart from her. "Okay, bread, eggs, milk. Peanut butter and jelly. Snack foods. You always need snack foods. You mentioned salads? Well, they have premade ones here. Can't say they are great, but it'll do the job."

"Are these products safe and green?"

"Green?"

"Organic. Not grown with hormones or pesticides."

"Ah, well, they have a small organic section." I ran a hand over my face. Looking for *organic* food at a supermarket was the last thing I wanted to be doing. She didn't seem to listen though. She walked up right next to some guy, not abiding by the unwritten rule of not getting too close to strangers, and she bent down to examine the cucumbers. She tapped her finger to her lip and nodded to herself before reaching over to rub her finger over it.

What was so interesting? They were goddamn cucumbers.

"Nora," I said, my voice a little harsher than I intended. "Fifty minutes. Stop wasting time staring at a cucumber."

"Hm." She stood up, grabbed one, put it back, and then picked it up again. She held it up and eyed it like it had all the answers to her problems.

It was green, just like the last two she'd held.

She clicked her tongue and set it next to an identical one, her gaze darting between the two. "I mean...how do I decide?"

"This one." I grabbed the one on the left for no other reason than it was closer to me. I set it in the cart, and she shook her head.

"No, not that one. Nope." She took it out, and my eyes about bugged out of my head.

"They are *all the same*," I said, my voice getting tighter. What a complete waste of time. "They are cucumbers. Pick one. This one, that one. It doesn't matter!"

She sighed like I'd told her plants were actually robots, but she finally put one in the cart.

The rest of the produce went about the same. She eyed all the pieces and couldn't make up her goddamn mind if she wanted them or not.

The next four aisles were a similar form of torture, but we made progress with fifteen minutes to spare. It was hard not to notice the blush on her cheeks and the way she seemed to study every single thing we walked by. There was no doubt we could spend hours here, and it was baffling to think she had never stepped foot in a place like this before. No late-night runs for snacks, or a one-stop-shop trip for food, clothes, and beer. The woman had everything handed to her, all the time, and while her privilege annoyed me...she wasn't entirely horrible. She held a green towel to her face and ran it over her skin, her lips turning down in a frown. Then, she set it back and tried a different one.

After letting out a contented sigh, she finally put it in the basket. Her toothbrush selection process was the same. She picked up a pink-and-purple one, and a white-and-black, and studied the back of each with furrowed eyebrows. As she read, she sucked part of her lip into her mouth.

Wait. What the hell was I doing? Watching her facial expressions? I shook my head to focus. I didn't stare at her at all as she perused the medicine aisle.

"Okay, time for the checkout."

"Checkout. Right." She swallowed and pushed her now full cart toward the aisles filled with people. It was a Sunday afternoon—right in the prime of shopping—and it would take forever. I sent a quick text to my buddy canceling our plan to play tennis and forced a smile at Nora. Her attention wasn't on me though. It was the outside section, and her already large eyes grew four times their size. "Oh," she said, sighing as she pointed to it. "I need to... Can I go look?"

I eyed the line. Eight people with full carts ahead of us. "Sure."

She didn't respond before waltzing toward the garden area, attracting stares on the way. It was hard to say why people stared. It could've been the hot-pink hair, the outfit, the overlarge backpack, the way she walked, the wild expression on her face, or the fact she clapped and let out a cheer when she walked outside.

Nora Atwood was a little bit...different. Weird. A total entitled oddball. Rolling onto my heels, I waited as the line slowly made progress. She still hadn't returned to the line, and while I could afford all her stuff, she needed to learn how to pay for her purchases. Her question about food being delivered still ate at me, and my irritation grew when it was our turn and I unloaded everything onto the belt.

I sent her a text.

No response.

The woman rang me up and smiled. "That'll be two hundred dollars and forty-seven cents, sir."

"Right." I chewed on the side of my lip as I swiped my own credit card. "Thanks," I mumbled and pushed the cart toward the greenhouse. She stood with about twenty different plants. "You owe me two hundred bucks," I said, making her look up at me.

She parted her lips, and her breath quickened before she frowned. "What?"

"You left. I had to pay for all of this."

"It doesn't...just...automatically come out of an account?"

"Your account. It comes from *your* account." My annoyance spiked. "Put the plants down, we're leaving."

"No, I need them." She stomped her foot, fully erasing any sort of relatively positive thoughts about her. "Plants are—"

"I'm leaving. I've missed my plans because of this, spent two hundred bucks, and don't feel like planting a garden. You can get plants another day." I started walking toward the exit, double-checking to see if she followed. She pushed the carts of plants behind me, and when I went into the parking lot, she did the same. "Nora, stop. You can't walk out with those."

"But you did."

"Because I paid for them." My god. This couldn't be real.

"Can't they just charge our account? Put them on yours?"

"This isn't your mansion. I'm not your parents. Push the cart back into the store, or pay for them."

She blinked, and the same worried, out-of-place look crossed her face before she pressed her lips together. She pushed the cart back inside and hung her head as we walked to my car. She got into the front seat while I unloaded them in the back, and her silence proved that the girl who once saved my ass when I dented a thirty-million-dollar car was long gone. She was replaced with a naïve, entitled princess who talked to herself and pouted. The same girl who wanted to marry *me* to get money.

It was best to stay far, far away from her.

Chapter Three

I BOLTED UP IN BED. THE SHRILL NOISE OF THE FIRE ALARM BLARED in my ears.

Fuck. I ran my hands over my eyes seeing it was five am and pushed the covers off to figure out. It wasn't the full building alarm—that was so loud my teeth would rattle. This one was a unit alarm. My pulse raced, and I slipped on shorts as I yawned, hard.

God, I was tired. Sleeping on the ground for a week in a tent wasn't the best rest, and now I'd lost an extra two hours because of *Nora.* Of fucking course. I exhaled, took a calming breath, and made my way from my door to hers and pounded on it with my fist. "Nora?"

I didn't hear anything on the other side besides the blaring, and a prickle of worry had my gut tightening. She surely didn't hurt herself. I frowned and hit the door harder. "Nora, open the door."

Another five seconds went by, and I took a step back to my unit to grab my master keys when her door swung open and Nora stood there in a lacy, *thin* bra and her short black shorts.

"Fritz! My goodness! The kitchen…I don't know what happened." Worry lines marred her forehead.

I marched directly to the scene of the crime. Smoke billowed from the microwave. I turned on the ceiling fan, went to her patio door, slid it open, and grabbed a cushion from the couch to wave the smoky air around. Her petite and curvy body didn't move a muscle, and her eyes went wide. "What…what are you doing?"

"Clearing the air to get this damn alarm to stop. Never had to do this in your castle, Atwood?" I grinned, the entire situation absolutely ridiculous. I had so many questions for her. Like why was she up this early? What did she try to make? Was that *foil* in the fucking microwave? Why was her bra so goddamn thin I could see the outline of her nipples? Why was she staring at me like I had three heads?

She blinked and crossed her arms over her chest, blocking the fantastic view of her breasts. Damn. Apparently, having a great body *and* being a headcase didn't have to be mutually exclusive. Batshit crazy or not, Nora Atwood was smokin' hot.

Much like her microwave.

"Uh, no. This is a first."

"It'll help if you grab a pillow and wave it around." I jutted my chin to her couch, and she licked her lips before picking it up and copying my movements. "So what happened?"

"I don't know. I put in the burrito packet, set it for four minutes, and the smoke started, and I couldn't get it to stop." Her voice shook, and by the grace of God, the alarm stopped. She perked her head up and smiled. "Oh! Thank God. My ears hurt."

I set the cushion on the couch and went to the microwave. It smelled horrible and had goo and eggs all over. Sure enough—there was foil, and I pointed to it. "You can't ever put foil in the microwave. It'll catch fire and break the whole thing."

"Really?"

"Yes. Metal, foil, Styrofoam. You can't put any of that shit in here. Why did you put the whole burrito in there?"

"Because it needed to warm up, and I've seen the staff put whole items in there before. I thought it would work." She pressed her hands together in front of her stomach, her bottom lip shaking as she looked from me to the microwave and back. "This is so much harder than I thought."

"Cooking?" I arched a brow and kept my face neutral. This couldn't be called cooking. Not in any universe, but especially this one.

"No. *Adulting*." She ran a hand over her pink hair and sat at the kitchen table. "Do you know when he'll be back in town?"

"Who?" God, this woman was all over the place. Why was I still standing here? I should go back to sleep or shower or get ready for work. Any of those. What I shouldn't do was remain in her kitchen that smelled like a Civil War battlefield and listen to Nora complain about her first-world problems.

"Anthony Carter." She tapped her nail on the table as a wild look crossed her eyes. "Is he still a womanizer? Last I read, he got around, but I don't mind. You're friendly with him, right? You must be since you work for the family and are probably his age. What are you... thirty-five? No matter."

She smiled and stared so hard at me, I was certain she would ask me to marry her then and there. But she didn't. Her comment, though, it caused a weird feeling in my gut. A womanizer? Was that what she thought about me? I wasn't near as bad as some of my friends with the one-night stands, and while Samantha was the only serious girlfriend I'd had in ten years, being called a womanizer was unflattering.

"I need to talk to Anthony to get this marriage set up and get me the hell out of this awful place." She winced when she looked around the unit—the one I owned and felt a sense of pride about.

My jaw hurt from how hard I pressed my teeth together to prevent myself from saying something horrible. Here I was, helping her out before I could even have my coffee, and she just proved she was batshit crazy. "I'm twenty-seven, not that it matters. He's out of town for a while."

"Could you arrange for him to call me? I tried searching for him online, but he doesn't seem to have a social media presence."

"He's overseas. Probably would be best to wait." I deleted all my socials after the bullshit with Samantha went down, and it was something I'd never regret.

"I can't wait, Fritz. Don't you see? I need to get out of this hell. I have nothing to wear for work today besides a gross acrylic dress from that horrible shopping center. I don't have my plants yet or my belongings." She flopped onto her couch and sighed for a full minute. She looked up at me and held her hands in the air palms, up. "This is *torture*. I've been dreaming about my business for a decade, yet it is just out of reach as my parents dangle the money in front of me. It's not my fault I was raised with privilege and didn't learn these things. I had no choice! I didn't ask to be born to wealthy parents!" She groaned and tossed a pillow onto the floor, almost hitting my foot. She narrowed her eyes and spoke in a deeper tone. "Marriage is the most logical way for me to get out of this...place...and for me make my dream a reality." She waved her hand in the air, her nose pointed up like I was beneath her.

Even though I still stood and towered above her.

"People like Anthony and I will never find true love anyway. Anything we feel for another person is always going to be tainted by the suspicion that they love us for our money, and not who we are. I know you can't comprehend this, Fritz, but trust me. Wealthy people have problems too."

"Right." That was the only thing I could say.

"I *need* Anthony Carter." She made the *need* stretch out to last four syllables. My skin crawled from the desperation in her voice.

She truly, one hundred percent, thought marriage was the way out. Fuck. I squeezed the back of my neck and felt unsettled at her mini rant. "Look, I'm heading out. Things are under control for you now. Don't put foil in the microwave again."

I marched back into my place, bothered by quite a few things, which only sent my annoyance level higher. I shouldn't care. Like at all.

But she never thanked me, which was dumb to be upset about. It was a certain type of privilege to expect things to be done for you. Her certainty that Anthony—me—would marry her baffled and worried me. Why the fuck was she so confident I'd agree to it? A sham marriage? One where she didn't care if I slept around? God.

I rubbed my temples. No way I'd be able to go back to sleep after that. For every step she took forward, she took eight back. She was weird as hell, but it was good to remind myself she was here because her parents had forced her. She had to prove she could be a bona fide adult, which so far she couldn't, or marry to get the money. She would be the type of wife who wanted everything done for her—just moving from being catered to by her parents to being spoiled by a loveless marriage to a rich husband.

Yeah, there was no way in hell she could know who I really was. Lying to her after the shit that happened with Samantha was hypocritical, but this was for the best. One woman had already tried to con me into marriage. That was more than enough. I needed to stop it. Somehow...I needed to get that marriage idea of out her hot-pink head.

BEING A CORPORATE LAWYER MEANT SELLING A LITTLE PART OF MY soul, and despite taking a week's vacation to clear my head, just two days back caused a familiar ache in my chest. This couldn't be it for me.

Gilly carried her joy like an accessory when she talked about her job. Our best friend, Grace, did too. They both found a passion that they made a career out of, while I became a lawyer because it was what I was supposed to do. It was expected. The clear-cut path paved for me, and while I was good at it—it never made me smile. Arguing cases, preparing dispositions, doing the back-end work to be successful on the day of trials. That stuff used to get my blood pumping. Now, it sucked my soul dry.

I parked my Beemer in the usual place, got out, and jogged into my unit to undo my suit and tie. Lying didn't feel so unethical when I considered Nora's motives, but my conscience nagged at me for going to these lengths to hide my identity. Could I lie to her about why I, a lowly errand boy, was dressed in a two-thousand-dollar suit? I could say the Beemer was the family car, because it was, since I was a part of the family, and she could assume it was given to me for being the twenty-first-century butler she so delicately described me as.

I changed into athletic shorts and an old college T-shirt as the buzzer rang from outside the unit. I hadn't ordered anything but went to let him in. "Hey, man, what's going on?"

"Got a delivery here for Ms. Atwood, unit one?"

I eyed the large cart he had filled with plants. Not like four or five. Like fifteen plants of all different sizes. There was so much green. "Uh," I said, counting up to twenty different pots. "Right. Ms. Atwood. She's not in, but I can sign for them. I own the building."

"Great." The guy unloaded all the plants right in the main foyer and waved after he set the last one down. "Have a good one."

"Yeah, you too." He left, the bell above the door chiming when he pushed it open, and I was left with a long silence. How the hell was Nora going to keep twenty plants alive when she could barely take care of herself?

I bent down and eyed the littlest plant—it was in a blue pot and had soft leaves and smelled a whole lot like mint, and I briefly recalled her saying she packed away a small plant to fly here. Who *packed* plants? I snorted and found myself smiling at all the greenery.

The bell chimed, and before I looked up, I heard my sister gasp. "Um. Love what you've done with the place."

I stood back up and laughed at the bewildered expression on Gilly's face. "Just arrived for our temporary guest."

"Nora? God, I cannot wait to see her. I stalked her after you shared the happy news. She is a social media darling, but never posts herself. Just pictures of a million plants and short clips on how to take care of them."

"Gil, she thinks dear Anthony will marry her since she covered for him when he crashed that car. She's mentioned me, well, Anthony, ten times." I ran a hand through my hair and sighed. "If you see her, do not call me anything but Fritz, no matter what."

"I forget your real name at least twice a year. Don't worry." She bent down and touched some of the leaves like I'd done. "Some of these smell really good."

"I know."

Gilly reached out for another one, and the sun hit off her engagement ring—reminding me that our mother had left when she and

Gilly had plans to spend the summer preparing for her winter wedding.

I had zero plans to ever get married, not after the breakup. Love was a waste of time for me, but my sister had found her match. Christopher was a good guy who didn't give a shit about her money. It was the best situation I could ever imagine for my baby sister. "Hey, Mom call you yet?"

"Oh, how she's gone all summer and wants me to reschedule all my dress fittings?" she asked, a tinge of pain in her voice. "Yes. She did."

"Grace and I will be there for everything."

"You'll go...*dress shopping?*" Her brows about disappeared into her hairline.

I resisted the urge to wince. "I'd do anything for you, Gil."

She smiled and gave me a hug. I knew she worried that her paying my ex to disappear had ruined our relationship, but the more time that went on from it happening, the more I appreciated my sister. My ex planned to use me for my bank account and Gilly discovered her real intentions. My sister would, without a doubt, do anything for me while our parents were more complicated. I would sit through dress fittings and drink champagne and get a manicure if that's what my sister wanted.

I patted her back and squeezed her tight for a second before resting my hands on her shoulders and smiling down at her. "I think you should continue doing all the things you want. It is your wedding. Not our parents'. They can be a part of it if they want or FaceTalk in."

Her shoulders slumped a little bit, but her normal smile returned. "That's what Christopher and Grace have been saying."

"And we are all in agreement because we love you, but you do what feels right, okay?"

Her expression softened just as the bells chimed again, signaling another guest. The loudest, high-pitched squeal echoed in the marbled foyer, and Nora ran to the plants and fell to her knees.

"Oh, my babies. Look at you. I've already started a spreadsheet with your names and oh, wow," she said, gushing as she touched every leaf on every plant. She hadn't glanced up once, and Gilly and I shared a look of *what the fuck.*

"Nora," I said, making her jump back. "Hey."

"I didn't even see you." She stood and dusted off her clothes. When I dropped her off at work that morning, she'd been wearing a tight gray cotton dress, but now she wore a bright-pink, curve-hugging dress that matched her hair. It fit her personality well.

"Did you order them online or steal them?" I asked, hoping she'd paid for them.

"Online," she said, not bothering to glance my way. "I called my father, and he helped me figure out how to put an order online for next day delivery! You just pay more. It's so easy." She beamed and picked up one of the plants and held it to her chest. "This is an aloe. One of my favorites. Roberta."

"Ro-Roberta?" Gilly said, causing Nora to whip around with wide eyes.

"Oh, another guest. Wait, you look familiar? Anthony's sister. Gilly Carter. Engaged to be married soon."

I bit my lip from cackling at the bemused expression on Gilly's face. My sister held it together and nodded.

"That's me."

"I must inquire about your brother. I've been telling Fritz I need to speak with Anthony, but he has yet to provide any contact information."

Damn, Nora wasted no time in her hunt to escape this simple life.

"He's hard to reach," Gilly said, eyeing the plants again. "May I ask a question? Why did you order so many?"

"I love plants. They bring me peace and are better than most people." Nora caressed the one in her hands, almost like a pet. "Did you know there are studies that prove plants grow better when they are talked to? I try to have a conversation with them every day. My father insisted it was madness, but it works. I've been thinking of a playlist for them all day as well. Oh! Actually, I want to try a podcast! A positivity podcast for plants. Yes. That would work." She tapped her finger to her lip as she nodded to herself.

The beat of silence following Nora's statement felt like a weight being dropped on my shoulders. That was the weirdest shit I had ever heard in my entire life. Gilly, who had a comeback for everything, stood there, mouth parted, with absolute shock on her face.

Nora didn't seem to care though. She set the small plant down and picked up another, eyeing it with the same expression Gilly wore when she was in the children's section at the bookstore. Nora *loved* plants.

"Um, wow. That's...something." Gilly's eyes bugged out of her head, and her lips curved. "Cool."

"I need to get them settled in their new home. Fritz, did the delivery person leave the wire shelving?"

"Nope. Just plants."

"Order me one. The sooner the better," Nora said, her attention moving toward the plants as she unlocked her door and carried them in one by one.

"Uh, why don't you order it online? Overnight shipping?" I said, flipping Gilly off as she covered her mouth with her hand. "Not a word," I whispered.

"Hm," Nora said, not paying us attention.

Gilly blinked a few times, and a little giggle escaped before she waved. "Well, I have a hair appointment, so I'll head out. I wanted to drop by with some errands for you, Fritz, if you would be so kind to get them done."

I glared at my brat sister. "Errands?"

"Yes. You'll be able to complete them, won't you? My car needs the oil changed." She smirked.

"Your fiancé can help you if you're so clueless about it."

Nora sucked in a breath and pointed a finger at me. "You shouldn't speak like that to the family who employees you. It is not a good look on you. Especially when they are so lax on the dress code." Her gaze dropped to my outfit, and her face twisted into a scowl, like I was the weirdo talking to *plants*.

Gilly's entire face was on the verge of tears—from amusement— and she spun around toward the door. "She's right, Fritz. Remember that."

"Wait! I have a favor, Gilly Carter," Nora said, waltzing up to her with her swaying hips. "Could you save your hair?"

"Hm?"

"The clippings. I would like the clippings, please. It's very hard to find human hair."

"Um, why?" Gilly paled and rubbed her knuckles together.

Nora's phone rang, and she dashed into the apartment, not answering Gilly's question, and my sister narrowed her eyes at me.

"Holy shit, Fritz. Holy. Shit."

"I know."

"I can't...this is..." She shook her head, laughing hard and waving. "Should I drop the car off for the oil change tomorrow or...?"

"Get out."

She cackled before the door shut, and I put my hands on my hips, torn between horror and amusement. Why did Nora need hair? Why was she so weird?

But the most terrifying question was—why did I find her so intriguing?

Chapter Four

ANOTHER UNFULFILLING DAY AT MY JOB CAUSED MY SHOULDERS TO be more tense than usual, and I stretched my arms as I walked from my car to the apartment building like I had every day since I moved in. I got the mail—nothing exciting—and was about to go into my unit when a very loud booming came from Nora's unit.

I hadn't seen her in twenty-four hours. I'd heard her, that was for sure, and the booming caused a prickle of worry down my spine. I got closer to her door when the booming shifted, and a loud, deep voice carried through the door, but it was muffled. Like someone was speaking on a megaphone through a pillow. *Did she have company?*

I knocked, just to make sure she was alive, but no one answered. The voice rambled on until I caught the words *James and the Giant Peach.* My entire body tensed for one second before the loudest, most absurd cackle overtook my body. It was one of those laughs that made my face ache from smiling and my throat hoarse from laughing so hard. It was a fucking audiobook.

She wasn't home but had an audiobook going, and I'd bet my entire inheritance it was for her *plants.* My eyes watered from amusement, and I unlocked my door, still laughing, and was about to kick off my shoes when the hairs on the back of my neck stood on end. Something was different.

It wasn't the bookshelf or the empty beer can on the table…it was the lighting. I loved the natural lighting in the place, but it was darker than the afternoon sun I was used to getting. I scanned the patio when it hit me.

There were plants in my fucking apartment. Six of them. Three were inside my living room, and three were on my patio. How the—what the—*why?* My amusement shifted to annoyance really fast, and I picked up the three plants in my apartment and moved them onto the patio where I was assaulted by green leaves.

They were everywhere. The only space uncovered was the two-foot area outside my door. Nora had claimed the *shared* patio for her plants, each of which had a name tag. *Kacie—loves Sara Bareilles. Colin—loves rock and guitar solos.*

I couldn't breathe. I pinched the bridge of my nose and tried to rationalize how this happened or why when the sliding door next to me opened, and Nora walked out—letting the audiobook blast the quiet air. She wore a large floppy hat, a tiny tank top, and cutoff jean shorts.

Whoa. The cutoffs were very *normal* for someone like her, and I wanted to comment on them, on the plants, on everything when she started singing. "Mommy loves you so much. You're the best plants in the bunch. She'll find you a home and a new life. I just need to be rich or get married."

I snorted. I couldn't stop myself, and she gasped, spun around, and knocked over one of the plants. She yelped and fell to the ground as *Justin* fell out of the pot and spilled soil all over the bricked patio.

"No, no, no," she mumbled, scooping up the dirt and rearranging the plant into a different pot. "It's okay. You'll root here."

"Uh, can I help?"

"No. Your negative energy is already doing enough damage."

"My negative energy?"

"Yes," she snapped, her tone darkening before she eyed me up and down. "You are a very uptight man. That is why I placed all these calming plants by your unit. You need their positive, absorbing energy."

"Nora, you went *into* my place. That's...not cool."

"It was unlocked."

"You took that as permission?" I laughed at her audacity. She didn't look ashamed at all. If anything, she looked mad. "You realize that's illegal, right?"

She rolled her eyes. "We share a floor."

"Yeah. Doesn't give you permission to *enter* my place. Did you touch any more of my shit?" I rubbed the back of my neck, wincing at the thought of her seeing a photo of Gilly and me and her piecing the truth together. "Did you?" I asked again when she remained quiet.

"Of course not. That would be rude to touch your personal things."

"But entering my apartment didn't cross that line?"

"You need these plants, Fritz. You're carrying around your stress in your shoulders, and these will bring a sense of calm."

"I'm not stressed or uptight or..." I said, hearing the words come off shallow and a little untrue. I had been more uptight than usual, and the lack of purpose in my life had been bothering me more and more. In college, I was laid-back, living the dream without real responsibility, always figuring I could figure my future out later. And now it was later, and something was still missing. "Much. Maybe a little bit."

"Ah, there it is," she said, pushing herself up to her full height and smiling. It was unnerving to see her lips curved up on both sides. It made her face softer, more feminine, cuter, even. "Here."

She shoved a piece of paper at me, into my chest, and arched one brow. I grabbed the sheet and pulled it back to look at it. There was a lot of green ink, and before I could ask what it was, I saw her writing.

WATERING AND MUSIC SCHEDULE

Irritation prickled along my skin, making my neck tense. Did she want me to tuck them in too? I groaned, but stopped when she narrowed her eyes.

She bent down and rubbed the leaves of *Jason* again, a line appearing between her brows, and she looked at me over her shoulder. "Stick to that schedule or they won't succeed."

"Um, okay."

"I mean it. If I come back here and they aren't taken care of, I'm going to lose my mind. Plants are therapeutic and can help your soul. Let them." She touched two of the other plants, the audiobook still carrying on, and headed through her patio door without another word, leaving me on the patio surrounded by leaves.

I tended to be quick on my feet and could banter with the best of them—growing up with Gilly had taught me that—but with Nora, she left me speechless all the time. I rubbed my palms over my eyes and sighed before taking the damn schedule and heading back into my place. Keeping the plants alive wouldn't be the worst thing in the world, and it didn't mean she was right at all. I just...liked nature.

DESPITE THE FACT I WANTED TO HEAD TO GILLY AND Christopher's place to escape my proximity to my neighbor, Gilly showed up early for our FaceTalk call with our parents. We both knew why: Nora. Gilly had texted about her no less than a million times since the hair incident, and my goddamn sister thought it was hilarious.

More than hilarious if there was a word for it. She waltzed into the foyer and into my place, but left the door open and wiggled her brows. "How is our dear friend doing, and *why* does your patio look like a zoo?"

"Nora thought I needed plants to help settle my negative energy." I shoved my hands in my pockets and eyed the plants. It had been two days since she broke in with plants. "There's a watering schedule."

"This shit is wild, Fritz." She walked over to the plants and touched the leaves like I had. "They look good here. It fits your vibe."

"You calling me a crazy plant person?"

"Nah, just saying the green livens up your place. I get why you moved—you needed a clean slate from Samantha—but this place doesn't feel like you yet. This works, somehow." She ran a hand over her jaw and nodded a few times. "Work any better this week?"

My shoulders tightened. It felt dumb to complain when there was no reason to be uptight. I didn't like what I did, but I made good money and had a job. "It's fine."

"Bullshit," she said, relaxing onto the couch and pulling up her phone. "I know you're lying, but let's get this call over with, and we can dive into that fine bottle of whiskey I spy on your counter. Where'd you score that?"

"A gift from a happy client." I sighed and joined her on the sofa as she started the FaceTalk call. It rang three times before our mom answered.

"Oh, my babies. How are you?"

"Hey, Mom," Gilly said, adjusting the phone to the side so we could see more of our mom. She sat on a small patio, and traffic moved behind her. "Where are you?"

"A café. Your father is dealing with a thing with the Ports. You remember them, yes? They are very influential, and your father wanted to partner up with them on a new venture that helps children with disabilities. Roland and your father…well, they ran into a legal thing. It'll be sorted though. Don't worry. How are you doing, Gilly, with the wedding? How is Leanora adjusting?"

Gilly slid me an amused look. "Wedding stuff is fine. Fritz, fill us in on Leanora, *please.*"

"Are you helping her? I assured her parents you'd keep an eye out so she wouldn't totally fail being on her own. She has a kind heart but is a little misguided. Eccentric, to be honest, but her parents insisted we could help. Now, are you seeing her every day?"

"Oh, he sure is," Gilly said, not bothering to hide her smile. "She's been over here all the time asking for favors."

Our mom relaxed and took a sip from a small coffee cup. "Good. That's good. Her parents are afraid they've spoiled her too much. I can't say I blame them. Your father and I tried to make sure you weren't helpless." She looked quite proud of herself, and I bit my lip to prevent myself from spouting off that yes, she was right about that, but they'd failed in other ways.

Parents were complicated.

"Oh, before I forget, I got an email from Leanora wanting to set up a time to meet with you. I assumed you've met with her already, so I'm confused why she's emailing me, but I thought I'd pass it along. She didn't say what it was about…" She trailed off and looked off camera, muttering a curse. "I need to go. Love you!"

She hung up, leaving Gilly and I both with mouths agape.

"Ah, another loving call with dear Mother," she said, rubbing her hands on her dress. "That was…fun."

"Sorry, Gil." I winced, hating how little our parents were involved in her wedding plans. "I know you wanted to update her on the appointments."

"It's fine. Christopher's mom, sister, and Larissa and Grace are more than enough women to be in a dressing room with me. We'll FaceTalk her, and if she can make it, she will."

"We need that whiskey." I pushed myself up and poured us two glasses before heading to the living room that now had plants everywhere. It did fit the room, but I'd rather shave off my eyebrows than tell Nora that.

Gilly took the glass and took a drink before sighing and giving me *that* look.

"What?"

"I had this idea. It's crazy but hear me out."

"Oh God." I wiped a hand over my face, like that would prepare me for whatever came out of her mouth. "What?"

"Grace and I were talking about your marriage with Nora—"

"Wait, my marriage? Grace knows? No." I shook my head and took another swig before pointing my finger at my sister. "This is a whole thing now."

"It is. She thinks you're the chauffeur." She cackled. "We need to set her up with someone else so she forgets about you—well, about dearest Anthony. If she falls in like, love, or lust with someone else, maybe that'll prevent her from hoisting you over her shoulder and running down to city hall."

"She's…a headcase."

"She's also cute as hell. Are you worried we can't find someone?" She snorted. "We can. There's yin to every yang."

I rolled my eyes. I wasn't so sure. The woman put foil in a microwave and made her plants listen to podcasts. My chest tightened at the thought of some dude taking her out. She'd probably ask what a fork was and demand to be fed. Or ramble on about the different type of leaves there were. But the thought of her dating someone agitated me, and I couldn't pinpoint why.

It's either this or her trying to marry me. "You're right, yeah. She needs a distraction that isn't me."

My sister squinted her eyes and tapped her foot on the ground. "Let me do some digging. Think about your single and open-minded friends. We can make this work. I can't have a sister-in-law who collects human hair. That's too far for me."

"Uh, you and me both."

We shared a good laugh before she finished her drink and put on her *battle* face. I knew better than to rush her. She'd ask what she needed when she was ready. I poured myself more whiskey before she exhaled. "I have a favor."

"Name it." Scary how well I knew my sister.

"Christopher's bachelor party. Would you help his buddy plan it? You know the area so well, and his friend is one of those who...goes over the top. He'll get like twenty strippers and cocaine, and Christopher is not on board, obviously."

"His loss. That sounds super fun," I teased.

Gilly didn't appreciate the joke. I held up my free hand and nodded. "Yes, I'll help out. Text me his info, and I'll call him. But you need to find a dude for Poison Ivy soon, okay?"

"You got it." She picked up my laptop. "I'll start looking on social media now."

There had to be single guys who'd be enamored with her pink hair and weird hobbies. She was cute and upbeat...someone might like her lack of life experience and rich-girl hobbies. I hated the tiny guilt making my chest tight, but it was for the best.

I was not going to marry Leanora Atwood.

Chapter Five

THERE WERE FLYERS EVERYWHERE. ON THE STREETLIGHTS, ON THE stop signs, on the front door to the apartment, and any structure that allowed tape to hold paper to it. Standing outside my car, I counted fifteen within view.

SAVE THE OCEAN—DONATE NOW!

Love fashion and *the ocean? You don't have to* choose! *Wear it as a reminder to reduce your plastic footprint, advocate for ocean-friendly legislation, and encourage others to take action to protect the ocean we all love so much.*

The bright-yellow flyers with large pictures of whales hurt my eyes. It was horrible, yet…something tugged at my chest. Despite all the reasons I hated people like Nora, this act was not typical of an elitist princess. None of my mom's friends would've taken the time to hang up flyers. They would've thrown a gala together or a black-tie event to dress up and showcase their home or their latest outfit. This was almost juvenile.

I pulled the one off our front door and folded it into my pocket. It had been a few days since the plants showed up in my apartment, and since Gilly and I came up with a matchmaking plan, and I had only seen her once for one second in passing. She crossed my mind more than I would've liked, but it was relaxing not to have errands to run for her or show her how to be a basic adult.

Like my mind conjured her, her doorknob started to turn as I walked into the foyer. Shit—I was still in a suit. I rushed to my door, ducking inside, where I stripped off the jacket and tie and tossed them onto the recliner.

"Fritz! I heard you." *Bang. Bang. Bang. Bang.* Silence for a few seconds. *Bang. Bang. Bang. Bang.*

"Were you waiting for me to get home?" I asked, replacing the slacks with jeans and making sure I didn't wear anything that screamed *lawyer* or *Anthony Carter.* When I opened my door, she smiled up at me. Her grin was so large, it caught me off guard. "You all right?"

"I have a tiny favor to ask you. It's small. The smallest. But as the Carter's chauffeur, I feel like this is something totally appropriate." She rocked back on her heels, and worry lines appeared on her face. She looked brighter than normal today. She wore a bright-yellow skirt and an off-blue shirt that somehow went together.

I didn't bother correcting her. "What's the favor?"

"I'm going out tonight. To some venue called Whiskers? Or is it Whiskey? Or Whisper?" She frowned and pulled out her phone.

"Whiskey Rose," I said, naming my favorite pub in town. I met my buddies there once a week for a happy hour, and just saying the name made me hungry. I'd marry their Reuben sandwich if I could. "You're going to Whiskey Rose?"

"Yes. You see, the people at the foundation said Anthony liked to hang out there a lot, and I figured there was a chance I'd run into him."

"I told you he's out of town," I grunted. "Why are you hoping to see him so damn bad?"

"Because, Fritz." She huffed and put her hands on her trim hips. "I have all these ideas at the foundation, but no one listens to me. I can't just be invisible for another eleven weeks. Ugh, *eleven weeks* seems like a lifetime in this pit." She closed her eyes, but it only lasted for a second before she set her jaw in determination. "I need money, and he's the answer. *Proving* to my parents is not the route I'm going. This place sucks."

I ignored the brief sting of her dissing my building.

"To recap: even though I told you he's out of town, you're hoping to run into him?"

"Someone said they saw him this weekend. I think he's here, and I think you don't want me to see him for some reason." She pointed at my chest. "You must be protective of your employer, but I assure you, he'll see me. He owes me." She shook her head, like she was pushing that conversation away to move onto another topic. "So can I ask my favor?"

Words escaped me. I nodded.

"I left a schedule for my plants. Depending on how tonight goes, maybe I don't come back for an hour, but some of my babies need to be watered and misted, and to listen to the audiobook I bought for them. It's very important." She narrowed her eyes. "I wrote down all the instructions here for you." She reached into a pocket of her sun-yellow skirt and handed me a sheet of paper.

It was a full map of how she had her plants arranged, each one labeled with their name, their favorite song, and how much water they needed. It wasn't every day like I'd have thought, and she had a misting schedule. And when to turn on fans? For what? This was beyond anything I could've imagined, and I snorted into my fist. This took the schedule she gave me and amplified it by a million. Color coded and everything. "Uh, wow."

"Is this a yes? George is high-maintenance and needs a lot of praise."

Two very conflicting thoughts battled for dominance in my head. I wanted to laugh at how weird my life was, but also, I wanted to tell her talking to Anthony wasn't going to solve her problems. She was banking on him—me—fixing everything for her so that simply wouldn't happen. That caused the same uncomfortable tightness in my chest. The clientele at Whiskey Rose would eat her up. They were rough, hard-working people who wanted a beer after a day's work. She screamed money and entitlement, and while a part of me wanted her to be knocked down a peg, she'd been here for days. Not even a whole week. It would be cruel to encourage her to go there. Alone.

"How about..." I said, running a hand over my jaw as Gilly's words repeated in my mind. *Finding a distraction for her.* "How about this? Let's have a night out."

I could set up something with a buddy, bump into one so she doesn't know it's a setup.

"Like on a *date?* With you?" she asked, making the word date last twice as long, like she wasn't sure how it sounded.

"Not like a date, no," I said, my face burning a bit. "Anthony is gone, and I want to show you that you *can* have fun living in this *dump.*"

She chewed on her bottom lip. "It wouldn't hurt to have fun until he gets back in town. A night out...hm. Yes, I don't...I should."

"Yeah, we can hang out at a different bar with some of my friends, some locals." There, that was casual. I was proud of myself for presenting it so smoothly.

Her eyebrows came together, forming a concerned line between them. "Are any of them wealthy?"

"Jesus," I barked, my jaw tensing as images of fucking Samantha intruded on the moment. Of course she wanted rich friends so she could use them to start her business. I opened my mouth to give her a piece of my mind when she held up a hand and furrowed her brows.

"Listen, I've been on dates, hung out with these *wealthy* men and..." She paused, made a face like she ate spoiled cheese, and shook her shoulders in disgust. "They are horrible lovers. Selfish. Think they know everything."

Wait. What did she say? "Horrible lovers?" I don't know why I pegged her for innocent, like she hadn't been with a lot—or any— guys. Why were we talking about her love life again?

"Yes. No one likes a selfish lover, no matter how big your bank account is." She rolled her eyes with an expression I read as *duh,* and images of her in her thin bra and short shorts crossed my mind, and I squeezed my eyes shut to erase it.

"Right." I cleared my throat and shifted my weight from one foot to the other. The front entrance to my place felt smaller than normal.

We would have a night out. I'd introduce her to a friend and distract her. That was the plan. Not thinking about her in bed with someone.

"So are your friends colleagues of the Carters?" she asked, concern still etched on her face.

"Uh, they aren't wealthy like *that*," I said, ignoring the way my face tensed from the half lie. "I just…think it'll be a good idea to do this since you're on your own. Maybe you'll make some friends, have some good stories to tell all your friends when you get back home."

"Hm, I see your argument. Fine. Yes. I'm in."

"You're not going to Whiskey Rose then, right?"

"No, I can focus on selling more bracelets since I'll have a few free hours."

"Your 'save the whales' bracelets and flyers, huh?" I smirked, jutting my chin toward the door and admiring how she stood taller, like she was proud of assaulting the doors and windows with the obnoxiously bright color.

"You've seen them!" She beamed at me. "The referral code has gotten two more people to buy one since I put them up! It'll make such a difference if I keep trying."

"You realize you could *volunteer* to actually help clean a lake. In fact…" I said, pulling out my phone and typing in volunteer opportunities in our area. There were lakes in every direction. Big, small, gross, wonderful. Picturing her attempting to clean up trash made me smile for real. *Plus, what a perfect setup for a date.* "Look at that. Next weekend there's an outing to clean Lake Brownstone. It's just a twenty-minute drive from here."

She curled her lips up on the side in disgust, and she shook her head. "I could donate money. That helps and is enough. That's what my parents said."

I clicked my tongue and made my face look serious. "The thing about donating money is you can never really be certain where it goes." I gritted my teeth thinking about the fake charities my parents had donated to because they trusted everyone without reason. They had so much money it didn't bother them, but it did me. It still stung knowing Gilly and I had donated our allowances for an entire year to the CEOs of the foundation instead of animal shelters. "You'd make more of a difference getting your precious hands dirty. But that's not your thing."

Nora tilted her chin up, eyeing me in the way Gilly did when she needed to be tough with her students. This heiress was trying to intimidate me, and it was precious.

"*Leanora*, stop. I shouldn't have mentioned it," I said.

Her eye twitched at the use of her full name, and she huffed. "You think I won't volunteer? I led all things philanthropy related for the Atwoods for the past five years. We've had record-breaking donations and have made a difference in a lot of people's lives."

"Yes, I have no doubt," I said, not bothering to hide the mockery in my tone.

She bit the inside of her cheek for a second before saying, "Fine. Sign us up."

"Us?"

"Yes, I'm not going *alone*. Plus, you seem like this is your sorta thing. Outdoors." She gestured her hand to my outfit. "You've got that whole lumberjack vibe."

I stifled a laugh. If only she had seen me thirty minutes ago in my suit. It was settled though—I was keeping the beard.

"*Chauffeurs* really don't volunteer on their off days." I shrugged, enjoying the conversation more than I would've thought. My monotonous days were so goddamn boring, and she was the opposite of that.

She blinked, taking a step back, and stood taller.

I couldn't take it anymore, and I laughed. "I'm teasing. I'll sign us both up."

"Really?" she asked, a hint of a smile on her face. "We're doing this?"

"Yup. If there's anything I've learned, it's that sometimes getting dirty and helping with your own hands is better."

"From seeing all the donations with the Carters?"

"Right. Exactly that."

"Hm, well, this will be a first." She put her hands on her hips again and nodded to herself. "What do I wear?"

"Outdoor stuff."

Her dark eyebrows furrowed, and she tapped her foot on the floor. "I don't…like slacks?"

"Clothes that you're okay with getting destroyed. Research what to wear online. You'll figure it out."

"Hm, okay, sure." She sighed, gave me a long look, and started walking to her unit. She glanced over her shoulder one more time and arched one brow.

She pursed her lips, but it didn't hide her smile. She waved before walking inside, and while I didn't exactly feel like spending the next weekend outside cleaning up trash, it'd feel good to escape the boring day-to-day routine that was slowly driving me mad. Plus, it'd be fun to mess with the heiress.

NORA INSISTED SHE COULD COME UP WITH OUTSIDE CLOTHES AFTER her five suitcases finally arrived from the airport. All five barely fit in the back of the truck my buddy still let me borrow. I wasn't sure what to expect when I knocked on her door the next Saturday morning. It wasn't her dressed in flats, jeans, and a skintight black tank top that fit her really well. It fit well enough that I cleared my throat.

Was I checking out this weirdo? Kind of. It was fine. She had a great body and a cute face…I shook my head a few times, refusing to go down that route. Like…at all. "Morning, Doc. You prepared to have your entire outfit destroyed?"

She chewed her lip and scrunched her nose, like this was a surprise to her. "You think?"

"I know. We will be in mud. Picking up trash that lazy assholes leave out. There will be glass, so you got any other shoes?"

"House shoes and heels," she said, her voice getting soft and her cheeks burning bright red. "I don't…I wear sandals when I work with my plants. I have gloves though! I brought like six pairs! You can borrow a pair if you want, but you seem big, so they might not fit you." She held out a bag with a lot of aggression, like she was excited to show me. It was cute.

"Gloves are a great idea. Shoes though, hold on a second."

I ran back into my place and went to the guestroom. Gilly and Christopher tried to do a hike—which made me laugh hard because Gilly didn't do anything that made her sweat—but her onetime worn hiking boots were here. I grabbed them and a pair of my clean socks. She stood outside my door, frowning at her phone. She looked up when I came out, and the frown shifted. It was nice to see her smile at me.

"You found me boots! Oh, thank goodness. I was low-key freaking out worrying about fungus and broken glass. This is, like, my first time seeing a lake, and I couldn't sleep last night because what if there are snakes? Or spiders? Or creepy-crawly bugs that go into my ears?"

I snorted. "Okay, for one, boots will prevent anything from getting your feet. So put these on and lace them up tight."

"Okay, sure. Yes." She nodded and took them from me. "Are these women's boots?"

"Yes, they are my s—my ex's. She wore them once."

"Did you guilt her into volunteering, too, and then she left you?"

"Are you joking with me?"

"Perhaps."

We shared a small smile before she bent down and started putting the socks and boots on. Her pink hair seemed brighter somehow. It was shorter than my own slop of hair, and I typically preferred long, dark hair on women. I liked how it looked and felt in my hands. But hers...I wondered if it was soft.

Which was weird.

I checked my phone to confirm if my buddy Steven was joining us when a ladybug landed on her shoulder. I reached over to grab it, but she must've sensed my hand because she smacked it with the reflexes of a ninja. "Uh, whoa."

"Don't kill it!" She stood, with one boot on, and got the ladybug onto the pad of her finger. "These are excellent for plants! Oh, Ollie was getting eaten alive. I'll be right back."

"Hm...now? Ollie?"

She didn't respond. She went into her place, leaving her flats and the other boot on the ground, and for the tenth time, Nora Atwood left me with so many goddamn questions.

Chapter Six

"Putting ladybugs on plants helps them fight off their enemies."

"The plants have enemies?" I asked as we were en route to Lake Brownstone. It was mainly country roads, and the crops still hadn't taken off. My dad always muttered *knee-high by July* when we drove around together in the summer, and there was something majestic about the landscape here. It was all greens and browns with trees in the distance and so overwhelmingly large.

I sneaked a glance at Nora and found her staring out the window with an awed expression. "People don't assume farm grounds are pretty, but—"

"No, they are *gorgeous*. I haven't seen anything quite like this. Look at the colors! The large buildings. The hay bales! The cows! Are those all farms?"

"Silos. They store seed."

It was totally inappropriate to think of driving around with Samantha, who complained how boring it was living surrounded by fields. She never would've said they were beautiful. I cleared my throat to rid myself of the unwanted intrusion. It just showed that falling in love was stupid. She had fooled me so damn much, played me, that my heart was off-limits. "I like the flat lands and how you can see it for acres."

"Yes, I agree." She pulled her knees to her chest and rested her chin on top of her hands. "Back to my plants. Aphids, mealybugs, leafhoppers, and mites. They are a plant's nemesis. They eat the leaves and damage the growth of the plant. Ladybugs feast on them. It is actually a sign of a very healthy garden when you have ladybugs there."

"Uh, we don't have a yard in our place, so when you say garden… you mean the patio?"

"Yes." She rolled her eyes, like that was the simplest answer to ever grace the earth. "I have them organized by size and who needs the most sun. The sunflower is struggling. Oh! Did Gilly happen to give you a bag of hair? I swore I saw her car there the other night, but I didn't stop by to check because I was watching a tutorial on the best ways to use the stove."

Good gravy, she was weird. I shook my head. "Uh, nope."

"Damn. Okay, I can find another way."

"You going to explain the hair thing, or let me think you're insane? It's not normal to collect people's hair. Just saying."

"Hair is high in magnesium, Fritz. It is a great natural fertilizer *and* can actually help break up clumpy soil. That's why I started cutting my hair short. I'd use the clippings to help my plants grow." She made a face and turned to look at me. "Did you think I just collected human hair?"

"Yes. You have some odd…hobbies," I said the words carefully, wincing when she remained silent for a full beat.

"But I don't collect hair."

"Thank God for that."

She hummed a response before gazing out the window again, and the rest of the drive passed in a comfortable silence. It wasn't until I turned onto the gravel road, where twenty cars lined the side, that she perked up. "There's quite a few people."

"I imagine there's Boy Scouts or high school kids volunteering here too." I squinted and saw a school bus for a local district. "I think sports teams even volunteer together for bonding."

"My parents would tell me to pick three places a month I loved, and they would donate large funds to them. I always thought..." She stopped and let out a long, sad sigh. "I assumed that helped."

"Money does tend to assist, but this is better sometimes, more gratifying."

She swallowed so hard the back of her throat clicked, and I parked the car, undid my belt, and got out. The ground crunched underneath my boots, and I fought a grin as she took her sweet-ass time exiting the car and looking around. Despite her wearing jeans and boots, she looked so out of place. Maybe it was her horrified facial expression, or how she walked like the ground wasn't worthy of her feet. I wasn't sure. But when a dog ran along the side of the parking lot and shook, spraying pieces of mud on Nora, she squealed.

"Ugh," she said, shaking her hands and sticking her tongue out.

"What's that, Atwood? I would assume you weren't afraid of some mud. You do spend lots of time with plants, right?"

She narrowed her eyes at me but remained quiet, despite her rosy cheeks giving her away. Flustering her brought me a lot of joy, and while I should probably have worried about why that was, I ignored that twinge of guilt. This was fun.

"Volunteers! Please check in at the table, get a bag and gloves if you didn't bring any, and we're going to break off into four groups. Each group will head to a different section of the lake and start collecting any debris. Restrooms are on the back of the trailer here. If you have any questions, find me. Name's Billy."

Nora tensed as she scanned the two porta-potties, and I smiled. "Ever used one before?"

"Dear God, no."

"Hope you didn't drink a lot then."

"Fritz," she said, her voice shaking a bit. "I can't...is this really necessary?"

"Is what necessary?" my buddy Steve Smith said, slapping me on the shoulder and eyeing Nora like she was the new kid at school.

She sort of was though. The fact he seemed interested in her was a good sign. All I told him was that I had a friend who was fun and wanting to date. He didn't need to know any of the details. She could handle that end.

All I needed was to get her off her hunt for Anthony.

"Nora, this is my pal, Steve Smith. He's a great guy. He'll be with us today." I jutted my chin in his direction and winked, hoping she could read social clues.

Nora blinked a few times before she twisted her lips up in a smile, staring at Steve. "Hello, Steve Smith."

Steve's grin widened, and he held out a hand. "Dope hair. Love the pink."

Nora blushed and ducked her head, looking at the ground after she shook his large hand. It was interesting to see her act this way, all demure and shy. This was not the chick I knew. Not at all.

They didn't have time to talk before Billy, the lead, shouted to the group to head to our section. The three of us checked in together so we were located on the southern part of the lake, paired up with the National Honor Society students from the high school. I snorted, imaging my Grace's students being here. Some people hated the small-town life, but I didn't mind it. There was something homey and familiar to it that just felt right. Especially when I'd never had that growing up.

"Tell me about yourself, Nora," Steve said, the two of them walking ahead of me.

Their voices carried over the wind, and I focused on picking up the trash near the water's edge. There was so much of it, and it pissed me off. There were literal trash cans around the lake, and people still just tossed cans into the water?

"I plant. I plant a lot. I love them. Plants are my dream."

Leapin' lobotomies. I shut my eyes and rolled my shoulders to rid the tension. Nora was weird, but that was not the best opening. Steve owned a bar downtown and was the definition of the average twenty-seven-year-old dude. He drank beer, watched baseball, and loved women. He was relatively clean, liked a good night out, appreciated his family, and was looking to settle down. But *"Plants are my dream?"*

Goddamn it, Nora.

"So what, you got a garden or something?"

"A huge greenhouse, actually. Well, not here. At my parents' location up north. I'm just here to show them I can survive on my own. It's not going...well. It's not horrible. But it's not wonderful."

Steven glanced my way with one arch brow, and the look in his eyes was easy enough to read. *What the fuck.*

I winced and pretended not to overhear. This was brutal. The worst. I regretted not bringing headphones, and the next hour was the same level of awkward. Steve asking *normal* questions, and Nora answering like she was competition to be the weirdest person on the plant.

"Nora, what do you do for fun?"

"Oh, I like chopping off my hair and collecting ladybugs to fight my plants' enemies."

If she was going to legit try to make new friends, or date, she needed to bring everything down to level two...not keep it at level-ten crazy. Needing to escape the awkwardness, I made my way over to the west side of the lake and started in on the newspapers and cups littered everywhere. Teens loved coming to the lake to hang out—and drink and smoke and hook up—but seeing all the legit damage made me want to do more to help. I could try to do this every other weekend. Get Grace and Gilly to come. Okay, Gilly would find an excuse, but still, there was more we could do.

The June sun beat on my neck, and I immediately thought of Nora. The poor woman never saw that much sun, and I didn't even think to offer her sunscreen. I'd figured we'd be done before the heat got bad, but shit. My skin was already sensitive to the touch, and I looked over to see if she had any redness.

Steve bent over to pick up trash while another woman—not Nora —stood next to him and laughed. I frowned.

Did my buddy just ditch her? That shit wasn't cool. I walked toward him, and he nodded in greeting when I got a few feet away. "Dude, where's Nora?"

"Oh, your friend?" he said, laughing and making his eyes go wide. "She asked me about marriage, Fritz. Marriage. Things got uncomfortable after that, and she excused herself to use the facilities."

"Christ. I know she's…she's different, but she's into volunteering and donating, and I know that's your thing."

He nodded and took off a glove and put his hand on my shoulder. "You meant well. Didn't work. At all. Like, no match. And honestly, not sure I'm up for you trying to set me up again."

"She's not…." I stopped. "You sticking around to help finish?"

"Hell yeah. It's gorgeous outside and plus…" he said, jutting his finger over his shoulder. He mouthed *hot moms.*

"Thanks for driving out. If you're up for doing it again, let me know. Pisses me off seeing all the trash."

"You got it. And by again, you mean you and me, right?"

I flashed a quick grin before heading toward the main area where the *facilities* released a horrible smell. It was unmistakable, and I leaned against the trailer for a few minutes waiting for Nora to come out, but she never did.

My stomach tightened. Was she crying or something? Shit. "Nora?"

No response. I went up the stairs, and both doors were unlocked, and units unused. Where the hell was she?

I scanned the area from the little lift I had on the trailer and couldn't see her black tank top or her pink hair. She wouldn't be stupid enough to jump into the lake, hopefully. Could she swim?

Oh God. Could she?

I immediately pictured her in the lake, asking me, *"Fritz, how do I float? Can I pay someone to hold me up?"*

"Nora!"

No response. *Again.* I pulled out my phone and groaned at the limited service I had, knowing calling her wouldn't be an option. My heart pounded against my ribs at how dumb of an idea this was—bringing her out here and leaving her with Steve. I was an idiot. She just didn't know common things that we did growing up around here. Like don't drink the lake water, or don't wonder off from the group…

I pinched the bridge of my nose and looked around again.

My stomach flip-flopped like I was on the descent of a ride at Six Flags when pink hair caught my attention. She was on the east side of the lake, bending onto the ground. Without thinking, I jumped off the tailer and jogged toward her, ignoring the pointed looks from the organizers because I certainly didn't stick to my area. When I approached her, I was expecting her to be upset or embarrassed.

She wasn't either of those things. She had a huge smile on her face as she stood up and walked over to the field filled with wild flowers. She touched each flower with a gentle embrace, bending over to smell it before she moved onto another with excitement almost buzzing from her.

It was mesmerizing. How she moved with grace, how she seemed lost in her own world, completely unaware that there were twenty bees around her or that she was off the path by ten yards. She was so focused, like she wouldn't be anywhere else. My chest got tight, trying to think about something I had done to ever have *that* expression on my face. That pure joy.

Music started playing from across the lake, making Nora look up, and her mouth formed a pretty *oh* shape when her gaze landed on me. "Fritz."

"Hey, Dora."

"Dora?"

"Yeah, like Dora the Explorer?"

"I don't understand." She stood up and wiped her muddy hands on her jeans. Mud covered her *everywhere,* and she didn't seem to mind one bit. "I'm Nora."

"Oh my God, never mind." I snorted. "You're off path, in the weeds, that's what I meant. What are you doing?"

"I haven't seen flowers like this. They are beautiful, and I was admiring them. Looking at their stems and leaves." She beamed, like she got a perfect score on a test. "Is that okay? Did I break...the rules?"

"Nope. Just got worried you ran off and got lost in the wilderness." I put my hands in my pockets and rocked back on my heels. A beat passed, and I smiled, hoping to ease the weird tension. Did Steve upset her? I hated knowing I might've caused it. "Uh, did things go okay with Steve?"

She shrugged and went back to the yellow wild flowers. "I asked him what he thought about marriage, and he stumbled and stopped talking."

"Nora, you can't...not the first time you meet someone. That's intense and will make people run far away. It's more a...fifth date type of thing."

"*Fifth* date? Fritz. Look at me." She stood up and put her hands on her hips. "I'm covered in mud. I had to look up how to make Pop-Tarts on my phone this morning because I didn't know how. Your friend laughed at me. I can't...this life isn't for me."

"You seemed to be enjoying yourself before I walked up," I said, not caring that the argument sounded weak. My annoyance at Steve spiked. He'd upset her. I didn't appreciate the tight lines around her mouth or the way she kept making a fist at her side. Instead of going over to call him a dick, I focused on the rest of her rant. "Don't let one awkward convo stop you from having a good time. You deserve it."

She crossed her arms over her chest and glared at me. "I'd like to go now."

"Fine. Great."

She marched by me, heading in the wrong direction. "Other way, Nora."

"Fine."

We made our way to the car, and I waved at Steve before we left. My plan didn't go as I'd hope, at all. My most easygoing, laid-back friend couldn't handle Nora, and if she wasn't distracted, she would try to find *Anthony* again.

My neck burned, and when I approached a stop sign as we left the country road, I noticed her arms and neck were also red, and I made a note to get her some aloe. Never mind. She already had a whole aloe plant. I wanted to ask her, but the tension seemed to clog the cabin. She had her phone in her hands, moving her fingers over the keyboard fast as her lips moved with soundless words.

The familiar sound of an email being sent filled the car, and she sighed, leaned back into her seat, and smiled. "Today was enlightening. That was for sure."

"How so?"

She sounded hopeful, and maybe the experience was good for her. I tapped my fingers on the wheel, anxious for her answer. My phone buzzed in my pocket against my thigh, and that was the only warning I got before she said, "It made me anxious to get my life started. The wild flowers there—they were beautiful. And the concept of volunteering...I want to organize trips through the Greenhouse."

"That's a great idea," I said, still skeptical of the glint in her eyes. "You could even help out with that from time to time."

"Sure, maybe. But I need to get started. Now. I don't want to wait."

Ah, there it was. I swallowed hard and adjusted my sweaty grip on the wheel. She sighed and tilted her head to look out the window with a smile toying on her lips. I hated that I wanted to know why it was there. "Thinking about your greenhouse?"

"No. I'm thinking about Anthony Carter."

I gritted my teeth. I knew it. Silence filled the cabin, and my pulse sped up, intruding on what I thought was a great moment. I liked hearing her talk about the greenhouse, her passion for it, but it shattered when she mentioned me. "Still trying to find him?"

"I found his email, so that's a start. I think he might be avoiding me because he's embarrassed about what happened, but I just need to talk to him. He'll understand." She pulled her knees up to her chest and wrapped her arms around them, a confident, happy look on her face. My phone seemed to weight a million pounds in my pocket.

She'd emailed me and looked way too confident about it. I had to read that email.

Chapter Seven

GRACE AND GILLY PASSED MY PHONE BACK AND FORTH, BOTH OF their faces scrunched in thought. Their silence was a worrying sign—they always had an idea or a plan for anything, but after dear Nora emailed *Anthony* in an urgent tone, I had no idea how to respond.

The distraction plan would have to be taken up ten notches, but how did that happen when she was…so different? I sighed and stretched my hands over my head, relaxing onto Grace's couch. It was our monthly Sunday get-together where we all met at Grace and Brock's house, and Christopher joined us now that he and Gilly were getting married. This tradition had continued since college and served as the family Gilly and I had always wanted. Roots. Routine. Consistency. These gatherings helped me after that shit with Samantha imploded, and now, it'd help me balance this fine line of lying while protecting myself from the spoiled wrath of Nora.

"What do I say? Saying *out of town* seems too shallow."

"Dare I point out how much of a hypocrite you are?" Grace said, narrowing her eyes at me and giving me that scary teacher look she'd mastered quite well in the last few years. "You gave Gil so much shit for lying to Christopher."

We all looked at Christopher in the kitchen, who held his hands up to his ears and turned his back to us. God, he was such a good dude. Gilly smirked at her fiancé before giving us her full attention.

"G, I'm not one to advocate for lying, but this chick is wild. Keeping her in the dark about chauffeur Fritz is the right move. Trust me here."

Grace rubbed her forehead and sighed, like she was an elderly woman and we were kids trashing her lawn. "Why do I put up with you both?"

"Because you love us. Now enough judging," I said, picking up a small blue pillow and tossing it at her face. "Help me respond to this email and come up with a better plan. She blew the secret date with Steve yesterday."

"Easygoing, cute Steve?" Gilly said, causing Christopher to look at us again, and she laughed. "Cute in a '*I love trees*' kinda way. He's an environmentalist."

Christopher shook his head and joined Brock on the patio. My chest tightened at how perfect Gilly and Grace's partners were for them. They understood our friendship, how close we were and how often we needed to see each other even when we talked and texted nonstop. These friendships were the longest and most meaningful relationships I'd had, and while my heart was still bruised from Samantha, I hoped that if I ever did find someone, they would fit in with this group as easily as Brock and Christopher. But it wasn't likely.

It was a frightening thought to picture Nora here—she'd fuss over the lack of plants or bugs or question what a grill was. The mental image made me laugh, and I focused back on Grace, who moved her fingers over my phone. "Hey, what are you saying?"

"I'm answering. I'm not lying because I think the Carter siblings have had enough of that. But I'm being creative in my answer."

"Anthony's answer, you mean," I clarified.

"Yes."

Gilly leaned into Grace as they penned what I hoped was the right answer. Her aggressive email was a little worrying from such a petite and naïve heiress, and when Grace was done, I reread the exchange.

From: LeanoraAtwood

To: AnthonyCarter

Dear Anthony,

I hope you're well as you are a very difficult person to find. I'm sure you remember what happened all those years ago, and there is no need to be embarrassed or anything. I don't regret covering for you, so I hope you're not worried about it or avoiding me. I haven't told a soul, and I never would! But I've found myself in a predicament, and I hope to cash in on the favor you assured me had no expiration date. We must meet soon. I insist. I've asked your assistant, Fritz, for your information, and he insists you are out of town. If that is the case, we can set up a FaceTalk.

This is important so please, let's chat soon!

xoxo

Nora

I could practically hear her voice writing this, her light laugh as she wrote *xoxo*. It was almost cute how she thought I was embarrassed. I wasn't sure what I expected after her confidence in the truck, but there wasn't a threat or something substantial there. Like she was trying to be tough and strong but didn't know how.

"Why does she think this favor is happening?" Grace asked, her furrowed brows making me realize I never told her the history between me and Nora.

"Well, shit," I said, causing both women to frown. "I wanted to drive her father's car and broke in, drove it, and crashed it twelve years ago. I was on my last strike, according to my mom. If they'd found out, they would've cut me off financially or sent me to some stuffy school abroad. Nora covered for me, and it was a thirty-million-dollar car or something."

"That's the underlying threat then." Gilly nodded as Grace paled.

"Thirty *million* dollars. Good god, the world you live in."

"Lived in, Grace," I corrected. "Past tense."

Her eyes softened, and I made a couple of tweaks to her response. It would work, for now, but it wouldn't last long.

Dear Leanora,

I've heard you're working at the Carter Foundation. That suits you. I'm afraid I'm unable to meet soon, but I will reach out when I'm able to. I do remember that favor, and I've always wondered why you covered for me all those years ago. I haven't forgotten.

Anthony

I hit send, hoping the brief email was not filled with lies. "There, sent. Why do I keep finding myself in these bizarre situations straight out of a reality TV show? What did I do in my former life for this shit? First Samantha, and now Nora." I groaned and pulled the end of my hair.

"All the broken hearts you left. This is payback."

"Wow, thanks, Gil."

"It's the truth. You've gotten around, and these are your consequences."

"Helpful." I glared at her and was about to grab a beer when my phone went off. "Shit, is that her?"

"I don't know. Are you fourteen? Answer your phone," Grace said, rolling her eyes and laughing. She picked it up and tossed it to me. "It's Nora."

"Shit."

I sighed and answered. "This is Fritz."

"Hi, yes. Fritz. I need assistance. I tried your doors, but you didn't seem to respond."

"Doors?"

"Yes. Your front and patio door."

"Stop trying to break into my place, Nora." I made my eyes bulge out, and Grace and Gilly snorted into their fists. "What's up? I'm not home."

"Oh. Okay."

She sounded sad. *Maybe it's about Anthony's email.* "What's going on?"

"I'll video it or something on YouTube. It's fine."

"I'm on the phone, just tell me."

She let out a long, frustrated sigh that had me making a fist at my side because for all the weirdness about her, I felt bad. "I have bills."

"Most people do," I said, fighting the urge to laugh. "Price of being an adult."

"I don't...I have three. Do I go to the store to pay them?"

Let her struggle. Let her. Let her learn. Don't offer to help. My mouth didn't follow my brain's instructions, and before I could stop myself, I said, "I'll be back later. I'll help."

"Really?"

God, her voice was filled with hope, and I pinched the bridge of my nose. "Yes, I'll help. I'm with friends, but I'll be back soon."

"Thank you, Fritz. Oh, I appreciate this. Okay. I'll see you soon. Enjoy your friends."

She hung up, and Gilly had a questioning look on her face. "Princess request your presence?"

Her question shouldn't have caused me to frown and feel the need to defend Nora. There was no reason to defend her. She was an heiress. And helpless. I shrugged. "Yeah, I'll head over there in a bit."

Gilly shared a look with Grace for a second, but I didn't have time to decipher it before Christopher came back into the house with hamburgers. My stomach growled, and thoughts of Nora left my mind. Most of them, anyway.

SHE SMELLED LIKE MINT AND FLOWERS, AND IT WASN'T THE WORST smell. Her overlarge pink shirt said *donate* on it in a small font, and it hung on her thighs like a dress. Her rainbow bracelets covered her wrists and her pink hair seemed brighter than the last time I saw her, and I couldn't explain the lightness in my chest when she smiled shyly and led me to her kitchen table. She had four envelopes and a sleek laptop open, and a credit card sat to the right. "Thanks for coming. I, uh, think I got it figured out. I'm not sure."

"Let's see." I sat next to her, and she scooted her chair closer. "What are you wanting to set up?"

"Um, I think paying bills. My parents sent me my phone bill and insisted that I pay for water and electricity here. I haven't opened the letters yet, but my father walked me through how to use the credit card."

"What did you do before? When you went out with friends or shopping?"

"It was always taken care of." She took a breath, and her cheeks flushed. "I don't know, okay?"

"Okay, that's *different*." I covered my mouth to prevent myself from laughing. Once I settled down, I jutted my chin toward her envelopes. "Let's open them, and I can show you how to set up autopay. You'll want to set an alert though to make sure it goes through each month. I used to set up autopay and not touch it for a while, but that can be dangerous."

"Autopay. Right." She moved her delicate fingers over the keyboard and stared at me. "What does that mean?"

"It'll make the payment each month and deduct it from your credit card or bank, so you never have to worry about posting a payment."

"Hm." She opened the bills, set each piece of paper down, and smoothed it out. "This is what I owe?"

"Yes."

"Okay." She read the directions and chewed on her very full bottom lip. It wasn't sexy and shouldn't have had me thinking about how full they were, but they looked soft as hell. Her tongue darted out and wet one before she went to the website and frowned. "It won't let me pay it."

"You have to create an account. Do you want my advice or want me to make sure you don't sell your soul online? I can do both."

She smiled, just a bit, and the worry lines around her eyes disappearing before she pulled on her earlobe. "You must think I'm ridiculous."

"Yes, I do, but there are many reasons. Why do you say that this time?" I teased, shocking myself. My phone burned a hole in my pocket knowing she'd sent me that email, yet I was here, with her, almost flirting. *Get a goddamn grip.*

"That I don't know how to pay bills." She squeezed her eyes shut. "This is so hard, and I *hate* that my parents are making me do this. How does this prove anything?"

"No offense, Atwood, but if you're wanting a large sum of money to start a business, and you don't even know how to pay bills...not really a vote of confidence. I'd be hesitant too."

Hurt flashed in her eyes for a beat before she pursed her lips and studied me for a beat. "Fine. I see your point, their point, about this. But I can *hire* someone to take care of all that. My parents' foundation has a finance manager, and he handles everything."

"Sure, I get that," I said, fighting the urge to roll my eyes. Money didn't solve everything. "But you need to understand how money is distributed, what it's spent on. What if you hired someone who stole from you? What if they mishandled money? How could you ensure all your funds are going to the right place? You can't fix all your problems by paying someone."

"Like how going out and cleaning the lake is better than donating money online?"

"Yeah, a bit like that."

We shared a small smile, and she pushed her shoulders back and jutted her chin toward the laptop. "Guess I'll create an account then."

"Accounts." I picked up the stack of envelopes and tapped them onto the table top. "Once you get done with setting them up, I can show you how to organize everything on a spreadsheet."

She scrunched her face. "Sounds horrible."

"Oh, it is. But there's a sense of pride in how I organize my finances, so I'm going to go on about them and you're going to take it. If I had to hear about ladybugs and plant hair and enemies, you're listening to me."

She bit back a smile and let out a tiny giggle. "Okay then."

Her laugh made me smile. I pointed at her. "Quit avoiding. You got me over here from my lazy Sunday afternoon. Get to work."

"You're awful bossy for a chauffeur." She eyed me before focusing on the laptop. She frowned, stared up at me for a beat, and then tilted her head. "Hey, you're not...you don't have to help me, right? You're choosing to be here?"

What an odd question. "Yes. I'm choosing to be in your plant-infested apartment where I get to talk about spreadsheets. Why would you ask that?"

"No reason." She grinned as a blush crept up her neck and face. The pink made her skin glow, and I sat there, transfixed.

She ran her tongue over her bottom lip and wet it, the movement captivating me in a way I wasn't prepared for. Her mouth looked soft, delicate, and her lips reminded me of a classic Hollywood starlet.

She ran a finger over her neck, scratching just below her ear, and I tracked the movement. My entire body tightened with need. I wanted to taste her, to kiss her mouth, see if she kissed like she did everything else—with gusto.

She leaned closer to me, her floral scent tickling my nose and making me all the more aware of how close she was. Her face was inches from mine. "Okay, is this a good start?" Her minty breath hit my face, and I fought every urge I had to *not* lower my mouth to hers.

She chewed on the side of her lip and stared up at me with so much trust, I wanted to fall into her. Lose myself in her. Set her on the table and rip off her too-large pink shirt.

"Fritz?" she said, her voice small. Her gaze moved from my eyes to my mouth, and she sucked in a breath. The air stilled between us as she leaned just an inch toward me, her nostrils flaring.

Her computer *dinged* three chimes, signaling an auto-update, but the sound brought me back to present. To normal. To the place where I shouldn't be thinking about kissing Nora Atwood.

"Let's take a look," I croaked out, my throat way too dry and my voice a little shaky.

I could be attracted to her—that was fine. But acting on my lust? That was so far off my game plan. She wanted to use me, and I was done letting that happen.

Chapter Eight

TO REDIRECT MY MOMENTARY BLIP OF ATTRACTION TO MY neighbor, I tasked Gilly to come up with a guy to distract Nora. She came through, fast.

Four days later, I was at a Throwback Thursday night at a coffee shop watching Gilly's friend, Victor, fawn over Nora. According to my sister, he loved the farmer's market and liked short-haired women. I didn't want to know how Gilly knew that or how my sister convinced me to dress up in a retro 90s shirt, but I was here and had a cold beer in my hands.

Nora wore oversize overalls, platform shoes, and a crop top that ended up showing a lot of skin—all courtesy of my sister—and Victor leaned onto the bar next to her. She smiled a lot, but I hadn't seen her laugh or heard her singsong voice. *If she starts talking about marriage, I swear to God.*

"Why the pink hair? I gotta ask. I love it. But it's not what I pictured when Gilly told me about you," Victor said, lowering his voice in a way that made me cringe.

Was this how he flirted? Deep voice? God, men were idiots. Myself included.

"It's after my favorite plant, actually. It's my favorite color, and when I was a kid, my aunt bought me this charm. It's of a petal and bright pink, and it was the only girly thing I let myself keep."

"You're not much of a girly-girl then? Could've fooled me."

Barf. His lines were cliché. She couldn't fall for that shit. She was smarter than that. I chugged half my beer and eyed the exit. Thoughts of her lips, and body, were in my head too often for me to sit here and listen to her flirting. She didn't need a babysitter, and I didn't have to sit through this. *Why am I here then?* The unsettled feeling in my gut had me rooted in place as Victor excused himself to the restroom, and before I could even think about analyzing why I hadn't left, Nora walked up to me with wide eyes.

"Okay, he's fun. He eats organic!" She clapped and ran a hand through her hair. "He mentioned the farmer's market. What is it? I nodded like I knew, but is it like a store where farm people go to the market and hire them? Or do we go to the farm?"

"No, but that's an interesting idea." I snorted into my glass. "It's every Saturday morning, where local farmers get together and sell fruits, vegetables, bread. You name it."

"Wow. Plants, even?"

"Yeah, and all the natural and organic items you could think of. Chocolate, milk, coffee. You'd lose your mind and spend your entire savings account there."

"I wouldn't. I don't have access to it all yet."

Oh God, was she teasing me back? Her face slowly shifted into a grin, and she elbowed me in the side like we were buds. It was adorable.

"There's one this weekend, actually."

"The market?" she said, her voice going up three octaves too high. "Could we go? Please?"

"Yeah," I said before thinking it through. It was probably the absolute joy and wonder on her face. The last time I was that excited about something was…a decade ago. "We definitely can go."

"Oh my God, Fritz, I'm so excited. Okay, yay!" She reached over and squeezed my forearm hard and shimmied. The movement of her made my throat tight. "He's coming back. He's interesting. I like him. Okay, I need to act cool."

"You're not cool at all."

"Hey," she said, smirking at me before swatting at my chest.

Her touch lingered for a second, and my skin tingled at the warmth of her fingers. She blinked up at me, her long lashes fanning over her cheek, and a lone piece of her hair fell over her forehead. Without thinking, I brushed it off her face. She sucked in a breath, and just like that, she stepped back. We stared at each other, the air thick with tension, but before I could say anything, she ducked her head and returned to her date. She turned her back to me, cutting off our conversation and *touch*, and I used the break to scan the room for any potential people to blow my cover. I went out often enough it wouldn't be crazy for someone to recognize me. My shoulders relaxed when I didn't recognize any familiar faces.

I'd finish my beer and head out, but I'd make sure Nora felt safe. That was the plan. It was reasonable, and I could go home and continue living the life of a seventy-year-old man. *God, what is wrong with me?*

Another bout of self-doubt, confusion, and annoyance crept up my spine, making me replay every regret I had, but before I could enter a full mental breakdown, Victor's question caught my attention.

"So you have millions of dollars?"

"Yes."

"Like, right now?"

"Not right now. I have this card that pays for things. Like I could order thousands of drinks this second, and it would go through." She pulled out the card and waved it in the air. "It's crazy."

"Yeah, right on." Victor's voice changed just a bit. "Your credit card."

"That's what it is, right? Fritz told me that. Credit card."

"So what are you into, Nora?"

"Plants. Greenhouses. Growing them and maintaining them— trimming and naming and all of it. What about you? Are you into nature?"

"Ah, I like jogging on the trail, watching basketball. CrossFit. Typical dude stuff."

"Oh, excellent."

"Do you run?"

"No."

Victor didn't ask another question, and the awkward silence weighed down the room. Nora was going *full* Nora. Not even pretending to be chill.

"So, uh, you're living here for a bit. You like it so far?" he asked, no longer leaning in closer to her, his posture stiff.

"No. It's tough living away from the mansion. I have to prepare my own food, do laundry, which, let's be honest…laundry is hard. I mess it up each time and ruined a white shirt already. Did you know bleach stains? I didn't. It also makes my hands smell funky, which I don't love at all." She laughed. "I'm learning how to use everything. Fritz had to show me out to use a microwave. I put foil in it! Could you believe it?"

"Wow."

Don't blame you, buddy. This was a train wreck, and I could feel Victor's mood changing from ten feet away. He got on his phone, and Nora's face dropped. She fiddled with the bracelets lining her arm. A dull ache formed in my chest, and I pushed myself off the bar. There was a line between supporting her and torturing myself, and I needed to go.

We made eye contact, and I waved before pointing to the door.

She nodded before turning her attention back to Victor, saying something about her campaign to sell bracelets at the high school.

Victor's phone went off, and he held up a finger to stop her "What? No, okay, yeah. Of course." He hung up, got up from his barstool and gave her a very insincere look. "My sister needs help. I gotta head out."

"Oh no, what happened?"

"She, uh, had an accident."

"What?" Nora stood up. "Where?"

"Don't worry. She's okay, but I need to go get her."

"Of course. Oh, I'm so sorry. I hope she's all right. Is there any way I can help?"

"No. Thanks though." He clicked his tongue and looked at me, and I knew just from the sneaky expression on his face, this was fake. A fake call.

He was ditching Nora. Asshole.

"This has been...well, see you, Nora." He waved and ducked his head down before taking off.

Nora's brows furrowed. "Fritz, I sure hope his sister is okay."

"He's lying. There's no accident," I said, my voice harsher than I intended. My anger wasn't at her. Not even a little bit. "He used the oldest trick in the book."

She tilted her head to the side and frowned even harder. "What do you mean?"

Sighing, I rubbed the back of my neck with my free hand and set down a ten on the counter to cover her drink. "Let's go home."

"Will you explain why he faked that accident? Why he tricked me?" She adjusted one of the straps of her overalls, and while I didn't want to dive too deep into why I could read her expressions so goddamn well, she looked hurt. Her eyes weren't as soft and filled with awe.

"People have a backup plan when they feel like a date isn't going well. It's been done forever. A fake accident, a fake emergency. I've done it before, I won't lie." I pushed open the door for her, held it, and enjoyed the slight floral scent that always lingered around her. It was nice.

"Why wasn't it going well?"

Shit. I had to be careful. We got to the truck—still on loan from my buddy who took payment in beer and getting to temporarily drive a Beemer—and she hopped in without a moment's hesitation. *Look at my little heiress, getting used to a beat-up truck.*

My little heiress? I wiped the smile off my face and started the ignition, choosing my tone carefully. "He must not have connected with you."

"Oh." She twisted her hands in her lap and let out a disappointed sigh. "I liked him, I think. Not anything profound, but he liked my hair and talked about how important being vegan was." She glanced out the window, and I sneaked a peek at her, admiring her long eyelashes. She was actually quite pretty once you got past all the... heiress nonsense.

"Does liking your hair and being vegan matter a lot to you?"

"Fritz, don't get me wrong, this might be outside your comfort zone since you work for the Carters, but I'm often mocked for my short, pink hair. I got pushed out of all the social circles because I'm too weird for them. He's the first person to compliment my hair in a year. It's vain, I know, and my hair is for me, but...it sparked a tiny bit of hope that was foolish. I should know better."

"What do you mean?"

"Love, relationships that aren't a partnership, none of those things are meant for me." She shrugged and pulled her knees up to her chest, resting her chin on them.

Her words hit me like a bag of bricks. Her sadness, her acute moment of clarity about how she viewed her life...it felt achingly familiar.

"I actually *love* your hair, not that it matters."

"You do?"

"Yeah. It's badass." I grinned, throwing in a wink to wipe that defeated look on her face, and she perked up. "Nora, you have a lot of unique hobbies and quirks about you. It makes you interesting. Probably the most interesting person I've ever met."

"You mean weird."

"Yeah, a little, but who wants boring?"

"You sound like my mom trying to give me a pep talk."

"It's not a pep talk. It's the truth, so you should listen to it. You'll find someone who will like you for you. Pink hair, and plant charts, and bracelets, and saving the turtles."

She snorted, and her cheeks turned a little red. "Thanks, Fritz."

"Of course. This is what friends do. They build each other up when they need a kick in the ass. They also help put out fires and show off their spreadsheet skills," I teased, expecting her to laugh, but she got quiet again. I approached a streetlight and looked over to see her staring at me with lips parted and wide eyes. "What? Did I say something wrong?"

"It's been a long time since I've had a friend, Fritz." She closed her eyes, sniffed, and when she opened them again, she gave me the biggest grin I had ever seen on her tiny face. "We are friends. I didn't realize. The workers never got too friendly with me at the house because my parents paid them, but this is different since you don't work for us!"

"Right." I scratched my chest as I digested her words. She didn't mean she didn't have friends at all, right? "We are friends though. It sneaked up on me."

Her entire demeanor changed, and she put her legs down. The worry lines on her forehead disappearing entirely, she laughed. "Me too! Gosh. I'm so used to people wanting my money or making fun of me. This feels different."

"Oh, I don't want a penny, but just to be clear, I will make fun of you. As you told Victor, you put *foil* in the microwave. Such a newbie adult."

She giggled and hit my arm, and I laughed. She was naïve, spoiled, and weird, but there was a huge heart under all that and a lonely soul that I totally understood. There came an added pressure of being her first friend in a long time, and instead of freaking out, I made a plan. If she was going to be here for only another two months or so, she could try to marry *Anthony* and go on dates, but I'd be there for her as a friend.

It was the least I could do.

"Now, tell me about this farmer's market. We're going tomorrow morning, right? What does one wear? Should I wear my overalls?"

I snorted, and just like that, we were back to her being clueless. Instead of rolling my eyes, I kind of, sort of liked it.

Chapter Nine

SHE WASN'T KIDDING ABOUT WEARING OVERALLS. INSTEAD OF A crop top, she wore a tight green shirt that said *plants,* and her entire outfit clashed with her hair. Growing up with Gilly taught me a certain level of vanity and style, and I wasn't ashamed of it. I was content with my masculinity.

Nora's outfit broke every single fashion commandment, and she didn't seem to care about the double takes people threw her way as we entered the farmer's market. "Fritz, do you see all the booths? This is like, better than any boutique I've been to. Ah! They have mugs! Oh, jewelry. No way. We must explore!"

She didn't wait before running up to the table covered in wooden jewelry. An older man stood behind the table and smiled at her as she picked up three pieces. "These are beautiful. Did you make them?"

"Sure did. I carved them. My wife loves flowers."

"I do too. Wow." Nora grinned widely at him, then at me. "Check it out. Isn't it pretty? It looks like Jeffrey."

Jeffrey was a plant. "Ah, you should get it to remember your times in Boringville."

She gave a slight frown before swatting at my arm. "You're teasing me, but I'll accept it because this place is magical. Can I buy this?"

"Absolutely," the old man said, jutting his chin to another pile. "It's two for ten if you want to pick a bracelet. All proceeds are going to help our granddaughter get a therapy dog."

Nora's entire body frowned. Her shoulders slumped, and she made the smallest noise of concern. "Oh, that's wonderful you're helping. I hope you raise enough. Hm, I could buy a few...maybe sell them to help. Do you have a business card?"

"Sure. What are you thinking?" the older man asked, reaching into in his back pocket for a second before pulling out a card.

"One day, I'm going to open my own greenhouse. I want to have therapy—maybe your granddaughter would even like it! But these are perfect to sell there."

The old man blushed and ran a hand through his hair. "I'd be honored."

Nora beamed at him, and the wildest, foreign sensation formed in my gut. Envy? That wouldn't make sense. Why would I be envious of Nora Atwood? I chewed on the side of my mouth and shuffled my weight back and forth, trying to find the source of the odd feeling. She was making connections without scaring people off. She hadn't sounded naïve or silly once, and instead of encouraging that, I was being moody.

I was getting really sick of myself.

"I'll just get the one for now, though. It'll be a nice reminder until I get the greenhouse up and running." Nora took out the credit card she now waved around like an accessory—I smiled, thinking about how proud she was she knew how to use one—and the older gentleman frowned.

"Ah, I can't take cards. I'm sorry. We don't have enough revenue to pay for those wireless card readers."

"Oh." Nora froze, her wide eyes filling with concern.

"I'll cover it, don't worry," I said, pulling out my wallet and handing him a five. "Put it on, Nora."

"Are you...are you sure?" Her voice lacked her usual upbeat tone, and she held the necklace to her chest and frowned. "You don't have to."

"I know. Consider it an investment in your future business." I shrugged and my chest grew warm seeing her and the older man exchange smiles. I ran a hand over my beard and cleared my throat, scanning the area for the coffee bar. The few times I'd been there, two women had the most delicious blend I'd ever had. "I'm going to get a coffee. Want one, Nora?"

"No, I'm quite okay. I don't need caffeine. Not with all this to look at! I feel like my heart is a butterfly in a tornado, spinning around without direction. I want to go everywhere all at once." She tried unclasping the necklace a few times and grunted when she failed each time. "My damn thumb is too calloused to get this."

"Come here." I sighed as I held out my hand. She stared at it, confusion swirling in her very brown eyes. "I'll put it on you."

She smiled again, this one reaching her eyes, and maybe it was the way the sunlight hit her perfectly, or how she had a little red on her cheeks, or the passion in her eyes, but it struck me how beautiful she was. Dainty nose, smooth skin, long lashes, and eyes that had stories to tell. "Thanks, Fritz. Best chauffeur ever."

And there it went.

She spun around, and I put the necklace around her neck, trying not to think about how close we were. Her back hit my chest, and despite her short hair, I could smell her floral shampoo. It was pleasant, and after two tries of getting the clasp, it was on. I ran a finger over the back of her neck, smoothing out the metal chain, and she shivered. Her skin was so soft and warm. Would she react like this if I pressed my lips against her? If I trailed my tongue along her jawline to her collarbone? Would goose bumps break out if I grazed her earlobe with my teeth? My skin heated, and my fingers lingered on her too long. Enough to make me take a large step back.

"How does it look? Does it go with my outfit?" She twirled around, looking like a maniac, and I couldn't stop my smile.

"Looks great."

She stopped, whipped her head in the direction of organic vegetables, and then she was gone. She reminded me of Gilly at a designer sale or the teacher store, where she would bounce around from item to item, unable to decide what to focus on. It was entertaining to see to Nora enjoying herself. Seeing her smile made me inexplicably happy. She radiated joy here, and I found myself walking with a little spring in my step. I'd brought her here, showed her this place. It felt good.

She spoke with the owner of the organic vegetable booth as she picked up about six different vegetables and held them against her chest. I could show her how to cook, how to make our family vegetable salad, but what if they didn't take credit cards? I pulled two twenties out of my wallet and walked them over to her. Her eyes widened, and she spoke loud and fast. "These are pesticide-free. All of them. Look at how clean they are. They smell so fresh. Wow. How does everyone not eat these? Why are they not at the stores?"

"They are, but not everyone can afford them." I held up the twenties and put them in the extralarge pocket of her overalls. "Go crazy. On me."

"Fritz, I'll pay you back, really. I didn't realize it was cash-only."

"Don't worry about it. I should've thought ahead."

She hummed in response and went back to talking to the couple.

I searched out the coffee booth. The women who ran it only did so on the weekends as they tried to get enough income to keep going. I got to talking to them about it about six months ago on a visit here, and their story had stuck with me. Their passion and patience were admirable. They were my favorite booth and by far had the best coffee.

They were tough, smart, and hopeful. They wanted to go green—all recyclable cups and lids, no straws, and bakery items coming from local shops to put revenue back into the community.

"Do you have a space yet?" I asked, taking a sip of the cold brew that was so rich and powerful, I coughed. "Basically, where can I stop every morning to get this?"

Carla, the older of the two women, laughed deep. "Not yet. Right now, we're just selling here and at a cart at the business center downtown."

"What's stopping you from going full-out?"

"Money, hon. Money." She sighed and clapped her hands before putting her arm around her partner and shrugging. "It's always money. I swear, if I won the lottery tomorrow, I'd open up this baby in a day."

An idea formed. It started as an itch, like a tiny annoying spot in my mind I couldn't quite reach or grab.

A woman and a young boy ordered a cookie and a hot chocolate. Carla smiled at them, filling their order without any rush. It wasn't just a grab 'n' go table. She talked to people. She cared. She loved what they did and had a vision for it. *Didn't our foundation have a vision?* Didn't we have a plan and put the right pieces in place to make it happen? We functioned off donations, but them...they could get funds.

What if they got a starter loan?

I knew people.

"Have you applied for a loan yet?"

She smiled like it was the dumbest question in the world. "Sure did, hon, but no one would take us on without experience or collateral." She shrugged, defeat evident on her face and shoulders.

I rubbed the back of my neck a couple of times, and my face got hot. If I used my influence, I could help them. I'd vouch for them, for sure. How did one exactly offer this? How did one say *hey, I have connections to help you start this?* Was that a power move? Was that too pompous?

Carla narrowed her eyes at me for a beat, and I opened my mouth to say something, anything, but I looked like a dope.

"You okay there, son?"

"How much would you need to get launched? Do you have investors? Have you thought about getting an investor? Do you have a business plan?" I asked all the questions in one breath, and I felt a little of what Nora did when she said she didn't need caffeine. This felt like a high. A buzz I hadn't felt in...years. "Forgive my intrusive questions, but I might know a guy who invests in local businesses and start-ups. I'd have to ask him, but this...your cart, your story you've shared with me, he might be interested. Can I mention it to him to maybe reach out?"

"What?" Carla took a step back.

"Yeah." I smiled and blew out a long breath. "It sounds insane, I know, but…"

Nora was approaching the table and *fuck*. I didn't want her knowing I had connections—what if she realized I was Anthony? Or this blew my cover?

"Look, do you have a card? Can I call you to potentially set something up?"

"Yes, yes, of course, I just…why are you doing this?" Carla blinked a lot and handed me a business card, her cheeks tinging red as her partner stared me down with mistrust. I didn't blame her. This wasn't the proper protocol.

"I want to make a difference in our community," I said, the truth grounding me in a way my job hadn't in years. Hearing Nora talk about involving the guy with jewelry, how she wanted to include small artists in her plan…it sparked something in me. She had so many obstacles to overcome, yet her passion and drive never wavered. Even when her idea seemed impossible, she never went off path, and I could channel some of that energy. "I'll call you and set you up with the right people."

"Fritz! Oh, is this the coffee you were all gung ho about?" She slid up to me and nodded to the card in my hand. "Did you grab the card for me? Are you looking to sell your coffee at a greenhouse by chance?"

Carla eyes widened in surprise, and I guided Nora away from the table. "I'll talk to you later, Carla."

She waved, and Nora frowned for a second before seeing another table filled with pottery. The large bag of vegetables swung on her side and hit me a few times as she went up to the table with plant pots and her eyes got all crazy again.

"New homes for your children?" I asked, totally messing with her, and I didn't expect her to throw her head back and laugh. She reached over to squeeze my forearm, like my comment amused her so much that she needed help with her balance. I wasn't complaining. I liked seeing her small hand on my arm. *Really* liked it.

"Oh, that was good. Very good." She cackled again and let go of me. She got closer to the table and ran a finger over the rim of a brown pot. "You're not wrong per se. They *kinda* are like homes for them."

"You name them. So…it's not far off saying the pots are homes."

"Hm."

She tuned me out as she studied the various sizes, and I couldn't help but smile at her as she touched every one and lifted it up, examined it, before nodding to herself. Her mind had to be a wild place with all those crazy thoughts. While she used another one of the twenties I gave her to buy a bright-red pot, I scanned the booths nearby and wondered how many of them were like Carla, dying to open a spot but needed funding.

How many of them tried for loans but couldn't get it for lame reasons? Why wouldn't banks take a chance on a small business?

My heart sped up thinking about the potential for them. An organic coffee bar. A totally green restaurant with zero waste. They would provide jobs for the community, a place for people to go, and there could even be partnerships with schools or animal shelters. They could have local artists perform there or sell work. Nora's eclectic greenhouse idea sparked a million thoughts about all the possibilities, and my mind raced with excitement. Something I hadn't felt in a while.

Nora joined me after she left the register and nudged her shoulder with mine. "You look very serious. A serious lumberjack, even with the beard and plaid."

"I'm thinking." I frowned, scrubbing a hand over my face, and when I gazed directly into her eyes, I forgot what I was going to say. Every single thought just evaporated out of my mind when her expression was curious and kind. Her full lips were so inviting I just wanted to *kiss* her, to thank her for inspiring me. For lighting that flame that had been extinguished a year ago.

"You're giving yourself worry lines. Not that it matters to you, but I try not to frown that much so my forehead doesn't wrinkle." She reached over and smoothed my forehead down. "Why are you stressed out? Could the Carters give you time off?"

I tensed. She still didn't have any idea who I really was, and the momentary gratitude I had disappeared. She didn't know the real me because of the marriage deal, and suddenly I was irritated. Privileged Nora didn't worry about her future. She didn't have to.

"How are you so damn sure what you want to do? How is that even fair that you have no real experience yet know exactly what you want out of life?" I fired at her, my envy turning to jealousy.

"Because it's where I'm happiest." She sucked one side of her cheek into her mouth, and a dark cloud crossed her features. I'd put that cloud there. I regretted snapping at her. These were my own issues, not hers. I relaxed my face and gently squeezed her forearm.

She stared at where my fingers touched her skin and spoke without looking at me. "When you go through what I did...finding comfort and feeling safe to be yourself is everything."

"Wait, what did you go through?" I racked my brain trying to recall a conversation with my parents about Leanora Atwood, an accident or something horrible. Nothing. Her words felt like a punch to the gut. She sounded...sad. Upset. Hurt.

I didn't like it.

"Let's not cloud this wonderful morning. Another time." She smiled again, this one a little forced, and she patted her front pocket. "I have five dollars to spend, and I'm going to use every penny. Just think of all the souvenirs!"

She walked off again, leaving all my questions unanswered.

I grinned, for real. The heiress was excited about five dollars. Who would've thought we'd get to this point?

Chapter Ten

GILLY: *I RAN INTO DAVID AT THE WINE STORE AND HE'S PERFECT for Nora*

Fritz: you think?

Gilly: YES! Set them up! Do it! Do it!

Gilly: I'm coming over tonight, by the way.

Fritz: Sure, invite yourself. It's your world, I'm just living in it. Not like I have plans.

Gilly: You don't. I checked your calendar.

Fritz: Boundaries, Gil. Jesus.

She replied with a cringe emoji, and I laughed. My sister was a lot, but also my favorite person on the earth. It had been three days since the farmer's market, and if Gil came over, it wouldn't be a horrible idea to chat through this insane idea with her.

Putting people in contact with the right people. It'd use my privilege for good. Green start-ups that gave back to the community. It'd be risky, from all the research I did all damn day. But I found a place and reached out to them, setting the scene for them to talk to Carla. It wasn't a no, and if I could somehow help them, God, it'd feel good. It sent an explosion of excitement through me to the point my heart raced thinking about the potential.

I paced my living room, making sure not to disrupt the plants that now seemed to fit in there, and let my mind wonder with the possibilities.

My blood hummed with the fantasy, and I was about to get out my computer to do more research when someone knocked on my door. Nora. It had to be. No one else got into the building without being let in, and my sister would've let herself in. I already changed into sport shorts and a T-shirt, thankfully. I opened it, and Nora stood there in a plain black dress and sensible black shoes.

I did a double take and not in the *is that blouse see-through?* kind of way. "Why are you wearing that?"

"What do you mean?"

"Is there a funeral?"

"I look professional," she fired back, her brows drawn together with worry. "I wanted to impress people at the foundation today and wore a power dress."

"Nora, you look like a storm cloud." I shook my head and hated to admit I missed the bright colors already. "You aren't someone who's meant to fall into the background or shadows. You have plenty of outfits that would've worked and fit you."

She opened her mouth a few times, but said nothing. Her cheeks got rosy for a second before she exhaled and ran a hand through her short hair. "You, the scruffy chauffeur lumberjack, are giving me fashion advice?"

Shit. My ears burned. "No, not advice. I'm saying you stand out. Your personality, your hair, your colors. Own that. It's a part of who you are."

She blinked a few times again and gave me a shy smile. "That was nice, Fritz."

"It can happen once or twice."

She laughed and held out a card to me while she chewed on the side of her lip and bounced on her feet.

"Why are you nervous?"

She clicked her tongue. "I'm not. Maybe. Just…open it. It's for you. A payback. A thank-you."

"Hm, all right." I tore open the paper and pulled out a thank-you note with green ivy doodles all around it. It was on a brown, recycled-type paper, and a gift card fell out. "Uh, why did you get me a gift card?"

"Read it first!" she yelled, making me grin even harder.

It had been years since anyone had given me a gift or written me a note. My cheeks burned as I read her loopy handwriting. She wrote how leaves grew off stems—messy and pretty and organic looking.

Dear Fritz—thank you for so much. Showing me so many things a normal twenty-two-year-old should know. The lake, the farmer's market, the store...you've changed my life. Now I want to change yours.

You eat so many sweets. All the time. But this place is known for vegan desserts that will make you weep. Enjoy.

N

"This is for spotting me the cash at the market. And just being a good friend, even though you're probably paid to do that." Her eyes were downcast, and she pushed her hands behind her back, refusing to look at me.

"Thank you, Nora. This is nice."

"Of course. I hope you eat there. Angelica at the foundation was telling me about it and how she wants to use them as the desserts at the big gala coming up, and she sent me there to taste test them. I almost cried."

"She sent you to taste test?" My warm feeling went away thinking about my mom's go-to gal when she was out of town. They had never once done a taste test in all the years my mom threw galas. Not once. This made me uneasy. "What else did she have you do?"

"Go select paper for the flyers, even though I believe our campaign should be on social media. We should go paperless for the entire event. Silent auction, raffles, tickets in the door. She insists she has that part under control," she said, her tone didn't agree with the stubborn set of her chin. It was clear as day that she disagreed with Angelica.

"Have you proposed the social media campaign?"

"Yes. Of course. I have this whole proposal together about a new look with a cleaner tagline and how to engage people online instead of just telling them information." She huffed a bit and took a step back, farther into the foyer. "When I get this damn money to start my own place, I won't have to try to convince people it's a good idea. No one cares to know that I've helped my parents' modest charity grow their platform."

"What else do they have you doing there during the day?" I asked, feeling a throb at the back of my head. It annoyed me because I would've done the same thing Angelica was doing—giving the heiress pointless work to keep her busy. Nora was more than an airhead though. Her ideas were creative and had merit. "Could you try another department besides marketing?"

"Mrs. Carter arranged for me to be there, so I imagine other departments will not be thrilled with the prospect of me being put there. It's...fine. Nothing I can't handle." She pursed her lips and jutted her thumb over her shoulder. "I should head back. I'm reaching out to Anthony again."

"I have another date lined up for you." I changed the subject, plotting for a way to get more information from Angelica without letting Nora find out who I was for real. "You down to get drinks tomorrow?"

She narrowed her eyes and tapped one finger on the side of her black dress. "The last one didn't really go as planned. Not sure if these night outs are helpful for me."

"It's all part of the experience. Plus, it'll show your parents you're giving this a genuine shot, right?" I pushed off the door frame, holding the note and gift card close to my chest, and needed her to say yes. I couldn't explain why I desperately wanted her to agree to this date. Partially because no one gave her a shot at the foundation, or the fact she was going to try to email *Anthony* again. She needed a distraction in more ways than one.

"Tomorrow."

"Yes. Whiskey Rose."

"Will you be there too?"

"Nope. You'll meet him there. I can drop you off if you want. And pick you up if you're more comfortable," I said, about ready to smack myself because what was I going to do? Sit in the parking lot like I was my dad waiting for me to get out of track practice? I scoffed but didn't take it back. "Your call, Nora."

"You're being quite nice and really want me to do this. Why?"

"I think," I said, taking a breath to buy an extra second, "you need to prove yourself at the foundation, and instead of being by yourself at night, you should experience things before you go back to living in your palace and plant world. You've missed a lot being sheltered. Not trying to harp on you, but you have. That's the truth."

"You're right. People see me as this spoiled, dumb girl with idiotic dreams," she said, her voice going low as her face twisted into a frown. "Maybe they'll trust me or view me as a normal person if I date. Yes. Helen talks about her dating life all the time, and people to eat it up. Maybe I can be more like Helen."

"No one should be *more* like Helen. You don't know her well enough yet," I said, laughing because Helen was a three times divorced hellion who wanted sex, a good time, and had a the kindest heart. She put her soul into the foundation, but her personal life was a mess. A whole trash fire of a mess.

"She is a bit much, isn't she?" Nora laughed. "Fine. Tomorrow, I'll meet this friend of yours for drinks."

"No marriage or plant talk, right? That's more second date material."

"Got it." She grinned and pushed a nonexistent hair behind her ear. "Get the desserts. Trust me."

"Didn't realize you knew about my sweet tooth."

"It's obvious. You're always eating," she teased, and she returned to her door before turning and waving. She raked her gaze over me, her face flushing, and my stomach tightened.

It was strange, but I didn't want to go back into my apartment alone. I liked being out here, talking to her, hearing her singsong voice and experiences at the foundation. I enjoyed watching her gestures and hearing her laugh, and I ran a hand over my beard, trying to prolong the conversation. Nothing came out. "Well, I should—"

"I'm just gonna go," she said at the same time, somehow making the moment even more awkwardly delightful.

With a slight chuckle, I went back in and closed the door,

rereading the note and smiling to myself. I put the note on the fridge and popped open a beer. Watching the Cubs play the Reds was the perfect way to zone out and keep my mind off Nora.

An hour later, Gilly and Grace walked in carrying tacos and margarita mix. My stomach growled when the aroma of carne asada hit my nostrils. Grace eyed the plants without saying a word, and I arched a brow. "Jealous?"

"Not even a little. They're named?"

"Obviously. Do you *not* name a plant? Grace, come on."

She snorted as Gilly poured three drinks, and we all sat on the couch.

While Grace and I took sips of our drink, Gilly tapped her toes on the carpet and looked from me to Grace a few times.

"Spill it. You're being strange," I said, tipping my glass to her. "Are you calling off the wedding? Getting a face tattoo?"

"Jesus, no." She stood and twisted her hands together in the front. "I'm getting married. To Christopher."

"Yes, we're aware, thank you so much," Grace said, a hint of a tease to her voice.

"Shut it, you." She narrowed her eyes at our friend. "We'd stalled on setting a date because of so many things with his sister in college and our parents, and well, we finally decided to just go for it. We chose a date."

"And?" I said, legit thrilled for her. "When?"

"September 25."

"Sounds perfect," Grace said, holding up her glass. "Cheers to—"

"No, not yet." Gilly took a deep breath and looked us both in the eye. "I kept going back and forth about this, but I'm not a traditional or conventional person. I'm weird and want this to be done my way. That's with both of you standing up with me. I'm not doing a maid of honor or a best man or anything like that. I want the two of you, my closest best friends on the planet, up there with me when I marry the man of my dreams. Are you in?"

"Um, oh my God, yes," Grace said, standing up and hugging her.

It took me a second before my face burst into a grin and I joined them. It was like we were in college again, a little too drunk and emotional from watching the entirety of *The Office,* and my chest filled with happiness for my sister. I hugged them back, hard.

"You guys are the best," Gilly said between sniffs. "Ugh, I was so nervous to ask."

"Which is dumb," I said, giving her shoulder a squeeze. "We'd do anything for you."

Gilly gave us a toothy grin as someone knocked on the door, and both of the women stared at me—Grace with curiosity and Gilly with amusement. "Must be your neighbor," she said, wiggling her brows.

"Plant lady?"

"That's the one," Gilly said to Grace.

"Shut up, both of you." I rolled my eyes and gave them my meanest glare. With one last look at my idiot friends, I opened the door and found Nora there with tears down her face. "Nora, what's wrong?"

"It's my dad. There was an accident."

Chapter Eleven

"What do you mean?" I asked, my soul hurting for her. Her dark-rimmed eyes and the utter shock on her face worried me. She had to have been crying for hours. "What happened?"

She hiccupped, and I put a hand on her shoulder, hoping it was comforting. She leaned into me entirely so her head rested on my chest as she sobbed. "Car accident. H-He rolled o-over."

"Is he...all right?" I asked, my throat tight and dry as I rubbed her back. Grace and Gilly were dead silent behind me. I gently guided Nora outside my door. I would tell them about this later, but this should be a private moment between Nora and me.

"I th-think so. He's in the hospital three hours away. I don't know how to see him. My mother is helpless. Oh, what if he doesn't make it?"

"You can't think like that." I rubbed my hand up and down her arm, hating the way her face twisted with misery. "Who have you talked to?"

"My mom sent a text with the information. I tried calling, but she broke down," she said, sniffing and clutching my shirt hard. It stung, but I didn't say anything. "What do I do? What do I do, Fritz? I can't just stay here. It's my father! He thinks he's young and does too much, and my mom fawns over him and…oh my God," she cried, her body trembling against mine.

"Let's go."

"Hm?" She looked up at me, her mouth just a foot away from mine, and her brown eyes swirled with pain and desperation. "Go?"

"I'll drive you there. Right now. You want to see him, right?"

"Yes. Yes, I do." She let go of me and took a step back. She stood straighter and met my gaze. "I didn't even think to ask you. It's your job! Duh!" She smiled and backstepped toward her place. "Let me change. We'll leave in two minutes."

The pang in my chest hung around longer than I'd like. *It was my job.* That's why she thought I volunteered to drive three hours for her to see her dad. That meant I'd have to call into work sick, miss part of the morning, and adjust my life. All for her. And she thought it was my job. I pressed my forehead with my fingers to rid myself of the negative cloud her words put over me. This was about her. Her family. Not my weird feelings.

I stepped back into my place, shoved my hands in my pockets, and sighed. "Her dad had an accident. I'm going to drive her up to see him."

Gilly's face fell, and Grace set her drink down on the table, frowning. "Oh, I'm sorry. Is he okay?"

"I think. She wasn't clear. I guess her mom is helpless right now." I chewed on the side of my lip, hating that I could still picture Nora's distraught expression. I blinked, wanting to get rid of it, and focused on my sister and Grace. "You can stay here as long as you want. Finish the food, relax. Maybe I can ask if you'll take care of Nora's plants if we're gone long?"

"Sure," Gilly said, nodding too fast as she moved over to me and pulled me into a hug. "You're such a good man, Fritz. I know we don't tell you enough, but you are."

"I'll keep you posted."

Nora had changed into black leggings and another oversize shirt that said PASSION. Her water bottle hung from the side of her goofy backpack. Exactly like the first time I'd seen her at the airport. Out of place, weird, yet still adorable in her *Nora* way. This time, instead of being put off by it, it made me smile.

"Did you get dinner yet?" I asked, my stomach growling at the uneaten tacos.

"Oh. No. I don't think I could eat right now." She clutched her phone against her chest and took a shaky breath.

"Well, I want to grab fast food once we get on the road. It'll be quick, I promise."

She sucked her lip into her mouth and nodded, and I couldn't stop myself from putting my arm around her shoulder as we walked outside to my car. The truck wasn't fit for the drive, and I unlocked the Beemer. Thank *god* my friend returned it yesterday. Her eyes widened for a second before I said, "Carter's car."

"Right."

It wasn't a lie. It did belong to a Carter—me. I moved toward her and held out my hand for her bag, but she stared at it, frown lines forming at the corners of her eyes. "I'll take your bag."

"Oh, sure."

She needed direction, and while Gilly would say I was very bossy, I considered it taking charge. I took the bag, put it in the trunk, and went back to the passenger-side door where Nora leaned against it with an unreadable expression on her face. "Get in and put on your seat belt. Come on, Nora."

She listened, not saying a word, and I shut the door once she was in safely. It felt right, somehow, taking care of her right now. I could be what she needed, even if she thought it was my fake job as the chauffeur.

I started the car, pulled onto the road, and sneaked a look at her, but she stared at her phone with her lips parted in an *O*. "You hear anything else?"

"No."

"Is there anyone you could call, to get updates?"

"No. It's just my mom and dad and me. There is the house staff, but my parents always kept a firm line of business between them and us." She pulled on one of her bracelets, and her tone got so sad.

It was like she reached into my chest and covered my whole heart with her hand and squeezed.

"We keep our circle close ever since we learned our closest friends were stealing from us in thinly veiled attempts at helping. They took millions over the years, and while my parents cut off contact with most of their social circles...I lost the only real friend I thought I had. I stopped trying after that because I couldn't trust anyone's intentions."

Fuck. The realization we had nearly identical stories was like a bucket of ice-cold water being dumped on me in the middle of a blizzard. It chilled my bones and made me shift uncomfortably in my seat. Maybe we weren't that different after all.

I tried to respond, but I had to clear my throat twice before words could form. "I'm sorry."

She shrugged, letting out a deep sigh as she typed on her phone, and a heavy silence filled the car. I felt no need to fill it—rather, I used the quiet to wrap my mind around her confession. Was that why she was so weird? Did she put up these bizarre walls to keep people out? Or was that how she got into plants—a way to distract herself from the betrayal? God, I wanted to know so damn bad.

But I wasn't going to ask.

God, how could I try to set her up with people when she clearly had trust issues too?

An hour went by before my stomach growled, breaking the comfortable silence. Nora slid me a look, and a hint of a smile curved her lip up. "Work up an appetite chopping wood today?"

"Yes. I chopped wood and started fires in the wilderness," I teased her right back. "I need food, or I might just wither away."

"No, you're way too meaty for that." She blushed as soon as she said the words and held up a hand. "I meant, strong. You know, you're beefy. Buff. You have muscles. That's what I meant."

"Ah, thanks for clarifying what *meaty* meant. I wasn't sure."

"Ugh, stop." She closed her eyes, but her smile crept out. "We can stop. I wouldn't want you to be frail."

"Thanks for your kindness, Doc."

"That's the second time you've called me that. Why?"

I pulled over for a fast-food joint and flashed her a grin. "Poison Ivy, Dr. Pamela Lillian Isley?"

"What?"

"Batman's occasional love interest? Obsessed with plants? Gotham's botanist? Nora, I refuse to accept you don't understand what I'm saying." I scoffed and shook my head as we pulled up to order food. I got two burgers, fries, and milk shakes. Even if she insisted she wasn't hungry, she needed something, and if she hadn't experienced the joy of dipping French fries into a milkshake, she'd learn on my watch.

The salty and sweet combination, the hot and cold, it was Midwest bliss.

"I've heard of Batman. I don't live under a rock."

"No, but you do live inside a greenhouse, so it's possible you missed the greatest comics of all time. Poison Ivy is iconic."

"Hm, well, I like that."

"She has wild red hair too. Yours is pink, but close enough."

"Doc isn't an insult then?" she asked, her voice holding the tiniest bit of hope. That hope flooded my chest, making me feel warm and weird.

"Not even a little bit, crazy plant lady. Just promise me something," I said, needing to lighten the mood. It wasn't heavy, but it was different, and I didn't like the way she was making me feel right now. Exposed. Like she saw beneath the charismatic persona I wore every day and liked me for who I really was.

But I couldn't forget the bottom line. She wanted to marry me to get her inheritance, and while I knew she wasn't a gold digger like Samantha, it was still manipulative. She wanted to use me. She wanted to be with me without getting to know who I really was— because I owed her a favor.

My gut twisted. I couldn't forget that was her goal. To marry Anthony. Repeating that over and over helped the ice form back around my heart, keeping it cold and safe like I preferred.

"Sure, yes. What is it?" she asked, her voice a little shaky.

"Don't try to kill me with any of those green babies of yours, okay?"

She snorted, like I wanted her to, and we got the food and were back on the road within a few minutes. I devoured the burger and fries before she'd opened her bag. "I need you to trust me."

"For what?"

"What I'm about to share with you."

Her face got serious, and she tilted her body toward me. I wanted to take a picture of how damn adorable she looked—brows set in determination, her mouth slightly opened. I let myself enjoy it for two seconds before I said, "This is the biggest secret I've discovered living here."

"What is it?" she asked, rather breathless.

"Dip your fries into your chocolate milkshake."

She blinked once and then again, not moving from her stance. "That's...that's not a secret."

"Yes, it is. Do it. You'll understand." I jutted my chin toward her drink and bag of food, and she groaned as she picked it up and did as I asked. She hesitated as she got chocolate goodness on the fry and put it in her mouth.

It was weird how much I looked forward to her response. Would she thank me for showing her the best dessert in the world? Would her large brown eyes widen with awe?

"Hm," she said, chewing in silence.

Hm.

That was her response? No. That wouldn't do.

"Hm? That's all you have to say about this magical combination? Nora, I might make you walk the rest of the way."

Her shoulders sank at the reminder of why we were in the car together. I was such an asshole. I'd wanted to tease her but missed the mark. Shit. I needed to distract her. Ask about plants? Her greenhouse? My heart raced in my chest as I stared at her grief-stricken face, and I panicked, unable to form words with my goddamn mouth.

But then she dipped another fry into the shake, and her eyes crinkled on the sides. "This is...I can't quite put a finger on it."

"Divine. Excellent. Amazing. You can use any of those words."

She laughed, and just like that, the tightness in my chest disappeared. It was crazy how emotionally invested I was in her happiness when I still wasn't sure if I liked the woman. We were friends, sure, but that damn story about losing her only friend hadn't left my mind since she shared it.

After this trip, I needed distance from her. But until then, I'd do whatever I could to keep that smile on her pretty face.

We argued about the best desserts for the rest of the drive, but when I got off the exit and neared the hospital in a suburb of Chicago, she quieted. The energy she had talking about organic chocolate evaporated like the mist on a hot summer morning, and I had no idea what would happen once we pulled up.

Did I get out with her? Could her mom recognize me? Did she want me to stay, wait for her? She'd have no way of getting back, and it wouldn't be the worst thing if I had to find a hotel for the night. I tapped my fingers on the wheel to the erratic beat of my heart. Once we parked, I tried to read her face.

It was blank. Just wide eyes, lips pressed together. Was she worrying about her dad's health or her mom? Probably both. "Hey," I said, unable to take the tension anymore. "It'll be okay. I know it."

"You don't." She took a shaky breath. "But I appreciate the effort." She unbuckled and got out of the car, waiting next to the door, and I jumped out to get her backpack.

In small moments like this, the lie between us came to light. It was easy to forget the lie, that I worked for my parents, when she laughed and shared parts of herself with me. But it was there, and it was just the thing I needed to put a barrier between us.

"Would you like me to wait for you in the parking lot? I can stay at a hotel and drive you back in the morning."

"Let me talk to my mom first. I'm hoping, honestly, that they'll say to hell with this plan and I can move home." Her eyes got all watery, and her throat clicked when she swallowed. "This will show them they need me there to help."

"Right." The sinking feeling in my gut meant nothing. If she moved home with her parents, I could get rid of all the plants and not worry about her burning the place down. It would be a good thing for her to return to her sheltered, protected life. But the feeling morphed into crushing disappointment, and I took a step back, like that would help construct the few walls she tore down. "Well, I'll wait an hour or so."

"Are you sure you don't…want to…" She trailed off, pointing her thumb over her shoulder, but she stopped and shook her head. "Yes, I'll keep you posted in an hour."

She walked toward the hospital entrance, and I ran my hand over my chest, willing the uncomfortable feeling to disappear. Nora and I weren't going to be lifelong friends. There was no way. It was for the best. I knew it.

But it still ate at me not knowing if I'd get to see her weird hair or mismatched outfits every day.

Chapter Twelve

It was ten, and I still hadn't heard from her. Surely, visiting hours would be over by now. I needed to take a leak. Really fucking bad. I turned off my car, locked it, and made my way into the hospital to find a restroom.

The last thing I wanted Nora to worry about was texting me, but it was killing me not knowing what was going on. I hated not knowing how she was doing. Was she holding it together? Was she doing all right? Was she breaking down because of how tough everything was? I could have gone to a bar to watch a game to pass the time, but I was compelled to stay close by in case she needed me.

It's your responsibility as a human, man, brother, friend, son to always look out for those who need help. It's not only your duty but a privilege. My mom's voice came into my mind as I washed my hands. They were unconventional parents in many ways, but they'd instilled in us the value of family, humility, and duty. Help took various forms, and while they preferred money and donations, Gilly channeled it by teaching and making change in the community by focusing on literacy. Christopher, too, had a passion for it.

Helping Nora through this crisis was the right thing to do.

I was getting a water from a vending machine when a familiar voice carried from the hallway. *Nora.*

"Let me come back, please. I can help with the care and the grounds. I belong at home with you both," Nora said, her voice shaking at the end, and the same overwhelming disappointment hit me. She hated her life here. Even though I'd tried to make it bearable, had I done enough?

"Leanora, this isn't up for discussion. You heard your father. He'll be fine."

"He's getting older, and you can't do everything."

"I can handle things just fine. It's you, dear, who need to learn to live! You're doing so well down there and—"

"No, I'm not. Most of the Carters are all out of town, and it's just me with all these people who think I'm ridiculous. They don't listen to a word I say and laugh at me when I leave. It's horrible. I want to come home. I'll just…wait five more years until I'm of age to get the money."

"Nora, stop. Listen to me."

Footsteps thudded closer, and I froze. If they came in here, I could pretend I wasn't listening, but there was no way to prove that. The only way out was to walk by them.

"Mom, please. I'm not made for this type of life. I can't do it."

"You will. You will see this through. I don't care. We spoiled you despite our best intentions, and you have the biggest heart and best soul, but you need to grow up. Away from us."

Nora sniffed, and my face burned for her. This was brutal to overhear. I could only imagine how embarrassed she'd be if she knew I was right there. But it sounded like her father was doing okay, so that was the best news possible.

"You and Dad are all I have."

"That's the problem, sweetheart. That's a not a life."

My muscles tensed, waiting to hear what Nora said, but no sounds came from the hallway. I sneaked a peek and found them gone. I sighed in relief and made my way back out to the car, replaying her words over and over. Nora thought her life was just with her parents and the mansion, and her plants. Maybe that stemmed from the issue with losing her only friend, or...it was fear. She was outside her comfort zone in every way possible, and that was terrifying.

Like if I quit my job. Would that be the same thing she felt right now? Without direction, but the spark of a maybe? It was tough. I scrubbed my hands over my face and got my phone out of my pocket when it pinged.

Nora: He's okay. Heading to your car now.

Fritz: glad to hear it.

I tapped my fingers again, my anxiety over how to act when I saw her building. She would probably be sad or even annoyed at her parents. Her mom pushed her out of her bubble, again, while she was already worried about her dad. She might double down on trying to find Anthony or shut down completely. I know if my parents forced me to do anything...I'd shut them out. I'd rebel against everything they said.

A rebellious Nora. I liked the idea of that. Doing all the things most people got out of their systems as teenagers. Staying out late. Watching R-rated movies. Maybe a few X-rated ones, even. Skinny-dipping. Going to second base in the back of a dark movie theater. Fuck, I'd love to corrupt her.

Had she ever steamed up the back seat of a Beemer? Heat prickled my skin. I adjusted my growing erection.

Knock. Knock.

I jumped.

Nora stood outside the car.

What the fuck was I doing? Fantasizing about the nightmare next door? I'd lost my mind, clearly.

I got out, refusing to analyze the lightness in my chest that coincided with her return, and took her bag from her. "I'm so glad he's okay."

"Me too." She chewed her bottom lip as I set her stuff in the trunk and held the passenger door for her. Her floral shampoo wafted my direction, and I breathed it in. "Thanks for, uh, waiting. I didn't know it took that long."

This was the first time she thanked me, really thanked me, and I smiled, reaching out to squeeze her hand because she looked so damn sad. Resigned. Like she'd signed up for her defeat.

"You're welcome. Are you up for telling me what happened, or do you want to listen to a podcast on gardening?"

"Did you download a podcast on gardening?"

"Maybe I researched them. I became a plant dad recently, and I need to take care of them." God, what was I saying? Who was I? *Plant dad?*

She smiled, staring at me under her long lashes, and she blushed. *That* was why I'd said it. That look. To make her smile. To make her happy. "Let's listen. Maybe I'll be up for talking later."

"Sure. Sounds good, Doc."

She smirked again, and we got into the car, the weight in my chest gone and I had the weirdest urge to hold her hand. I did no such thing because how would I explain that? Instead, I rested it on the gear shift and relaxed knowing I'd have more time with my interesting neighbor.

Chapter Thirteen

MEETING ANGELICA FOR LUNCH TWO DAYS LATER WASN'T TOO OUT of the ordinary. In the past, I would've brought lunch in for her or my mom, maybe have Gilly tag along, and it'd be a nice social lunch. But I couldn't risk going into the office and having Nora see me.

Not after her sad reply to my email. It appeared that after her parents banished her to *living on her own,* she was set on talking to Anthony, determined that he could help solve her problems. A part of me hated that she wasn't trying to succeed on her own. She could do it. I'd seen how focused she could be when she put her brilliant yet weird mind to it. Relying on *Anthony* seemed like giving up.

"Thanks for asking me out of the office," Angelica said, grinning after she took a bite of her salad. The woman had eaten like a bird the entire time I'd known her. She dabbed a napkin on the corners of her mouth before leaning back into the plush red chair at the Italian bistro three blocks from the foundation office. "This is nice, even though I have a million things to do."

"You deserve an hour break." I meant it. She worked her ass off for my parents, and with their constant globe-trotting, Angelica was the backbone of it all. "I wanted to ask about Leanora Atwood."

"Oh." Her eyes dimmed, like the question offended her. "What about the heiress?"

"Why the tone?" I tilted my head and forced my voice to come out nonchalant. Gilly and I were also recipients of a huge sum of money, but the way she said *heiress* bothered me. She was misguided and sheltered, but the disgust in Angelica's voice was unmistakable. "How is that going?"

"Well, no one wants her here. I'm not sure what your mother is doing. She called and demanded we find a place for her, which put me in a weird spot. Our marketing and branding teams already had a plan for the year, and this pink-haired airhead comes in talking about plants. It's... Why are you frowning at me?"

"I don't know her well," I lied, running the pads of my fingers over the white tablecloth, planning my next move. I wouldn't offend Angelica. She was family, but she wore the same expression I had the first week I knew Nora. She was an odd-colored onion who needed ten layers ripped off before her heart showed. "But I did hear she actually helped her family's foundation increase donations and engagement online. Last I checked, we needed help on both those fronts."

"And I'm supposed to just give her this job? We spent months hiring a VP for marketing. I can't just ignore Ned's entire outline." Her face twisted into impatience, and she leaned forward, like she had a secret to tell me. "She wants to incorporate Pic Clock, FlashGram, all these social media apps that cater to the younger crowd. It's not a horrible idea, but our target audience is upper middle-class, middle-age."

"Angelica, young people care about making a difference in the world. Millennials and Gen Zs are constantly searching for purpose, to have a legacy. Statistically, these age groups are more likely to get involved and help. Engaging them and reaching out to them could bring a whole new element to the foundation."

She huffed, clearly annoyed I was right. "So I should let her in?"

"I'm saying you shouldn't have her going to *taste test* food."

She blushed and took a sip of water, avoiding my gaze. "That wasn't my call—that was Peter's. She made a comment about how horrible he was to the environment after he tossed a ton of plastic into the trash. She went into the garbage and rinsed it all off before putting it into the recycling. It…left an impression and might've rubbed people the wrong way."

"Peter should recycle."

"Fritz," she said, her motherly tone making me sit up straighter. "You don't get involved all that much with how things are run. Why this time? I'm not complaining but this isn't…you."

She was right. I broke the piece of bread in two, pulling apart a bite and chewing it. I wasn't quite sure of the answer myself, why I was getting involved on Nora's behalf. Hearing her break down in front of her mom, hearing her ideas that were actually good, and if I were honest…I did owe her. She'd covered for me, and I wasn't going to marry her to return the favor.

This could make up some of that debt.

"Over a decade ago, Nora helped me out with something serious. She's weird, but brilliant. Don't let her quirks overshadow her talents. Give her a shot."

Angelica's face softened, and she nodded. "You're right. I have been letting her oddities cloud my judgment of her."

"It's hard not to, but try. That's all I ask."

"Deal. Now, why hasn't your sister stopped by in weeks? I want all the wedding details."

I rolled my eyes and was thankful the subject had changed now that I'd done what I'd set out to do—clear my conscience.

Damn it. Why did I set this up at a bar where all the workers knew my name? I'd set my own trap, my own demise. If she heard anyone call me Anthony, the entire thing was done. Over. Everything would change, and that couldn't happen. No favors, no weddings, no women wanting me for their own agenda. My anxiety was getting ridiculous—no one ever called me Anthony, and I had to stop freaking out for the sake of freaking out. It wasn't productive.

I wiped the back of my neck. The humid summer air was heavier than normal, like it might rain. I scanned the patio covered with lights. It smelled like spilled beer and nachos—one of the worst- yet best-smelling things ever. It reminded me of college, of the glory days, and I grinned at Dave.

He held up his beer from his spot in the booth. "Hey, man."

"Dude, your sleeve looks sick." I jutted my chin toward his arm covered in bright colors and wicked lines. "You design this yourself?"

"Sure did. Took forever, but it's done." He twisted his forearm, and the images from his favorite album covers took over his skin, coming to life with the color. He'd wanted to finish that for three years. I clapped his back.

"You look cool as shit."

"Cooler than you now, even with your beard. You going for a lumberjack look? Chicks find your clean-shaven face too pretty?"

"Fuck off." I laughed, welcoming the shit-talking. I lived for this. The escape after the office. Even my meeting with Angelica caused the same unsettling feeling in my gut. She had purpose, a mission, something she worked every day toward. I didn't.

I ordered a Moscow mule and was about to ask Dave about his sister when Nora walked in. I had to do a double take. My pulse drummed in my ears. She wore bright-red lipstick, a skintight, half see-through, half lacy black shirt that showed every single curve, and tight, dark-green jeans. She spun around, frowning as she scanned the room, giving me an eyeful of her back.

It was like she forgot half the shirt.

Fuck. I swallowed hard at all the thoughts swirling in my mind. Her smooth back, the fact she couldn't be wearing a bra, the way her jeans hugged her ass. My throat got tight, and my gut tightened at the aggressive wave of lust. *Jesus.*

Dave whistled. "Damn, please, for the love of God, tell me that's your friend?"

His jaw hung open as he stared right at Nora, and I had the strange urge to reach over and slam his jaw shut.

This is what I wanted.

"Nora," I said, my voice way too scratchy. I took another drink, already counting down seconds until this was over. But what did *over* mean? Listening through the wall as Dave gave her an orgasm? Or her staying at his place and me worrying if she knew how to get back.

She turned at my voice, and a toothy, real smile formed on her pretty pixie face. I couldn't remember the last time a woman looked at me with that much joy. Genuine joy. "Fritz! Oh my gosh, hi!"

She jogged, not walked, *jogged* over to our booth, and her gaze never left my face. "Guess what?"

"What?" I asked, like I wasn't absolutely desperate to know what she was going to say. She slid into the seat next to me, and I had to make a fist to keep myself from touching her. Her body radiated heat, and every one of my senses went into overdrive.

The feel of her next to me. The way she smelled. How she looked me in the eye when she spoke, utterly ignoring Dave. The curiosity to know what her lips tasted like eating at me. I needed to get it the fuck together.

I took a breath, holding the drink up to my mouth so I wouldn't smell *her.* "What is it, Nora?"

"The foundation. They are letting me finally try one of my proposals. I was about to pull my damn hair out, well, even more of it." She laughed and only then noticed Dave. "Hello, hi."

She blushed when Dave flashed her his *pickup* smile. I'd seen it countless times, and it worked almost every time. She chewed on the side of her lip, staring at my friend, and I regretted this entire setup.

"Nora Atwood," Dave said, the want in his voice obvious to anyone in earshot.

God, it was hot. I downed the rest of the drink and flagged the waiter to order another.

"What should I try, Fritz?" she asked, looking at me again with the same wide eyes. I liked the trust reflecting back at me, and just as I was about to respond, Dave cut in.

"Oh, you need to try the special."

"Why?"

"Whiskey sour. It has egg in it."

"An egg? No." She set her hands on the table, her bright-green nails covered in dirt. It annoyed me I'd noticed.

I needed to get that tattooed on my goddamn face so I wouldn't forget.

Nora bounced in her seat, smiling at the waiter as he took her order, and once he left, Nora leaned over the table, giving me a full view of her back.

It shouldn't affect me. It was a back. Everyone had one. But…the smooth skin teased me when the light flickered over it, and I focused on the bowl of nuts in the center. That was safer.

"So how are you liking living here? Fritz said you're here for a few months, right?" Dave moved, and I knew the second Nora spotted his arm.

She let out the smallest gasp. "Your tattoo." She reached over the table, but her fingers stopped before she touched his arm. "Wow, can I?"

"Absolutely." Dave smiled, hard, and I couldn't blame him. Nora's voice was filled with awe, and I could only imagine the expression she wore as she trailed her soft fingers up his forearm.

Sweat beaded on my forehead and the drink tasted bland. I needed to leave.

"These are so beautiful, Dave. I love the patterns."

"I designed it."

"No!" She grinned at him, and his expression softened into awe.

My knee slammed into the table as I tried to get up.

Nora narrowed her eyes and tilted her head to the side. "You all right, Fritz?"

"Yeah, need to use the restroom. Can I slide out?"

"Of course, yeah." She moved, her back right in front of my face, and I finally took a breath. Not being right next to her helped ease my thoughts from going down a path that was non grata. She licked her bottom lip as she stared at Dave.

Dave arched a brow, and *Jesus*. Did they have to eye fuck right in front of me?

"You two seem to have hit it off. I'll be at the bar for a bit." I forced a smile and winked at Nora, hoping that made her feel safe. She looked at me too intently, and I excused myself.

I sat at the farthest part of the bar, out of view from their booth, and pulled out my phone. Maybe getting laid would help rid me of this weird, unwanted attraction. There were a million reasons why this wouldn't be a goddamn thing. A million and more.

But.

It was the *but* that made me look up to try to see what they were doing. Was he sitting next to her, hearing her talk about her plants and plans? Did he know her heart was golden even though it came in a weird package?

I needed to go. Distract myself from my distract Nora plan.

Fritz: hey, you okay if I head home? Not feeling well.

Nora: Oh no! yes, I'm good. Sorry you don't feel okay.

Fritz: If you need help, let me know. Anytime.

Nora:

There. I'd freed myself, and she could be smitten with Dave. He was a great guy, and I should be happy. Yet as I got a rideshare to head home, I kept hoping the date turned out to be a disaster.

Chapter Fourteen

I wasn't waiting up for her. It was eleven o'clock, and papers covered my coffee table, my laptop open, and a list of small businesses who focused on being green. There were six, including the coffee women—Carla and her partner. Worrying about Nora took too much effort and energy, so I channeled it to focus on being a middleman.

She still wasn't back. It was fine. They could be getting more drinks or at his place. Fine. Great. I pinched the bridge of my nose and tried to relax. I eyed the plants, refusing to *talk* to them, but if I were to, I'd ask them to give me some of those relaxed vibes she insisted I needed. The air did seem lighter in my place, but I pushed thoughts of plants, Nora, and her lips out of my mind.

If I were going to consider networking on behalf of Carla, I couldn't flail around without purpose. My ambition kept me up at night, making me constantly overthink my next steps, what else I could do, and I still had that, but it was pointing me in the direction of helping Carla.

I reached out to Sam at Fast Financial. Terrible name, great business, and he agreed to give me a call to hear me out. I'd tell him about Carla, their business, and get the gears in motion. Starting with Carla was the best option. See how that went, and then maybe try it with other small businesses.

Yes, that would work. I got her card from my wallet and sent her an email, hoping to set up a time to meet next week. My blood pumped like it was the bottom of the ninth inning and the winning run on third. Maybe she'd take me up on it, maybe she wouldn't. Either way, it was a start. I fell onto the couch, not straining to hear any movement from the hallway. *It's eleven fifteen.*

She had to work the next day, so she'd be back. I smiled to myself before it turned to a frown. I was a hypocrite. How many times had I gone out, hooked up, and still gone to work the next day?

Annoyed with myself yet again, I opened the patio door and sat on the one chair I had out there. The scent of an impending storm had grown stronger since I'd left the bar. I rocked the chair back on the legs and looked at the sky. Stars littered the ink-black color, and a sense of longing hit me out of nowhere. It'd be nice to have someone to share these moments with.

When did I become so melancholic?

A knock sounded at my door, and I frowned. The only person it could be was Nora, but I hadn't heard her come in. I bolted up, my stomach in knots. Did something happen with Dave?

"Nora," I said, swinging the door open and assessing her to see if she was hurt. Her brows were furrowed together, and she had a brown bag clutched against her chest.

"I brought you soup." She pressed her lips together tight as she held the bag out with a stiff arm, almost pushing it against me. "You said you didn't feel well, and you came to the bar with me, and well, chicken noodle soup is the best cure."

"Yeah?" Fuck, my heart almost skipped a beat, and I smiled way too large for someone who was supposed to be sick. I took the warm bag from her. "Thank you."

"I tried to find the best soup in the area, and most of them were closed, but this came from Soupo Loupos." She fidgeted with the edge of her shirt, her cheeks tinging pink at the top.

"Love that place."

"Good. Good. I'm glad." She flashed a quick smile and then looked at the ground. "Well, I, uh—"

"How was Dave?" I had to ask. I needed to know, or I'd obsess over it all night.

"Oh." She blushed even deeper and pursed her lips to one side. "He was great. Very charming. We're getting dinner on Saturday."

"Great." God, saying it was akin to swallowing rocks. It should be great. It was what I wanted. One sexy outfit wasn't going to cost me my sensibility. I was smarter than that. I cleared my throat and nodded, like forcing myself to be positive. "That's wonderful to hear. He's an awesome guy."

"Oh!" she said, her voice getting louder and clapping her hands together. "We should go on a double date!"

"No," I said, way too quickly. She flinched at my harsh tone, and I hated how I made her frown. "I'm not—I don't date."

She tilted her head to the side, her almost too-large eyes assessing me with warmth and curiosity. "Why not?"

"You're not the only one who has a betrayal story." I scratched the back of my neck and tried not to stare at her lips. They were still red, cherry red, so maybe he hadn't kissed her. She could've reapplied it— Gilly put on eighteen layers a day. *This isn't helpful.* "Thanks for the soup, Nora. Really. This was really nice of you."

"Of course. If you need anything, let me know. Like tissues or a blanket. I have those."

God, she was something. She looked proud, like having those two items was an accomplishment, and I refused to pop her bubble. "I should be okay, but I appreciate it."

Lightning flashed, brightening the entire door lobby, and a thundering boom followed. Nora jumped before recovering and giving me a small smile. She jutted her thumb over her shoulder. "I should get back. I'm not a fan of storms and prefer to hide under the covers."

"That doesn't surprise me in the least." My tone was softer than I meant it to be. I held the bag up. "Thanks again."

She was going on a date with Dave again, but she clearly thought about me being sick at the end of their night. That had to be a good sign. But a good sign for what? What the fuck did I want from this? I shut my door, hard, and set the bag of soup on the counter. Rain started coming down hard outside, and my mind now pictured Nora hiding under a blanket, worried about thunder.

This was unacceptable. She was weird. Level-ten weird. Thought I was a chauffeur because I had a beard. Just because I found her interesting, and attractive, didn't mean shit. Maybe a double date would be a good idea, to make sure she knew I wasn't letting her take up all this time in my mind.

Jesus, this was a lot. I got ready for bed, leaving only my boxers on. Before I slid under the covers, the power went out. Aside from the few flashes of lightning, it was pitch black. And quiet. No whirring, no fans, only silence and rain.

I went over my plan to talk to Carla three times, tossing and turning and unable to find a comfortable position. Every thirty seconds, I worried about Nora but shoved the thought away immediately. She'd be fine.

Right?

I'd check on her, make sure she had a flashlight. That was normal. Yeah. I got up and threw on some athletic shorts and found an old flashlight that I'd never put away after camping. I hit it twice, and it turned on. I made my way to her place. Maybe this would help me settle down and sleep.

"Nora," I said, knocking my knuckles on the door. I didn't bang, just in case she was asleep, but if she was afraid of storms, I doubted it. I waited thirty seconds, not hearing a thing. "Nora," I said louder, hitting the wood twice as loud. "You okay?"

Something thudded. Then another crash. "*Shit*" carried through the door, and I bit back a smile when she finally unlocked it. She rubbed her hip, and the flashlight illuminated her outfit.

Or lack thereof.

She wore a tiny gray tank top and even smaller boxer shorts. Jesus, her legs were longer than I'd imagined, and her chest was downright distracting. "Fritz, hi."

Thunder boomed, shaking the entire building.

Nora sucked in a breath. Her pulse hammered visibly at the base of her slender neck.

"I brought you this flashlight. Just in case."

"Oh, thank you." She took it from me, and the whole thing trembled in her hands. Now that I had a better view of her face, she looked pale. Really pale. "My phone died, so I didn't have light."

"Did you hurt your hip?"

"I ran into something, yeah. This will help. Th-Thanks." She forced a tight smile, the false bravado doing something to the knot in my chest, and I sighed.

"Want to stay in my place until the power comes back on?"

She gulped. "It's okay, I'm fine."

"You're trembling."

Fuck it. I reached over and put a hand on her bare shoulder. "You brought me soup. I can sit with you until the power returns. It's no big deal, really. I can't sleep anyway."

Her entire body relaxed under my touch, and she nodded, already moving past me with the flashlight pointed at my door. My anxiety spiked at the papers all over my table. *My finances.* "Uh, let me pick up real quick."

"No, don't even worry. It makes me happier knowing you're messy." She grinned at me as she climbed onto the couch. "You seem too stiff most of the time."

"I'm not stiff," I fired back, sounding mature as a teenager. "Maybe a bit."

She scrunched her nose and met my gaze, and I swore her attention dropped to my chest. Her teeth grazed her bottom lip, and heat entered her eyes as she stared at me, hard. That was going to be a legit problem if that heat was desire. A serious problem. One-sided attraction was one thing, but if she felt it too...no.

I shook my head and pointed to the blanket. "You cold?"

"No, it feels nice in here."

Well, there went my plan to cover up all her smooth skin. Her shoulders, collarbone, neck. All of it was silky, and each flash of lightning drew my attention to it. We sat in silence, the air thick with humidity and *spark.*

Was she thinking about me?

Did I want her to be?

God, this was why I didn't date. This shit was exhausting.

She let out a little sigh as she pulled her knees up to her chest. Thunder shook the place again, and she hugged herself tighter. "I've hated storms since I was a kid."

"Yeah, they freak my sister out too. When we were younger Gi— Gerry." I stumbled, almost saying Gilly and ruining it all. I cleared my throat. "Gerry and I would build these forts, and I'd pretend to be a weatherman to calm her down."

"What do you mean?"

"Forts. You've made a fort before, right?"

"I'm not an alien," she said, narrowing her eyes and holding up a finger. "No, I set that one up way too easy for you. I'm not! I've made a fort. I don't understand the weatherman part."

"I haven't thought about this in so long. I'd, uh…" I paused, remembering a time in Kansas where there was a tornado that did a shit ton of damage. That night, I did a bit about a weatherman who forgot what clouds were. Gilly laughed so hard she cried. "I'd do a bit. Like a skit."

"I want to see."

"Nora, no." I scoffed. "I'm not twelve."

"Oh, please!" She almost bounced on the cushion, her eyes wider than normal as she clasped her hands together. "I'm having a hard time seeing you be so goofy, and I need proof."

"I'm goofy, sometimes." I used to be, that was for sure. Hearing her say it was like a sledgehammer to my mind. When did I stop being goofy? Samantha? After or before her? It didn't matter. I'd lost a part of myself, and if being an idiot in front of Nora Atwood helped me find myself again, I'd do it.

And it had nothing to do with how happy she looked or the fact I might make her smile. I stood, grabbed the remote like a microphone and made my voice high and whiney as I went to the window. "Good evening, this is Wet Willy on Channel 4, and I'm reporting on the incredible rainfall we have in Champaign."

Nora covered her face with her hands, and my face heated like I'd shoved it in an oven, but I channeled my inner dorky self, the one with way too much confidence and nothing better to do than entertain my sister. "It's raining buckets! Buckets, I say!"

I pressed one hand to the pretend earpiece and nodded. "Hope you're not made of sugar because you will melt. Wet Willy has seen it happen before, I swear! You need a raincoat made of rubber so the water will bounce right off you! Can't have someone as sweet as you dissolve from a little rain, no sirree."

Nora cackled a full belly laugh, throwing her head back and releasing the most obnoxious sound in the world, like a goose and a car horn combined into one sound. That was her laugh. "Fritz. Oh shit. Oh shit." Water came out of her nose, and she stood, covering her nose with a hand. Her eyes watered, and she still let out that awful honking laugh sound, and I smiled so much it hurt my face.

"The restroom's right there if you need to clean up." I pointed to the door, not at all checking out her ass when she ran in there. God, that was freeing. Hearing that horrible laugh, not taking myself too seriously, it felt good. More than good.

"Uh Fritz," she said. "I didn't bring the light."

"You need that, huh? You need Wet Willy to bring it over there?"

She snorted like I'd wanted her to, and I brought the flashlight to the bathroom, sliding it inside for her just as the power kicked back on. The air conditioner started, the lights above the stove and cable box blinking at me, signaling the end of Nora being over here.

I sighed, the pang in my chest growing heavier. I couldn't recall the last time I didn't want the night to end like this. I turned the lights on and paced the living room until she came out.

"Yes!" she said, bursting out of the door with a huge smile on her face. "The power is on, Wet Willy. Can you believe it? The storm must have passed. The forecast says this is the last time it's going to rain all year, but I drought it," she teased.

My lips twitched, but I was too knotted up inside to fully appreciate her pun. If it'd been hard to keep my eyes off her in the dark, I was screwed with the lights on. So very screwed. Her thin shirt showed the outlines of her pebbled nipples, and her face was clear of any makeup and so pretty. Smooth skin, large eyes, long lashes. Full lips that got more distracting each day.

"Fritz," she said, the smile leaving her face, and she frowned. "What's wrong?"

"Nothing." *Get it together, asshole.* "Maybe just a bit embarrassed you saw Wet Willy's return after fifteen years."

"I'm glad I was here for it. He's a swell guy." She smiled again and chewed on the side of her lip as she placed one foot on top of the other, making her look a bit like a flamingo. "I'll get out of your hair. Thanks for letting me stay."

"Of course."

She walked up to me, and I froze, my gut tense.

I waited for her to reach out and touch me, but she never did. She gave me a shy smile, the same one I had seen her give Dave. My growing erection was becoming a problem.

"Keep the flashlight," I snapped, hating how my control dissolved around her.

She narrowed her eyes, and she hit the flashlight on her chest twice as she walked by me. "Thank you. I'll get my own and get this back to you."

"No rush. I have a few. I need them for camping."

"Camping?" she said, her eyes going wide as she turned to face me again. "Oh. You camp?"

"Yes."

Mental images of her in a tent, asking what a fire pit was for, and trying to sleep in a sleeping bag made me cackle. God, that would be a trip. She clicked her tongue, and fierce determination came over her face.

"Camping."

"It's this thing where you sleep outside in tents. Hike, swim, eat s'mores. You'd—" I took a shaky breath. "It's not your thing, Doc. I swear."

She let out a deep sigh, like she, too, was trying to find ways to delay her leaving my place. Once she got to the door, she tapped on the frame with her pointer finger before giving me one last look. A million questions swirled behind her dark-brown eyes, but she didn't ask a single one.

Her floral scent lingered in the air even after she'd shut the door behind her.

I had no idea what to do with my attraction to her, but at least she wasn't spending the night with Dave. But in two nights from now, after their second date, she might be. Unless I doubled with them like she'd suggested.

Chapter Fifteen

ANOTHER SOUL-CRUSHING DAY IN THE CORPORATE WORLD WHERE the most exciting part was a coworker accidentally clicking on an ad and moaning filling the office.

I walked from the Beemer to the front of my building while loosening my navy tie. Coming home to this brick beauty was my favorite part of my day. Where I shed the corporate lawyer skin and became me again—the change from Anthony to Fritz that I looked forward to all damn day. Inside the foyer, I checked my mailbox, and Nora's singsong voice carried over from her unit. The front door was cracked open, and a sliver of irritation hit me. Did she not realize the door wasn't closed?

"I'm so glad you're doing well, Dad. I wish I could've come home. Uh-huh. Yeah. Sure."

I couldn't hear what he was saying, but it pleased her. She laughed, and the sound got louder when she pushed her door open. Her gaze landed on me and her eyes widened, and I was pretty sure she was happy to see me. The knot in my chest loosened at her warm expression.

"I gotta go, Dad. I need to tell you about my experience with ordering a cable guy. Yeah, I love you too."

"A cable guy?" I asked, moving closer to her with the mail tucked under my arm. She moved within two feet of me and eyed my forearms like a kid at the candy store without a budget.

"Fritz, you look so handsome. Wow." She grinned and swatted at my sleeves rolled up on my arms. "You look so businessy and professional. Were you on the job? Or an interview?"

"On the job," I said, the lie running off my tongue like butter. "When did you call a cable guy? I could've arranged that for you." I didn't like the thought of some guy coming in there, seeing her and the plants, her not knowing what to do…

"Oh, it was no big deal. Angelica gave me the afternoon off, and I wanted to install cable so I could watch news and sports. Everyone talks about sports at the office, and while we didn't entertain the idea of them at the house, they are pretty popular."

"What sports do you intend to watch?" I asked, unable to help myself. These moments used to annoy me. Now, I loved them. I liked seeing small parts of her out of her element. I liked that I got to share these learning moments with her, so her calling a cable guy made me feel cheated. Experiencing her firsts had become a secret obsession.

Which—Wait, what? I blinked at the hard truth and took a step back. Then another.

"What are you doing?" she asked, making my heart rate spike.

"Nothing." I stepped back again, my shoulder hitting the wall with our mailboxes. It stung, but I ignored it. "So what sports?" I asked, hoping to bring her attention back to the conversation and not me.

"Um, baseball. That's what's playing right now, yes?"

"Well, NBA playoffs too."

"Right. NBA."

"Basketball."

"There's also golf, NASCAR, and rugby if you want to watch international sports. Really, the sky's the limit here."

"Wow." Her lips—pink today—formed an *O* before they curved into a smile. "I should stick to baseball."

"It's my favorite sport."

"Maybe we could watch a game together? My dad was telling me

I need to get *'real life experience'* besides the foundation, and it seems sports are big around here."

"And watching a baseball game with me would be experience?"

"Maybe?" She scrunched her nose and trailed her gaze over my face, chest, ending on my forearms. I swore she licked her bottom lip for a second, and a piece of my mail fell onto the floor, name up.

I bent down too fast, the same time she did, and we bumped heads as my pulse raced in my chest.

"Oof!"

"Shit, sorry." I snatched the mail up, hiding my name, and rubbed the top of my head. "You all right?"

"Yeah. Dang, Fritz. Your head is like a rock." She winced and ran a hand over her pink hair.

Without thinking, I reached over to make sure she didn't have a bump. Her hair was feather soft, smooth, and my god, my skin tingled with want as I made sure her head was okay. She grimaced when I ran my fingers over the top part, and my stomach sank.

"I'm so sorry. Come on, I have an ice pack." I let go of her hair, unwillingly, and gripped her elbow to drag her into my place. I set the envelopes on the counter and got an ice pack from the freezer and handed it to her. She gave me a weak smile before placing it right on her noggin. "Need some painkillers?"

"No, I'm okay. Not the worst thing I've had happen to my head."

"What's that?" I leaned against the counter, admiring how her bright-red sweater was tucked into her black skirt. It flared at her hips, and I really wanted to touch her curves, run my hands along them and see how she'd react. Shit. I thought I'd tamed my attraction, or at least got a hold on it, but that blew the fuck up.

She giggled, and my mood improved by a million percent. She tugged at one of her ears, this time lined with red jewels that resembled flowers, and she blushed. "I tend to get involved when I'm around plants. If I'm busy trimming or cutting them, I can forget my surroundings. One time, I was tending to seedlings under a table, and I stood up so fast, forgetting there was a huge oak table on top of me, that I gave myself a concussion."

"Nora," I said, frowning at the thought of her lying unconscious in a greenhouse.

"I know, my parents ripped into me."

"Christ." I wiped a hand over my face, and in that ten seconds, Nora leaned over the counter with her face set in a hard frown. She had one of the envelopes just out of reach, ANTHONY CARTER in big black letters, and my lungs contracted. *No.*

"Oh, you get Anthony's mail for him while he's gone?" she asked, her voice no crisper or interested than usual. She could've been asking about the weather, and I took the easy lie she handed to me on a platter.

"Exactly."

"Mm." She pushed the letter back into the pile and glanced up at me with a goofy grin. I expected her to ask about Anthony again, and I tensed.

"Fritz, I cannot get over how you look in the suit and tie. You are so handsome, like a fancy lumberjack."

"Uh, thanks," I said, my damn ears heating. I took care of myself and was just vain enough to know I was attractive without being a total asshole, but her weird, Nora-like compliment seemed to make my insides hum.

"I'm so used to you in baggy shirts or shorts. This is nice." She smiled, her eyes closing slightly as she sighed and set the ice pack on the counter, and then stood to her full height.

Tell her you have plans.

Go out and do something to distract yourself from her.

"There's a Cubs game on tonight if you don't have plans." I shrugged, hoping it looked natural and not at all desperate because that's how I felt. Desperate. Pathetic. Trying to hang out with a woman who not only wanted to marry so she could get her inheritance, but also a woman who assumed I was a chauffeur. I picked up the ice pack and put it on my head.

Perhaps the collision knocked my brain loose.

"Cubs. Chicago Cubs." She got a hazy look in her eyes, like she was going through her entire mind searching for the answer. Then she tapped her finger against her temple. "Baseball."

"Atta girl."

She beamed at me and eyed the couch. "I can stay? Are you sure? Don't feel obligated. I take up way too much of your time. You should be with friends or lady friends or something. Not—Well, you said we are friends, right?"

"We're friends, Nora." I sighed, my chest feeling tight at her worried expression. "We agreed on that already."

She swallowed, and something flashed across her face. A look. One I couldn't decipher. It was dark and sad, but it didn't last long. "You, uh, aren't hanging out with me because...it's your job?"

"Fuck no," I said, way too fast, but I didn't regret it. My sudden answer pleased her a lot, and the storm cloud disappeared from her face just as fast as it arrived. She was worried I was hanging out with her because I had to? Jesus, did she not realize I was a mess?

No. Probably not.

Good. Okay, cool.

"Yeah. Let's watch baseball!" She put her hand in the air and cheered, and I couldn't stop myself from snorting. Her mouth parted, and she pointed a finger at me. "You just snorted."

"Yeah, because you're a fucking dork."

"But that sound was horrible," she said, laughter bubbling out of her.

I shook my head, undoing my tie and tossing it on the back of a barstool, then undoing the top button of my shirt.

Nora sucked in a breath.

It thrilled me to no end to see her physically react to me.

Shit. No. This wasn't what I wanted.

"Okay, Doc, get comfortable," I said, jutting my chin to the couch. "You wanna order food?"

"Sure." She padded over to the couch and sat, a worried look overtaking her face. "Angelica always orders food at the office, and I'm not sure how she does it."

"Ah, never done takeout or delivery before, Atwood?" I said, grabbing two bottles of water and sitting next to her on the couch. It made sense to sit right by her and had nothing to do with how good her perfume smelled.

She picked up a pillow and put it on her lap, tracing her fingers over the sides of it where it frayed a bit. Her hands were always moving, always touching something or twisting together. Was she thinking about how the fabric felt different than leaves, or maybe she was nervous? I couldn't be sure.

"Okay, Fritz. I need you."

I blinked, taking a quick breath to make sure oxygen was flowing to my brain. *She needs me. Needs* me. A ringing started in my ears, and my limbs got a tingling feeling when she faced me on the couch, her pink lips pursed and on display, begging to be kissed.

She chewed the side of her mouth and leaned closer to me.

My heart slammed against my rib cage, and my mind raced in every direction.

She opened her mouth, her lips moving, but her proximity stopped my brain from understanding English.

"Fritz?" she said, frowning and lifting her hand to my forehead. "Did you hit your head too hard? Did you hear me?"

"Hm?" I cleared my throat, sat up straighter, and wiped a hand over my face. This was embarrassing. I wasn't a teenage boy about to touch a boob for the first time. "What did you say?"

"I need you to help me with this experience. Baseball and takeout. What should we eat? My dad made a good point that I should try harder to *enjoy* my time here."

That's why she needs me. Not to kiss her. I was an idiot.

I stood and went to the junk drawer that had takeout menus, bottle caps, pens, and random shit I threw in there. Space from her was good. I knew just the thing to give her the experience. "You like pizza, Doc?"

"Yes." She leaned over the back of the couch so she could see me, and her voice was high. "I love it."

"But you've only had fancy, rich pizza." I wiggled my brows, and she scoffed. "What? Am I wrong?"

"Pizza is pizza, Fritz."

"I'd argue with you, but you'll know I'm right once it gets here. Monicals, along with their dressing, is another divine gift. You haven't lived until you've had this combination. Trust me."

"I do trust you."

Her warm voice pulled at that string in my heart that seemed to be wrapped around her. That was a problem. The trust. It unsettled me to have that part of me slowly repair after Samantha, and the hypocrisy that I was lying to her twisted my stomach. I was going to have a goddamn ulcer.

"Great," I said, after the silence went on for a beat too long. I ordered a large thin crust pizza with the dressing and joined her on the couch—this time sitting as far away from her as I could. The game started in thirty minutes, and I did my best to focus on the pregame show. If she thought she was being discreet, she wasn't. She kept looking at me and studying me from the side, and a prickle of irritation made its way down my spine.

She was only checking me out because I wore a suit. That was a red flag. I *looked* richer in this outfit, and that changed her attraction to me. It was superficial and bullshit, and I stood, not even glancing at her. "I'm going to change."

I didn't wait for her answer. I went to my room and traded my work clothes for an old T-shirt and shorts that would seem more *on brand* for a chauffeur. My mouth had a sour taste, but I welcomed it. I didn't want to be into my weird-ass neighbor.

When I walked into the living room, she was on her knees near the plants she'd put in my place, humming to herself as she ran her fingers over the leaves. She was lost in her own world again, in Nora Plant World, and it was captivating.

Lingering curiosity made me ask, "Why plants? What made you so involved with them?"

She sighed, pushed herself up, and shrugged. "I didn't have a lot of friends, and when my best friend was ripped away from me, plants were all I had. My parents had each other, but going to school, small-talking with people who knew all about the scandal, it was too much. Clarissa, my former best friend and the daughter of the embezzlers, she told all these lies about me, and as a fourteen-year-old, it almost killed me."

"So plants and your greenhouse…"

"They helped me move on, heal from the heartbreak of being

betrayed by my best friend. After that, I stopped caring what people thought and put all my energy into things I loved. If life could be that cruel, then I wanted to do everything I could to find the things I enjoyed." She glanced at the ground, her shoulders slumping.

I needed to fix it. Her sadness. And I knew just the thing.

"I'll teach you how to keep score, and if you learn it, I'll consider getting another plant."

"That I get to choose?"

"Obviously."

She grinned, hard, and clapped her hands. "Let's learn baseball then."

Chapter Sixteen

I DIDN'T HAVE TIME FOR REGRETS, BUT TONIGHT PUSHED THE LINE. Agreeing to a fucking double date with Dave and Nora, along with Tessa, was dumb. It wasn't a great plan like I'd thought two nights ago. It was a slow form of torture. That's what it was.

"So he brought out a scorebook and showed me how to do it! It was so nerdy," Nora said, gesturing toward me from across the booth. Her gaze met mine, and she smiled. I wished she wouldn't look at me like *that.* Like our inside jokes made her feel special. She was on a date with Dave.

"You two hang out a lot?" my date asked, scooting closer to me and putting her hand on my forearm. Tessa was laid-back and gorgeous and liked sports. Totally my type. A month ago, I might've enjoyed her company and possibly asked for a second date.

Tonight, I was wasting her time.

"Sort of," I said, reaching for another chip from our shared nachos. Dave stared at me, too, questions swirling in his eyes, and all the attention made me sweat. Was I that obvious? Did they both know that I had unwanted feelings toward Nora? I chewed the chip and swallowed before answering. "We live across from each other, so we run into each other."

"And you help me out a lot, Fritz," Nora said, beaming at me as a blush took over her face. "I know it's embarrassing, but I've always lived with my parents. Learning how to *adult* has been hard."

"Girl, I know." Tessa laughed. "No shame in staying at home and saving money. I just moved out last year."

"Really?" Nora lit up.

"Yeah. My sister is still there too. Rent is stupid high, and I can't afford a mortgage yet so I'm tossing away money each month. That's nice Fritz is helping you out though. That first six months, I must've called my parents four times a week."

Nora nodded, and her shoulders relaxed as she stared at Tessa. Her face was so damn expressive with all the lines and curves of her features, and my gut tightened thinking about her damn lips. Her gaze landed on mine, and I winked.

I would rather be in my apartment, secretly lusting for her and answering all her questions about baseball. *"What is his role? Why do they change the throwers? Is the music necessary?"*

"Nora," Dave said, moving his arm around the booth to rest it on Nora's shoulders. "You said you had questions for us."

"For us?" I asked, my voice way too tight. His hand rested on her, just inches away from her neck. Her soft white shirt and jean jacket were nothing fancy or revealing but fuck.

She glanced down, chewed on her lip, before placing both hands on the table, steeling her gaze at all of us one by one. "I'm new at some of this, and I looked up questions to ask when on a group date. As a wise person said"—she paused, looking at me before continuing —"I need to experience all sorts of things away from home, so let's do it."

"Oh, this is fun, huh?" Tessa knocked her shoulder against mine and laughed, but it wasn't with malice. Tessa seemed to enjoy Nora's weird.

"Let's do it," Dave said, moving closer to her. Their sides touched.

My neck heated. She wasn't pushing him off or trying to squirm away.

She must like him.

"First question." She pulled out her phone and typed on it, her fingers moving fast as she said, "What is an ideal weekend for you?"

"I can go first," Tessa said, grinning up at me. "Ideal weekend. Drinks with friends or my sister. A hike, jog, or walk. A good book, a big loud meal with people I love."

"Oh, how lovely." Nora grinned like a Cheshire Cat. "Fritz?"

My ideal weekend. Hm. "Camping. Unplugging from life without phones and just admiring and being outside."

"Yeah, dude," Dave said, holding up his fist for a bump. "When are we camping again, by the way?"

"Name a weekend, I'll be there."

Dave nodded before giving Nora all his attention. "I like drawing. So some hot coffee, a sketchpad, some music. Good company. That's all an ideal weekend."

Ugh. *Good company.* Please.

Nora scrunched her nose and reached over to touch his forearm covered in tattoos, and her lips parted. "Mine would be spent in a greenhouse."

I waited for her to finish the sentence. In a greenhouse…talking to her plants, naming her plants, singing and playing podcasts for her plant babies. But she didn't add anything. She stopped and went to her phone.

"Okay, next question. If you were given a million dollars right now, what would you do?"

Tessa chuckled and said, "Pay off my parents', sister's, and my debt. Buy a house. Travel the world."

Nora nodded, a bit too much, and I finished my beer before I answered. "Invest in businesses that are organic and green, focus on helping the local community. Provide jobs for our town while keeping the earth safe."

"Damn, dude." Dave looked proud of me for a second. "Why don't you just do that?"

Shit. *Shit.* "Uh, well, I can't."

"Yeah, Dave. It's *if* he had a million dollars." She spoke to him, but her large brown eyes softened as she studied me. Even as Dave talked about opening a tattoo shop, hiring local artists, her gaze never wavered from mine.

"What about you, Nora?" Tessa asked, leaning forward.

I knew what Nora would do in a heartbeat. I waited for her to say it, for her to share her passion for a therapy greenhouse where she'd sell jewelry from the old guy at the farmer's market, but she clicked her tongue and tilted her head to the side.

"I'd open a business."

"What business?" Dave asked, nudging her shoulder. "You gotta be more open than that, Nora. We all shared details."

"A greenhouse, specifically." Her cheeks reddened, and my irritation wound around my mind, squeezing it until I got angry.

Why was she hiding this?

"More than a greenhouse," I said, my tone harsh. Everyone turned to look at me, and I forced my face into a neutral, playful expression and leaned back into the booth. "Don't be shy, Nora. I've heard you talk about this a million times."

She narrowed her eyes at me, fire spewing from them as she gripped her phone tighter. "No, it's just a greenhouse."

"Sick," Tessa said, holding up her beer. "Maybe we can all play the lottery and get really, really lucky?"

I cheered her glass, keeping on the façade that this was normal and a good time when really, I counted down the minutes until it was over. Until I could ask Nora what was up. This wasn't her. The shy, soft-spoken woman who only shared small bits of herself. She was loud, an explosion of color, and wore her emotions on her sleeve.

Did she think this was better? Pretending to be someone else?

"I'm going to use the restroom, excuse me." Nora slid out of the booth, and without thinking of how it looked, I motioned for Tessa to let me out.

"I'll get the next round." I gave Tessa a quick smile and made my way through the restaurant toward the back hallway where the restrooms sat. One thing I liked about this place was that they didn't have gender specific signs. Just one-person restrooms. Nora twisted the handle, and I followed, marching next to her into the room.

"Fritz, oh my God." She put a hand to her chest and jumped back. "What are you doing?"

"Why are you pretending to be someone else right now?" Jesus, I could hear the fucking hypocrisy of my voice. *Pot meet kettle.*

"What do you mean?"

I moved closer to her, forcing her to tilt her head to look up at me. "Just a greenhouse? That's not you. It's so much more than that."

"You told me not to freak people out talking so much about my plants," she said, pointing her finger at my chest, hard. "I was trying to tone it down. Be cooler. Experience this shitty life in every way I can."

"Yeah, by still being you!"

"I'm still me, just not talking about my plants. I get too into it— you told me. That guy ghosted me because of it." She blinked a few times, and her cheeks were totally red now. "I don't understand why you're angry."

"Because I hate seeing you *think* you need to change to be interesting to someone. You don't."

"But you told me to!" She threw her hands in the air, frown lines forming on her forehead as she stepped back.

"I was wrong, Nora. I like hearing you gush about your plants and dreams. I like you that way." I moved closer again, needing to be near her. Her pulse raced in her neck, and I wanted nothing more than to kiss her, show her without words how amazingly weird she was and how I found it charming. I swallowed, my throat tight and uncomfortable with how much I wanted her, and I cupped one side of her face. I ran my thumb over her smooth skin and almost groaned when she trembled at my touch.

God, the things I wanted to do to her.

"Oh shit," someone said, pushing the bathroom door open and backing out. It was a harsh reminder we were in the bathroom, at a restaurant, on a date with other people.

I dropped my hand like her face had caught fire. "Sorry," I mumbled, rushing out of the room like it was my damn job. My entire body flushed with embarrassment and want, and I didn't know what to do. My insides twisted with confusion, rivaling how I felt in junior high around the first girl I kissed.

It was like the last fifteen years of my life hadn't happened, and I was the same awkward tween dealing with insane hormones without a plan. I ran my hand over my face, took a deep breath, and went to the bar to get the next round. After this drink, I'd offer to take Tessa home and be honest and polite. It was the least I could do.

My heart still raced when I brought the drinks over to the booth and found Nora sitting there, no trace of the blush or what just happened in the bathroom. Conversation flowed with Nora and Tessa taking lead, and I survived the whole thing by sheer charisma. I was excellent at bullshitting people and had been doing it for years.

So that's what I did.

I laughed when prompted, answered when asked a question, and didn't look at Nora once. I couldn't. It would give too much away.

My body sagged with relief when the date was over.

Tessa slid out of the booth, and I followed.

"Want me to take you home?" I asked, giving her the choice since she used a rideshare to get there. "I really don't mind."

"Sure, that'd be great." She smiled up at me, and I wished, more than anything, to feel a pull toward her. She was beautiful, insanely so, but she didn't have pink hair.

Fuck. What did this mean? I was stuck on my neighbor?

I led her to my car, opened the door for her, and glanced up as Nora and Dave walked out together. After avoiding her for the last hour, I met her gaze, and it was like she sucker-punched me right in the chest. She looked at me with the same expression I felt on the inside. Confused. Mad. Worried.

Would Dave kiss her? Do more? Invite her inside? Did she want him to? Would he treat her right like she deserved or laugh when she talked about plants in her sleep?

I waved, nodding to Dave before pushing all thoughts of them out of my mind. I'd drop Tessa off and drive around for an hour, giving Nora plenty of time to either go home with Dave or invite him in. I'd rather not hear or see it.

ANGRY, RAGING ROCK MUSIC BLASTED OUT OF THE CAR'S SPEAKERS, and the evening air had the slightest chill to it. It smelled like summer. Like pool parties and lightning bugs and milkshakes after the sun went down, and all I could think of was showing Nora how to live. It was like my mind didn't care that she was only here temporarily or that she hated it. And worse! She wanted to marry Anthony Carter so she could get her inheritance. There were so many red flags, but I didn't care.

She lit something up inside me that had been dormant for so long, I was desperate to see it come to life again. I tapped my fingers on the steering wheel as I pulled into the driveway. *No sign of Dave's car.*

That could be a good sign.

Could also mean they were at his place.

I parked and took my time getting out and locking the doors. I wouldn't be able to sleep, so I had nothing to rush home for. Just more worry and thoughts about Nora. My stomach knotted as I walked into the main foyer and unlocked my door. No sounds came from her place, solidifying she was with Dave, and the disappointment and ache in my chest were the worst.

I tossed my keys on the counter, yanked off my shirt, and threw it on the floor. I needed to run, work out, do something to burn off this angry energy when a very loud, urgent knock sounded outside my door.

Just wearing jeans and shoes, I opened the door and couldn't help the huge smile on my face. She stood there, wearing her overlarge white shirt that said *THE PLANT LIFE* and slippers. "You're back," she said, her hands fidgeting like crazy in front of her.

"As are you." I arched a brow, fucking elated she wasn't getting naked with Dave.

"Did you mean it?" she asked, her gaze moving toward my chest and heating. I'd seen glimpses of her checking me out, but this was more. She wet her bottom lip with her tongue, and there was a hazy look in her eyes. *Fuck yeah.*

"Mean what?" I asked.

"You like me this way?"

I laughed and closed the distance between us, forgetting all the reasons why this shouldn't happen. I was done pretending. Done fighting it. If she wanted me, she had me. I stopped just short of touching her. "Yes."

Her breathing picked up as she reached one hand up to touch my chest. She trailed her soft fingers up and down my pecs, over my stomach, and up my collarbone. The innocent touch was potent, setting my skin on fire and sending all my blood south. "Fritz," she said, her voice raspy and deep and full of lust.

"Yes," I said, swallowing hard and seconds away from picking her up and carrying her caveman style to my bedroom. My hands rested at my sides, letting her take the lead being more important to me. I wanted her, but she had to want me too.

"Um, did you..." she said, parting her lips when she traced her fingers up my neck and over my mouth. "Did you kiss Tessa?"

"No."

She sucked in a breath and continued dragging her fingers over my skin. My heart raced at her warm touch, and she stepped closer, her floral scent surrounding me.

"Ask me why, Nora."

Something like panic entered her eyes, and I understood the feeling. Answering this question would change everything. It would shift the air, tip the balance. There would be no hiding it anymore.

"W-Why didn't you kiss Tessa?"

"Because, Nora." I put my hand over hers and stilled her touch on my face. "She wasn't you."

Chapter Seventeen

Nora blinked a few times. "I waited for you. I wondered... you're a very handsome guy, and Tessa...well, she was into you, and I didn't know..."

"Nora?" I said, unable to stop smiling at how flustered she was. She wanted me. I knew it.

"Yes? Hm?" she said, her chest rising and falling fast, straining against her shirt.

"Shut up so I can kiss you."

She sucked in a breath as every muscle in her body tensed. It didn't last long though. She swallowed as I lowered my face and pressed my lips against hers. My hands still rested over hers, and I let go, moving my hand to her lower back and pulling her closer to me. We were chest to chest, our hearts beating against each other, and she gasped when I dug my hands into her lower back.

"More, Nora. I want more," I said, bending lower to capture her mouth with mine. Her lips were softer than I imagined and were so fucking warm and full. I kissed her once, twice, and then slid my tongue into her mouth, wanting to have every part of her. Her timid kiss wouldn't cut it. Not with how much I wanted her. I wanted all of her.

She tasted like whiskey. My mouth tingled as she kissed me back, hard. It was messy. Teeth and tongue and lips all clashing together, trying to get every drop from the other person, and I cupped her neck, tipping her head back to kiss her more, kiss her deeper. This wasn't enough. My soul sprang to life as I tasted her. My skin prickled from head to toe as she kissed me back. Couldn't she feel how savage she made me? Didn't she know that she took up every single thought of mine?

She let out the tiniest moan.

It sent me spiraling through a torrent of lust. I hoisted her up around my waist, moving her legs so her ankles hooked behind my back. Nora arched her hips just enough, pressing against my hardening cock and trembling.

"I thought it was just me," she said in a husky, sexy-as-hell voice against my ear.

I guided us into my apartment, slammed the door, and pushed her back against it as she bit my earlobe.

"Just you?"

"I didn't know you…wanted me too."

I pushed my erection into her, arching a brow as I looked down at her. "I've thought of nothing else but you the past few weeks. Nothing else. Your lips, your skin, your body." I pulled her bottom lip between my teeth, letting go and running my nose down her neck.

She smelled so damn good. I bit the spot where her neck met her shoulder, and she arched her back, letting out a deep guttural sound that went straight to my dick. *Fuck.* "Fritz, wow."

I laughed against her skin, and using my weight to hold her against the door, I ran my hands over her legs. I gripped her thick thighs, enjoying the feel of her against me, before moving to cup her ass. *God.*

It was heavy and full, and she wore the tiniest little pair of panties. As I brought my mouth back to hers, needing to kiss her again, I moved us from the door and down the hall. "Naked," I said, sounding a bit deranged.

"I need to see you," I barked out, using my foot to shut my bedroom door, and I set her on the edge of the bed. She looked up, wide-eyed and flushed cheeks, and my fingers fucking shook with how much I needed this. Needed her.

"You're panting," she said, nervously playing with the edge of her shirt.

I pushed her thighs apart, so I stood right in between them and moved my hands along her thighs and up her hips, slipping my fingers under her cotton shirt. She trembled as I caressed her stomach, moving up over her ribs and the center of her chest.

I gripped the edge of the shirt and tugged it up a bit, and Nora paused. I stilled and looked her in the eye. "Hey, is this okay?"

"Yes," she said, her voice shaking. "My mind is racing right now."

"In a good way, right?" I kissed her again and traced her rib cage under her shirt. She sucked in a breath, and I inched the shirt up more. If she'd been with guys who didn't appreciate her wonderful idiosyncrasies, I wanted to make up for it. Show her how amazing she was.

She nodded.

"I want to hear you say it," I said, pulling her earlobe between my teeth, causing goose bumps to explode down her neck.

"Yes. In a good way." She pushed herself up and stared at me for a beat before removing her shirt.

Seeing all her skin, and her red lacy bra, short-circuited my brain. I didn't get to admire her long before she reached behind her back to unhook her bra, leaving her tits right in my face.

I groaned. "Nora, my god," I said, admiring her perfect full breasts with pink pointy nipples. I cupped each one, my dick throbbing with how much I wanted to slide into her right this second.

I wouldn't. She deserved all the pleasure, first. That was for sure.

"What do you like?" I trailed my finger and thumb over each nipple, tugging them a bit as her mouth hung open. "This?"

"Uhm, yes." Her raspy voice was sexy as hell.

"What about this?" I leaned down, still standing between her legs, and flicked one nipple with my tongue. She bucked off the bed, and I laughed, using my other hand to hold her hip down. I took the whole tip and sucked, and then flicked it in alternating patterns. Nora went wild, and my entire body hummed with pleasure just hearing her sounds.

I repeated the process on the other breast, and she reached up and dug her fingers into my hair, making my scalp sting. I loved it.

She dragged my face up to hers and kissed me again, this time wetter and sloppier than before, like she would die if she didn't kiss me.

It sent another wave of crazed lust to my dick.

"Fritz, shit, I …I don't know. Need you." She sounded deranged, just like how I felt, and she awkwardly pulled my weight on top of her as she ran her fingers up and down my back.

So I lay on top of her, enjoying how she squirmed beneath me as I kissed her slow. We figured out a rhythm, and each stroke of our tongues got me hotter. Needier. But Nora's tells were too obvious for me to go fast. She was nervous but trying to hide it.

She reached between us to undo my jeans and fumbled with the button.

I pushed myself back up and finished the job for her. I stood there, butt-ass naked, hard as a fucking rock.

Only problem was she still wore panties.

I grinned at her, and I put my hand between her thighs and took the damp material and pulled it down. I nudged her legs wider, giving myself the perfect view of her. "Jesus, Nora."

She shivered and sucked her bottom lip into her mouth. "Are you —you going to do it?" Her raspy tone was replaced with worry, and I stilled.

"Do what?" I asked, moving my gaze to her face. She sounded nervous, and I frowned, refusing to do a damn thing if she wasn't ready. "Nora, sweetheart, what's wrong?"

"Nothing! Nothing!" she said, way too fast. She positioned herself up on her elbows and gave me a goofy smile. "It's just been so long since someone's *licked* me down there, I'm not sure I could…go, you know?"

"Ah," I said, smiling wide at the clear challenge she set on the table, just for me. "Do you want me to try?"

"Uh, maybe?"

I licked my lips and sank back down to my knees, pushing her legs apart and dipping my head between them. Her musky scent and clear arousal was the perfect aphrodisiac, and while I wanted her to enjoy every second of my mouth on her, I was losing control.

I hummed into her, swirling my tongue right on her swollen clit, and Nora let out a bunch of incomprehensible sounds. It made me want to coax this orgasm out of her more than I needed to breathe. My knees hurt from my position, but I sucked and teased and nibbled more. Sweat coated her stomach and her upper thighs, and she said my name over and over, but I didn't stop.

I slid two fingers into her, and Nora reached to grab my hair.

"Yes, Fritz," she grunted, sounding so untamed and turned on, it got me harder. Her abandonment. She ground against my face and whimpered, and her muscles tensed as I slid my fingers in and out. Her legs wrapped around my head, trapping me against her, and it was so fucking hot.

"Shit!" she yelled, really fucking loud, but she fell apart as she came against me. Her orgasm went on and on, her body sliding against my face, and I grinned up at her when she finally stilled. "Fritz, my god."

"That was the sexiest thing I've ever seen."

"You," she said, staring at me with her wide, expressive eyes. "Your beard."

"Like it?" I flashed her a grin and pushed myself up again, over her body, kissing her stomach. I smelled like her now, her pleasure and arousal, and it only fueled my want for her.

"Yes," she said, her face lighting up. "Can you kiss me again?"

"Yeah, baby. That I can do."

I moved to place my lips over hers and kissed her. I could do this for hours and not tire of her taste, the way her small hand dug into my skin. Now that I'd tasted her, I wanted to feel her on top of me. "I'm going to flip us over."

"Oh, okay. Are you sure?"

"Yes." I smiled as I rolled onto my back, holding her tight so she ended up straddling me.

Her body on top of mine, her warm thighs clutching me, her tits grazing against my chest. *Fuck.*

She grew bolder the longer we made out, and she sucked my tongue into her mouth and touched me everywhere except my dick. She teased my chest and arms with her soft fingers, and I was going to die if she didn't touch my cock. I was sure of it. "Touch me, Nora."

She froze for one second before she took me in her hand. "Christ," I moaned, squeezing my eyes shut because it felt so good.

"Wow, Fritz," she said, moving so she could stare at her hand pumping me up and down. She parted her lips, and my entire body jerked with bursts of lust.

"Nora," I said, my voice breaking at her increased speed. I wasn't going to last if she kept at it like that. "Stop. I need a condom."

"Oh, right." She let go and watched me with wide eyes as I opened the side table drawer and got a wrapper. The way she stared at me, ready and excited and nervous, I paused.

"Are you sure about this? We can fool around other ways."

"I'm sure. I want you."

Those words made my ears ring and my cock throb. "Put it on me and then slide onto my cock."

She sucked in a breath and grabbed the condom, ripping it open, and staring at it for a second before sliding it on me. "I don't think I've ever been this turned on, Fritz."

"Me either," I said, not feeling a lick of shame at telling her the truth. The most gorgeous and fascinating woman I'd ever met stared at my dick, her perfect tits just out of reach. I gripped her hip. "Show me how you like it. The pace."

She nodded and put one leg over my hips, bent down to kiss me again. It was slow at first, like she was getting used to me, and she stopped and smiled. "I taste myself on you."

"It's hot, right?"

"Yes," she said, moving back and forth on me, not quite taking me yet.

Something told me she needed guidance here, someone more experienced to show her the best parts of sex, and I grinned at her. "You want me to show you what I think is hot?"

"Yes." She nodded eagerly.

I gripped her waist, lifted her up a bit, and guided my cock through her warm folds. I wasn't quite inside her yet, her warmth teasing me to the point I had to grip her ass to keep from slamming inside her.

I eased inside her, and *holy shit.* I almost saw stars. She felt so fucking tight and good. She sat all the way up, her body a goddamn vision. "Roll your hips on me."

I had to touch her.

I cupped her breasts and kneaded her gumdrop-like nipples in my fingers, wanting to take everything she had to give. I arched my hips up to go deeper, and she gasped and fell forward. I grabbed her neck and kissed the hell out of her as she fucked me. She didn't go hard enough or take me as deep as I wanted to go, but I let her continue the languid pace. Sweat covered our bodies, and the combination of our arousal smelled earthy, but that was Nora.

My muscles tightened when she squeezed around my cock, and I snapped. "On your stomach," I said, my control gone. "I want to *fuck* you now."

She giggled in a weird, sexy way, and she rolled onto her stomach and I slid in between her thighs. I used the headboard to hold most of my weight and used my other hand to go underneath her stomach and play with her clit.

Fuck.

I pumped into her, needing to go deeper. "Arch your hips for me." She did, giving me the angle I craved. "Jesus, Nora."

"This feels good. Yes." She fisted the sheets on each side and whimpered as I played with her clit. Her movements jerked and her body tensed, and I slowed my thrusting, going as deep as possible until she fell apart. "Fritz, shit, oh wow, yes!"

I laughed against her neck as she trembled around my cock, and I waited for her to catch her breath before I went hard again. My skin slapped against hers, the sound of our fucking filling the room between our grunts. This woman. She made me wild and *shit.* My spine tingled, and my thighs tensed as my release closed in on me.

I bit the back of her neck, needing a taste of her, and that did it. I pumped three more times before white-hot pleasure swallowed me whole. My mind spun, and my limbs went numb. Stars danced behind my eyelids. I rolled onto my back, my ears ringing and time standing still.

It must've been too long since I'd had sex because that was something else.

I took a deep breath, my pulse still racing, and pushed myself up to toss the condom out in the bathroom trash. I wasn't gone more than thirty seconds before I came back and found Nora quickly putting her shirt on. Normally, I'd be the one ready to head out after a hookup. I didn't cuddle or talk or want to grab a snack. But with her...I couldn't just kick her out. Not after she told me we were friends or that most of her past dates were selfish.

"Nora," I said, ready to ask her if she wanted ice cream or something. Anything to keep hanging out.

"Wow, this was, um," she said, her face turning beet red as she put her arm through the hole for the head. If I had to guess, my little neighbor was nervous and embarrassed. Which wouldn't do.

"Nora," I said, seconds away from laughing. She looked ridiculous.

"Hm?"

"What are you doing?" I reached into my dresser and pulled on a pair of boxers before walking to her and helping her with the shirt. Once it was righted, I tried to read her eyes.

She looked worried, sad even.

"Hey, whoa." I cupped her chin and forced her to look at me. "What's going on in that pink-haired head of yours?"

"Um," she said, biting the corner of her lip. "I'm not sure."

"Was that okay?" *Please say yes.*

"Yes. More than okay. Yes." She eyed the carpet like my floor was more interesting than me.

"You running away from me?"

"No! Well, I'm not...Yes?"

"Oh good, that cleared it up for me."

She snorted, and the worry disappeared from her face. "You're being cute right now. I appreciate it. I wasn't sure...*thank you.*"

"I'm not *cute.*" I rolled my eyes and helped her put her panties back on. "And why are you thanking me?"

Her answering silence put me on edge. Her cheeks reddened, and she twisted her fingers together. Was she hiding something from me? Embarrassed? "Nora?"

Her big brown eyes swirled with shame, and she looked at my nose, not my eyes. "This is hard to say, okay?"

I swallowed the lump in my throat, not having a clue what she was trying to get out. I relaxed my face into a smile and nodded. "Hey, you can tell me anything. What is it?"

"Um, it's not exactly cool to admit you're still a virgin at twenty-two, and uh, I didn't mention it. Not to keep it from you, but I was embarrassed."

Virgin. Nora was a virgin. The same buzzing sound I'd got in my ears earlier returned, but not from lust. From protectiveness. From shame. If I was her first...damn. But this was about her, not me, and my chest tightened at the way she frowned and blinked too much, like she was trying not to cry. I ran my thumb over her bottom lip and smiled, for real. "There's nothing to be embarrassed about. I wish I would've known beforehand, so I could've gone slower or——"

"No. That's the thing, Fritz." She spoke louder, with more emotion. "I want to experience everything, and holding back? I'm sick of people doing that. It was...amazing."

"It was, yeah." I moved my hand to the back of her head and kissed her quickly. Not sure if the kiss was to reassure her, or myself. We both smiled at each other. "If we're being honest with each other, I'd like to do that again as often as possible."

"With me?"

"Um, yeah. Was that not clear?" I threaded my fingers through hers the way I'd seen couples do. And we weren't a couple. No matter how protective over her I felt, we weren't together. We were...I frowned until an idea hit me. A brilliant one. "As long as you're here, I want to make it my personal mission to show you all the things you're missing out on when you live in the mansion. And that does include crazy wild sex."

She narrowed her eyes as I ran a hand over her neck and massaged her shoulders. "So we hookup."

"Yes."

"And remain friends?"

"Of course."

"So we're dating?" Her brows scrunched together in the cutest way, making me forget and ignore the red flags waving in the back of my mind. I could worry about all the *what ifs* later, like what if she found out who I was or what if she still wanted to get married.

"Ah, I wouldn't say dating." I smiled down at her, caught under her weird plant spell. "We're enjoying each other in the short time you're here. Only each other, by the way. I wanted to punch Dave when you touched him."

She gave me a shy, cute smile and nodded fast. "Okay. Yes. I'm in."

"I can't wait to show you all the things, Nora Atwood."

"Are you talking just sex right now or...?"

"I'm talking everything. In the bedroom, out of the bedroom, all of it. Camping, movie theaters, painting fire hydrants, the county fair." I cupped her face in my hands, admiring how petite she was. "All of it."

Chapter Eighteen

"So wait," I said, unsure if it was a joke or not. "You want strippers to pop out of a fake book?"

"Yes. Callahan will think that shit is hilarious," Justin said, my sister's fiancé's best friend. He had a good heart but was kind of a doofus.

"Ah, I'm not sure, man."

"Is this cause he's marrying your sister? Dude, come on."

"No, Gilly would be down for strippers." I laughed, thinking about the time her and Grace took a prank a bit too far. "Christopher would get flustered and all worried. Couldn't we go ax throwing, tour a brewery, golfing? That seems more his style."

"We need titties."

Okay then. I sighed and took a sip of the coffee, unsure how to make progress with the guy. Gilly wanted my help, but the guy clearly had his own agenda.

Fritz: How is Christopher friends with this guy?

Gilly: Justin? LOL. They go way back.

Fritz: There will be titties.

Gilly: Thanks for trying. You able to shop with me and Grace next weekend?

Fritz: Will you clap for me if I find the perfect tux?
Gilly: Possibly.
Fritz: Then yes, I'll be there.

I pocketed my phone and tried to give Justin my full attention. It was hard when he refused to listen to a single suggestion, and I tapped my foot on the floor waiting for him to be done. The bachelor party wasn't for another few weeks, and at least the guy was planning ahead. Poor Christopher might not enjoy his last hoorah as a single man.

"Keep me posted on the planning," I said, shaking his head before he left. I didn't have high hopes, but it would be fun to see Christopher sweat. Smiling, I finished my cup of coffee and got the folder out of my bag. There was a reason I chose to meet him here. The small café was just a block away from the business center where Carla and her partner ran the coffee cart.

Here goes nothing.

Sweat pooled on my neck as I walked in the midday heat toward their location with my heart racing against my rib cage.

I researched a location right in the heart of the college campus. Connecting her with Joseph Sweets would be a right step. He did business with our foundation and was a solid guy, always helping. It felt weird to be this nervous, but with all my connections, I could've done this sooner. If it worked out, they could afford rent for one year, hire part-time employees—probably students—and have enough to invest in some ads.

If only Nora could help them.

Hm.

That was an idea. Social media...marketing...Nora would be excellent as a consultant. Maybe a small fee. It was about a hundred an hour, I learned after some googling, but if she would do it for half that, yes, that would be incredible.

My palms dampened as I pulled open the doors and walked toward their cart. Carla knew I was coming and gave me a huge smile when she saw me.

"Anthony, hello," she said, shaking my hand with a slight tremble. Her eyes lit up despite her nerves, and I returned her grin.

"Hey, Carla. You ready to meet Joseph?"

She guided us to two lounge chairs in the west window. The business center's first floor was cafes, shops, all stores geared toward the working people of the tall building. Sounds of people chatting and eating lunch filled the area, and it smelled too much like garlic from the Italian place nearby.

But I liked the chaos.

"This is a bit nerve-racking, huh?" she said, smoothing her hands over her dark jeans.

"Yes. But I'm fairly confident this could work. He'll come through so you could get started."

She nodded as I handed over the folder. It had contracts, legal explanations, short-term and long-term goals and plans. I offered to look over her plan when I emailed her, and I combed through it Sunday. It was the perfect distraction after spending the night with Nora because *damn* that woman was something else.

I cleared my throat and waited as Joseph approached like I asked him too. He was a short guy, with dark-black hair and pale skin. "Joseph, I'd like you to meet Carla."

"Anthony, hey, thanks for setting this up." He shook Carla's hand and jutted his chin toward the folder. "Coffee is a weakness of mine."

Carla grinned and wiped her hands over her pant legs before she pushed the folder toward him. He clicked his tongue as he looked through the first pages, and I knew I should leave. This wasn't my place. I set up the connection and made sure Carla was prepared as much as I could. They needed to talk.

But leaving meant going back to the real world. Reluctantly, I got up and held out my hand. "I also know someone who I think would be an excellent marketing consultant for you."

"Please, that's one area my partner and I don't have a lick of sense." She had the same goofy smile, and she looked from Joseph to me. "Give me a call and we can chat."

I grinned, and a quick flare of panic danced along my spine. "Oh, one thing."

"Sure, yeah?"

"I don't want people knowing I'm involved at all. Not yet anyway."

"I can respect that."

I nodded and put my hands in my pocket. It was time to leave, yet I didn't want to.

This was so damn different from my job, it was tough to go back into the office for the rest of the day and pretend like my mind wasn't elsewhere. At least I had the thought of Nora to get me through the day.

COMING UP WITH NEW THINGS FOR HER TO TRY OR DO BECAME MY favorite part of the week. Last night, I took her to get barbeque. Tonight was Taco Tuesday.

"Nora?" I said, knocking on her door with bags of groceries. I had all the ingredients to cook bitching margaritas.

She flung open the door and gave me the biggest smile. "Hi!"

She waved me in, her floral scent clinging to the air, and I took a deep breath. I didn't take things too far last night. I just kissed her once after dinner. Tonight though. Shit. She wore rainbow earrings on her ears and a stiff white button shirt and a black skirt.

"Damn." I set the bags on the table and pulled her toward me. She melted against my chest, and I ran my hands up and down her sides before kissing her. "Seeing you look all professional makes me want to mess you up."

She bit her lip and giggled against me. "I've never been called professional in my life."

"Yeah, you need some dirt on you or something."

She laughed and broke our embrace, her eyes lighting up at the bags on the table. "You brought food?"

"Taco Tuesday, Doc. It's a thing here." I got the ingredients out one by one, and she watched like a good student. Her hair was getting longer, the soft pink growing out. I reached over to take a part of it in my fingers. "Will you keep it pink?"

"Oh, shit." She sighed and swatted my hand away. "I forgot I needed to make an appointment. My mother would be ashamed of me, letting my roots grow like this. It's unladylike and not proper."

"I think it looks cool. Dark hair, the pink. Just another layer of your intrigue, Nora."

She pursed her lips, almost looking bashful, before she busied herself with the ingredients. "Okay, Taco Tuesdays are a thing."

"Yes, and we know I take my food seriously. Now…" I picked up the pan and cooking spoon I'd brought with me. "You're going to learn how to make them."

"Oh, yes, please!"

She didn't bat an eyelash as I showed her how to cook the meat and drain the grease, or when I made her chop up the avocado and shred cheese. She did everything I asked and smiled the entire time. She didn't seem to care her shirt was covered with evidence of our cooking, and it reminded me of her in a garden where she didn't realize how messy she got.

"You have salsa on your shirt." I jutted my chin. "That might stain."

"Hm." She chewed her lip and unbuttoned the stiff material, resting it on the back of the chair and wearing a very thin silky tank top that I wanted to rip off her skin. "I read that I could put dish soap on it to keep it from getting ruined."

"Ah, learning all the adult tricks?"

Her ears turned red, and she nodded. "Uh-huh, pretty much."

I'd been with a lot of women, but her skin, her floral scent, they just drove me insane. I grinned so large my face hurt and ran a finger over her collarbone, enjoying the way goose bumps broke out over her flesh.

She giggled, and I let go, reluctant to finish cooking when her tank top and bra barely covered what I knew was underneath. Was it only three days ago that I had her?

Get it together.

The food was ready, and the spicy, strong scent of the onions, rice, guacamole, tacos, and sizzling meat filled her kitchen. She set plates at each end and hummed to herself when I brought the drinks. Gilly bought me a bullet blender for smoothies, but it ended up making the best frozen margaritas. Not her intention, but it worked.

"To experiencing adulting," I said, holding up my glass. She clinked hers against it and widened her eyes at the first sip. "Oh, yeah, it's strong," I added.

"Whoa, you're not joking." She coughed a bit.

"Another adult trick," I said, continuing to caress her neck and shoulder, "is to make the margaritas strong when you're at home. No driving, better drinks."

She reached for a tortilla shell and used her fork and knife to cut it.

"Stop it. Right now."

She tensed. "What—"

"Eat with your hand, good lord." I made my taco and showed her how to take a bite, and she blushed before modeling it. In moments like these, I was glad we were together. Temporarily. Not, *together-*together.

Maybe that drink had gone straight to my head.

"I have a favor to ask you," I said, reminding myself why I thought tacos and a drink would be a little bit of a bribe. She could say no, and I wouldn't push her hard, but I wanted her to say yes, really badly.

"What is it?" She reached for the salsa and put some on a spoon before dropping it over the taco, and she looked up at me with nothing but curiosity on her open face. The light streamed from the window just right, showing all the different shades of brown and tan in her eyes, and I had the wild urge to take her picture.

"Uh, it's about a business." Shit, my head got hot, and I unbuttoned the top button of my shirt to fan myself. I might've put too many jalapeños in the salsa.

"Okay. How so?"

"I have a friend, wait, no. Well, she is a friend. A colleague. Yes." I paused, hating myself. I sounded like an idiot.

"No need to be nervous, Fritz. You've seen me at some low moments."

My chest tightened when she reached over to squeeze my forearm, like she was comforting me. Damn it. I liked it.

"Carla—she owns a small coffee cart—is growing her business and will be in need of some marketing advice. She's starting off, so they can't afford a full consultant, but if you could only charge half your fee, just for a month or so. I think you're brilliant when you talk about what you did for your parents, and at the foundation. I heard Angelica tell my—me, she told me the other day how creative your ideas are."

Nora hung on my every word with hope and pure joy radiating from her, and I made a note to have Angelica tell her good job. It wasn't her style, but Nora needed the validation. "You think I'm brilliant."

"Yes. I do." I took another sip of the margarita, willing it to cool down my face. "Weird, but brilliant."

"I'll take it. And yes, of course I'll help your friend slash colleague."

"You're teasing me," I said, narrowing my eyes. "Not very ladylike or professional, Nora Atwood."

She laughed and shrugged, the nonchalant look coming across really sexy. "What ya gonna do?"

Damn. With the light and the tank top and the smile, I'd never want to leave her place. "Okay, I'll let Carla know. You'll make her year, really."

"I'm not being a saint." She looked a little wicked and spoke in a lower tone. "I do have an ulterior motive of seeing if we can partner up when I get my greenhouse. Once that money comes through, it's on. I'm thinking it'll be sooner rather than later too."

The mention of the money deflated the balloon of happiness and hope I was naïvely living in. She must've emailed Anthony or figured something out. My shoulder slumped, and I hated how my gut twisted. She still didn't know who I was, and I needed to tell her. Soon.

I took my last bite of food, preparing myself to do the right thing, when she slid off her chair and stood between my thighs. "Nora?"

Heat entered her eyes, and she unbuttoned my shirt one by one, teasing my chest with her fingers, making me forget about all the things I *should've* done. She straddled me and guided my hands up her thighs, going under her skirt, and when her lips met mine, and her greedy tongue slid into my mouth, lust took over.

A beautiful, wild woman wanted me? Yeah, I could hold off on the truth. Just a bit longer.

Chapter Nineteen

I IGNORED THE GUILT AS I CLEANED MY PLACE TO MAKE SURE ALL evidence of *Anthony* was gone before Nora arrived. No photos of Gilly and me, no mail. Every time I took a part of me and hid it, a sharp pang pierced my chest. Finding the ring I bought to propose to Samantha reminded me that Nora wanting to marry me had nothing to do with who I was as a person.

To her, Anthony was just a means to get what she wanted.

She wanted Fritz for…something else. I scrubbed my palms over my face and eyed the clock. *Six p.m.* We agreed to watch the Cubs play and order Chinese food, another must-experience. I wore sport shorts and an old T-shirt and double-checked my hair in the mirror as she knocked on the door.

The same cheerful-like feeling that formed in my belly when talking to Carla returned, but this time it was because of Nora. She beamed at me as I swung the door open.

"Hey," I said, matching her smile. She wore a bright-purple dress that hugged every curve of her body. Her earrings and lips matched the color, and she threw her arms around me in an aggressive hug. "Oof," I mumbled into her neck.

"Fritz, you brilliant man. Carla! Carla!" She pressed her lips on my neck, cheek, and mouth before she pulled back and narrowed her eyes at me with pleasure. "She's amazing. Her partner's amazing. I can't believe you recommended me to help them!"

I grinned against her mouth and yanked her into my unit. She tasted like cherries, and I wanted more. I cupped the back of her head, dug my fingers into her short, soft hair, and tilted her head back to kiss her deeper. She parted her mouth, matching my fervor, and groaned. She kissed so wildly, so passionately, it made a normal kiss seem boring. My blood started heading south with her mouth on mine, so I slowed down. "I like kissing you," I said, sounding like a dorky teenaged boy.

I like kissing you. Cool. Good one.

She bit her moist bottom lip and looked at me through her lashes. *Is she getting shy on me?* I tilted her chin up so I could see her large brown eyes. "This is when you say, '*I like kissing you too, Fritz.*'"

"Of course I do." She pursed those lips and ran her finger over one of my eyebrows, almost like she was studying the shapes of my face. I swore I felt her soft touch all the way down to my toes, which was silly. It was one finger on my eyebrow of all places. The least sexiest thing I could think of.

"You seem happy," I said, finally figuring out what was different about her. It wasn't the color of her lips or her hair or her nails. It was her vibe. The genuine sparkle in her eye. I still held her tight against me as we chatted. It would have made more sense to move to the couch. But then she could sit on the other end, and I liked her soft curves and warmth pressed up against me. I twirled a piece of her hair between my fingers and the tightness in my chest loosened.

"I might be, Fritz." She shook her head and let out a little chuckle, like she couldn't believe it herself. "I realized today I wasn't counting down the weeks until I go back."

And the tightness returned like Thanos's hand had gripped my heart and squeezed. *Weeks.* She'd be gone in weeks. It wasn't news, but I forgot to keep that fun fact at the forefront of my mind. I let go of her, needing a bit of distance. If she sensed a change in me, she didn't show it.

We went to the barstools in my kitchen, and I slid a takeout menu toward her. "Pick carefully. My treat."

"I can buy one of these nights, you know." She winked at me and nudged her shoulder with mine. "If you don't remember, I'm made of money."

"I don't care give a shit about your money," I said, a bit too fast, too aggressive. My tone was harsh.

She frowned, and wrinkles formed on her forehead. They looked out of place on her. Her smooth skin wasn't meant to be frowning so much.

"It's just...I don't want to get into it, but I have a story similar to yours. Someone turned out to not be who I thought they were."

"Oh." She rubbed her lips together as those damn wrinkles deepened. "I'm so sorry."

"It's fine." I cracked my neck from side to side. "I've moved on from it, really, but it still stings."

She leaned closer to me and ran her small hand on my forearm, then up to my chest and over my heart. She had to feel how it raced when she touched me, but she didn't say anything. She continued frowning and eyeing me with that glint in her brown eyes. "I'm glad we're friends then. We'd never do that to each other."

Fuck. *Fuck.*

My jaw was going to crush into dust at the rate I ground my teeth, and I tapped the menu with my pointer finger, needing to navigate away from this situation. "Food, Doc. Pick your food."

The wrinkles disappeared, and she asked a million questions about every dish. After fifteen minutes, I finally ordered beef broccoli and sweet-and-sour chicken. Two classics. Delicious classics. It'd be a good thirty minutes before it arrived, and the game didn't start until then. It felt hotter than normal, and I fanned myself with my shirt.

"Hey," she said softly, drawing my attention to her. "I can tell you're uncomfortable, so I won't pry, but I'm a really good listener. Your secrets are safe with me."

"You could tell your plants."

"True, but since I control their food, they wouldn't ever betray me." She grinned, her eyes crinkling on the sides, and she moved to stand between my thighs. She barely came up to my shoulders even with me sitting on a stool, and she cupped my beard. "One thing I learned from that ordeal was that we can really only control what *we* can control. Not that wise, but it doesn't make it less true. I couldn't help that someone I thought a friend played me. I couldn't control her parent's choices. But I could control my feelings and what I did after. I made sure that emotions and money never intertwine again."

My throat was sandpaper. Rough, hard sandpaper. She ran those delicate fingers through my beard and scruff, supporting me, when she had no idea I had to do the same thing. Keep it separate. But then it hit me. "That's why you're so adamant about Anthony."

"A *real* marriage makes me break out in hives." She laughed. "A contract? An agreement? That means no one gets hurt."

Bleak understanding weighed me down. Her reasoning wasn't as crazy as I thought. If she could *control* who she married to get what she wanted...but...wait. "Wouldn't you be using him for money though? Not his, but to get *yours*?"

A sliver of bitter resentment passed through me.

"I would be upfront though." She twisted her lips into a scowl. "It's the manipulating that bothers me. He won't be surprised or anything."

"Hm." My mind reeled at all the similarities with Samantha, but also all the things she spoke about that I was doing. Lying. Keeping secrets. The sadness about my ex-fiancé paired with the guilt caused a horrible pressure in my body that grew by the second. I needed to change the subject. Move on. Deal with it. "Tell me more about Carla," I demanded, a bitter edge to my voice. "Please."

She arched one brow and let go of my beard and stepped back. "Ready to change the subject?"

"Am I that obvious?" I forced a tight laugh and guided us to the couch. She didn't sit on the opposite side like I assumed. No, she sat right next to me and put her legs over mine, giving me access to her thighs. I caressed her legs over her dress a few times before sliding my hand under the edge to tease the skin right above her knee.

She sighed and leaned her head on the back of the couch, her lips curving into a lazy smile. That curve of her mouth was addicting, and if I focused on her joy, her laugh, her body, I'd forget about all the negativity brewing in my mind.

Plus, her skin was so damn smooth.

"She pretty much said I can have free rein with all socials and online presence. This is a dream of a job, really. She has a logo and a font she likes, but the rest is up to me. I'm thinking of starting small, using greens and whites and browns. Not like Starbucks, but a darker shade of green." She stared off at a distance when she spoke, her words stringing together and almost sounding lyrical.

I sat up straighter, brimming with pride. I *knew* she'd be great for this. "What else?"

She met my gaze, and excitement burst from her eyes. "She's paying me a decent amount for it and recommending me to a friend if this goes well. I'm tracking usage and numbers and all clicks for a month. Then, we'll meet to go over any changes and adjustments."

"Hey, Nora," I said, needing to kiss her. Her joy and comfort when talking about it pulled me toward her in a wonderful way. I leaned in, and she bit the side of her lip as I neared.

"Yes, Fritz?" she asked, a little breathless.

"It kinda, maybe sounds like you might not *hate* it here." I brushed my lips over hers once. Twice. "You sound *happy*."

She didn't respond, which was okay. Instead, she kissed me back, hard. She grazed her hands all over my body, but I made no moves to progress this. I just wanted her mouth on mine and to feel even an ounce of the joy she had.

She squirmed beneath me and let out the tiniest moan as our teeth and tongues clashed together. Everything about her should've put me off, but instead, it created an intoxicating pull to her. The sounds she made, the way she smelled, the softness of her hair and curves of her body. I reached up and trailed my pointer finger over the shell of her ear, feeling all four of the earrings there, and grinned against her mouth.

"Why are you smiling like a goon?" she asked, looking up at me with wet, swollen lips.

"Your earrings," I said, clearing my throat because despite my attempts at just wanting to kiss her, I was rock-hard. "Why so many?"

"I like how the light reflects off them."

What an odd answer.

But she was odd, in so many ways. She was a beautiful woman who thought I was a chauffeur, who wanted to negotiate a contract to marry Anthony, and was incredible in bed. I wasn't one to get caught up in emotions or feelings, but I needed to tread carefully. My job was to help her learn how to adult and to experience things, so when time was up, we'd go back to what we were before—just a memory.

But when do you tell her the truth?

That was the question I didn't have an answer to.

Chapter Twenty

Gilly spun around on the pedestal-like thing and arched a brow at Grace and me. "Well?"

"You look good in anything you wear, Gil, but how do you feel in this dress?" Grace tapped her finger against her lip, the sun hitting her wedding ring just right and reflecting into my eyes. The unexpected weight grew in my chest at seeing my baby sister try on wedding dresses. It wasn't a painful feeling, but definitely uncomfortable.

"Fritz, you have more opinions than any man ever deserves. Thoughts?" my sister asked, and the slight lilt to her voice forced me to let go of any weird feelings. She needed us present, for her, and if I weren't mistaken, she was nervous.

"I echo what Grace said, but…" I paused, studying the very traditional white dress. "If I may add some thoughts?"

"Stop being weird, yes. I want your thoughts!" She huffed, and the tips of her cheeks pinked. A part of me wondered if the fact our mom wasn't here bothered her. She said she was *fine* with it and *understood,* but this was a milestone for a woman—so I had read. My and Grace's duty was to make it fantastic.

"What did you wear to prom junior year?" I asked, hoping to guide Gilly in the right direction.

"Uh, a fire-engine-red dress with a lot of sparkle and poof."

"And senior year?"

She narrowed her eyes at studied me for a beat before her lips quirked up. "A hot-pink froufrou dress."

"So why in God's name are you trying on dresses that are so boring? That's not you."

Grace smacked my arm and shook her head. "Yes, that's exactly it. I couldn't pinpoint my issue with the last ten you've tried on. We need va-va-voom. We need to see *you* up there."

"Fuck." She pointed over our shoulder, and I swore my sister salivated. "That one. Grace, you know my size. Bring me that baby."

I craned my neck and watched Grace walk toward the most obnoxious, beautiful, off-white sparkly dress. It had feathers and fluff and beads and tiny shiny things that reminded me of Nora's earrings.

Nora. She'd be having a ball if she was here. I smiled briefly, before rubbing the back of my neck and wincing. We might connect in the bedroom, but she was after marriage. Not a great idea to think about her *here*.

"This thing weighs way too much." Grace huffed and carried it toward the dressing room door. Gilly yanked both Grace and the dress inside the room, and all I heard were laughs, *oh shits,* and the click of the door opening.

Grace met my eyes with *a look*.

My pulse sped up as that same weighted feeling came back and the wind knocked out of my lungs when Gilly stood there in *the* dress.

Her eyes watered and her hands trembled when she raised her arms up and said, "Well?"

"Christopher is going to melt onto the floor. This is *perfect.*" I stood and walked toward her, my own eyes prickling a bit at how grateful I was to be here with her. "Gil, yes." I grinned down at her, and she wiped under her eyes.

"I-It feels weird to cry."

"Who gives a shit?" I got my phone out and took some photos of her. I'd send them to our mom later, but I wasn't going to darken this moment with memories of her. "This is *you.*"

"Yes, it is."

"Did you find your dress? Oh!" A red-haired woman looked over at us from the counter and picked up a large brass bell. She held it over her head and slammed it back and forth, the clinging sound just making the moment more funny.

I was sure women loved that bell, but it reminded me of cowbells…specifically, the SNL skit *more cowbell.* I covered my mouth with my hand, and Gilly's lips twitched. Maybe there was a method to the bell madness because the weighted feeling lifted, and all I felt was utter joy for my sister and her wedding with Christopher.

Grace and Gilly went back into the dressing room, and I sat back in the chair and checked my phone. Two emails met me, one from Carla and one from a Peter Dubowski. My pulse raced at seeing Carla's name, and a million thoughts crashed together. *Did it not work without Nora? Did they need more help?*

Fritz—I can't thank you enough for putting us in contact to get a loan and with Nora. Things are moving at a rapid pace. I have a friend who is in the same boat, wanting to start a business that is an organic and vegan café. He's run into some road blocks, so I gave him your email. I hope that's okay. Please tell me if you'd like me to not share your information.

I hope you're well and hope to see you next week at the market.

That was the one minor annoyance about Gilly wanting to do the dress shopping this Saturday morning. No farmer's market. No Nora in her overalls and too-large smile and no checking in on Carla to see how it was going. But another guy needing to start a business?

My blood hummed. I wanted more details. I clicked the email and read it so fast, I had to read it twice.

Hope you don't mind me reaching out. Carla spoke highly of you and your connections. My brother and I want to start an organic and vegan café that uses local ingredients and supports the community. Do you have time for a call?

Peter Dubowski

Yes. Yes, I did.

"Fritz, you're bouncing your leg so much you're shaking the floor." Gilly walked up to me and put a hand on my shoulder. "You good?"

"Great actually." I slid the phone in my pocket and smiled, for real. "Are you good? You better not back out of our dress and mimosas plan."

"I would *never*."

She bought the dress and made all the appointments for alterations. I tuned out and thought about the email. Another local business. Man. That would be something else if I could help two small start-ups in our community. So much better than my day job.

SHIT, I WAS TIPSY. FOR SURE. MY HEAD BUZZED, AND THE ground swayed beneath me. I could always have a beer or two and be fine, but the mimosas were stronger and unlimited. Gilly charmed the waitress like she always did, and now here I was, stumbling back home at noon on a Saturday with a slight wobble to my step.

I could nap or eat or watch baseball or buy a beanbag chair. Oh. That's a good idea. They had adult ones now that weren't that weird Styrofoam. A big-ass beanbag chair. I could see it fitting in my living room. I hummed to myself, picturing how comfortable it'd be, and walked into the foyer of my building.

What if I got beanbag chairs for the entrance area?

"You're back!" Nora said, her door flying open and her wonderful scent tickling my nose. I grinned at her hard, the same buzzy feeling in my head moving toward my chest.

"Nora! What do you think of beanbag chairs? What if I got a million colors to match your earrings? Or pink! Like your hair?"

She ran a hand through her soft hair, and her eyes twinkled like she was about to tell a really funny joke. I wanted to know the joke. A lot. "You have quite the spring in your step today."

"I do, don't I?" I skipped. I literally lifted my knees and skipped in the foyer, and by the time I realized how foolish I looked, Nora laughed, and that sound made it all make sense. *That* was why I was an idiot. For that laugh.

"What has gotten into you?"

"Ideas, Nora. I have a lot of them. But if you're thinking specifics, mimosas."

"Ah, yes. That explains it." She smiled at me, her brown eyes going all gooey and warm, and visions of her in that wedding dress place assaulted me.

Her wearing a white dress with lots of flowers. Stupid amounts of flowers. She could even grow her own plant babies and use them as accessories.

"You're frowning. You need some food, which is perfect because I brought you something from the market."

"You went to the market without me?" I asked, on the verge of pouting. I didn't know why I was frowning or why thinking of her going to *our place* without me bothered me. She was a free woman. An adult. She could do anything she wanted.

Nora bit the side of her lip and narrowed her eyes before walking up to me and running her dainty fingers over my beard. I hummed and closed my eyes. Oh, her fingers felt good. Very good. "Are you saying you missed me this morning?"

"Yes, I thought that was clear."

"Nope. You never said it."

Her voice got closer, and her warm breath hit my face. Tingles spread from head to toe in a terrifyingly *wonderful* way. I leaned into her and captured her mouth with mine and sighed. Her full lips tasted like cinnamon, and I reached around to pull her closer to me. I needed more.

Her sounds and joy and smells.

"Fritz," she said, putting a hand on my chest and letting out a little giggle. "You taste like you need some water."

"You taste so good." I nipped her bottom lip again and enjoyed how her eyes darkened with lust. God, our chemistry was unreal. "I need you."

She might not have realized it, but she leaned closer to me like my words mattered to her, and I kissed her again, slowly. My goal was to just *kiss* her and taste her joy and smiles. She kissed me back and slid her tongue into my mouth, and I groaned, not getting enough.

The moment wasn't lost on me despite my very tipsy mind. I didn't make out with women in my lobby. That wasn't who I was. I also didn't skip around or picture women in wedding dresses, but things had gone sideways.

"You're insatiable," she said, pulling back and rubbing her thumb over her wet bottom lip.

"It's you." I trailed my fingers over her shoulders and arms. She was petite but strong. Her tank top showcased muscles earned from all her plant business, and I loved how it shaped her curves.

She blushed and looked at the ground, shifting her weight from one foot to the other. "Come on, buzzy. I bought you some gifts today."

"Gifts! For me?"

Was it a beanbag chair?

"No, it's not a beanbag chair."

"Did I say that out loud? With my mouth?"

"Yes. Why are you…you know what, doesn't matter." She laughed and took my hand to drag me into her unit. "I'll get you some water."

"Water, schmater. Do you have orange juice and champagne? I recommend it very much."

She pushed me onto her kitchen chair with more force than I would've known she had and set a brown bag in front of me. "Eat."

"Yes, ma'am." I opened it up and found a very sexy brownie. I took one bite and crossed my eyes. "What the fuck is this sorcery? It's magnificent."

"A brownie from this cart at the market. He takes his food cart to markets and small gatherings, but he was talking with Carla today about starting his own business."

Bells went off in my head. Loud fire alarms. *Did that mean Nora knew my name?*

"Oh." I swallowed. It hurt. She wasn't looking at me with suspicion or anger, but that didn't mean it wasn't a trap. Samantha trapped me, and I didn't even know it. Her stare grew and grew, and the silence was stifling. So I said, "It's very good."

"I thought so too." She beamed and patted my hand. "I also brought you this." She handed me a little gray pot with a large pink flower growing from it.

A flower baby for me!

Okay, maybe I did need some water.

"Another plant, how thoughtful," I said, hoping my voice came out teasing and not confused and worried. "Is this a plant version of you?" I held it up and found I liked the little flower lady. She was bright and pretty, independent but still needing some care.

She blinked, and her eyes looked misty. Oh no. Did I say something dumb? Or wrong? I couldn't remember what I thought versus what I'd said, and this was why I rarely got drunk because I could be a real doofus. "Nora, I'm sorry. Whatever I said, please, ignore me. It's the mimosa."

"No, you didn't do anything wrong." She sniffed and patted my hand. "I like all these new things you're showing me. I didn't think I would, but I'm having more fun than I would've imagined. The lake, the market, the bars…life isn't so bad."

"There is still so much more!" I set the flower down as my adrenaline spiked. "There are protests and camping and tubing in the lake and volunteering at animal shelters. We can try to fit it all in before—"

Before you leave me and go back to your palace. I managed to *not* say that. I took another bite of the brownie to shut myself up.

Her eyes widened. "Hm, maybe not all of those."

"Yes. All of them. This isn't up to you. I'm your tour guide here, Doc." I winked and made sure to close my mouth when I chewed because I did have manners. "Get ready. I'm packing your itinerary tight."

Chapter Twenty-One

SHE SLEPT OVER.

Nora Atwood was in my bed. Wearing one of my shirts.

My head pounded, and my throat begged for water. While the day drinking caused my hangover to start in the evening, it lingered. *Damn mimosas.*

I watched Nora sleep for a minute. Her long lashes fanned over her cheeks, and her lips parted slightly as she breathed a heavy sigh. I scratched my jaw as I studied her smooth skin, the way her hair fell over her forehead, and her pixie-like face. She was my little weirdo, and my stomach fluttered with something like butterflies. Which was weird. I didn't get those. I wasn't a teenage girl at a boy band concert.

But the feeling was definitely there. I slid out of bed and tossed on shorts before using the bathroom. Mouthwash was a must. I tiptoed toward the living room. This wasn't exactly new territory of having a woman in my bed, but Nora was…Nora. We might've been sleeping together for the past couple weeks, but staying over in each other's beds was next level. I grunted, trying to figure out what it all meant, and made coffee.

Caffeine would certainly help my head on *and* help get rid of this damn hangover. I chugged water and stared at my phone, the unanswered email to the café guy. My fingers flew over my keyboard as I sent him the phone number of my finance buddy and quickly sent him a text to give me a call.

The same warm feeling I got hearing about Carla's success returned even more, and I made a fist of victory alone in my kitchen. Only, I wasn't alone.

"Do you always cheer yourself on in the kitchen or is today special?" Nora's husky voice was filled with sleep. God, I wanted to kiss that mouth.

"Confidence is a sexy trait for men and women," I said, arching a brow at her as she stood at just outside the kitchen. She twisted the edge of the shirt in her hands, and I jutted my chin at it. "You planning to take off that shirt, or are you nervous?"

She let go like it was a live wire, and a shadow crossed her eyes. "Ah. I'm obvious, huh?"

"I spend a lot of time looking at you, so yeah, I can read your face." *Shit.* My face heated at how lame that sounded. At least it wiped the worry from her face. "Anyway, why are you nervous? Is it because I'm so attractive you don't know how to control yourself?"

She rolled her eyes and joined me in the kitchen. "You're easy to be around, Fritz."

"Likewise, Doc." She walked up to me and trailed her fingers over my collarbone and down my chest. I sucked in a breath at her touch.

"I stayed the night." She looked up at me with clear brown eyes. "I crossed that invisible line we drew."

"I'm not mad about it." I cupped her face and pressed a soft kiss on her. I didn't get too heavy with morning breath and hangover mouth. I wasn't a monster. "Are you okay with it?"

"I…" She stopped and her brows came together in a hard line. "My lip balm fell into the side drawer, and I had to get it."

"Okay." I frowned, not at all understanding why we had a cute moment that shifted to worry. "Did you get it back?"

"Yes." She chewed her lip and stepped out of my reach. "I found a box in there. I was curious, and I looked. I'm sorry."

A box.

Samantha's ring.

I scrubbed my palms over my eyes and groaned, the familiar pang of her betrayal overtaking my body. Lies. Money. Marriage. I knew, rationally, that Nora did nothing wrong. She never lied about her goals or intentions. She was clear as hell about them. But how did I explain this?

Worry danced along my spine like little bolts of electricity, and I exhaled. She didn't actually ask a question, just apologized for seeing it. That meant I didn't have to acknowledge it.

Coward.

"Are you…you're not…that's old, right?" she asked in a small voice that reached into my chest and fisted my heart. Nora had no idea how much space she took up in my mind.

"Nora," I said, making my voice serious. "That ring is very old. The story I told you about also being betrayed? It revolves around that damn ring."

She nodded, and her lips formed an *O*. "Ah, I see." The concern left her eyes, but she was still curious. Tilting her head to the side and eyeing me up and down. I wasn't in the headspace to tell her the truth about any of it.

"Sit down. Let me cook you breakfast." I picked her up, enjoying the quick scent of lavender around her, and set her on the stool. "Bacon? Sausage? Eggs? Toast? Hash browns?"

"Do you have all of those items?"

I grinned at the surprise in her voice. "Yes. I like to eat, we've established that."

The awkward tension around the room dissipated as I got the ingredients out and started preparing the food. She wanted to learn how to make hash browns at home, and we chatted about all sorts of things as we navigated through the kitchen.

We talked about our families, our dream vacation, the plant we'd choose to be if we had to be one. That was her question, obviously. She wanted to be a *Monstera deliciosa*, and I chose an apple tree. That way, I could always eat them.

Conversation flowed as we ate, and it was just as I started cleaning up the dishes that my phone rang. My first thought was the café guy, and I jumped up with a half smile on my face. Maybe he already talked my finance guy, and it went through. It'd be a hell of a Sunday morning to hear good news.

But it was my *mom*. Opposite of good news.

Shit.

"Gotta take this. Give me a moment, would you?" I asked Nora, admiring how my shirt rode up the back of her thighs as she leaned into the sink. God, I could spend hours touching and licking her skin. *Not now. You need to talk to your mom.*

"Sure. I'll clean up." She winked at me over her shoulder, and fuck, if it wasn't the cutest and self-confident thing I'd see her do. Seeing her go back to her mansion would really suck.

I went into my room and shut the bedroom door before I answered. "Hey, Mom."

"Anthony," she said, the background noise almost too loud to hear her clearly. "—you doing?"

"What?"

"Sorry. Traffic is horrible here." She cleared her throat, and the noise quieted down. "Ah, better. I asked how you're doing? How's your sister? And we must talk about Nora Atwood."

"That's a lot in one question, Mom." I sighed and fell onto my back on the bed.

"Don't sass me, young man."

I rolled my eyes. Young man. I was almost thirty, but okay. "I'm fine. Gilly's doing well. And why must we talk about Nora?"

"Your sister found her dress and didn't FaceTalk me."

Ah, that was the reason for the call. My gut tightened with a fierce need to protect my sister. We were beyond thankful for growing up without lacking anything besides parents who wanted to be involved in our lives. We had zero complaints, but this was the issue. "It's a beautiful dress."

"Is she mad at me? Did she intentionally try to leave me out of the process?"

"First off, you should call her if you want to talk about this. She's not the one who hopped on a plane to go abroad. You did. Her plans never changed or went off course, yours did."

"Anthony Carter."

Oh shit. I got *full-named*. "I can tell you're hurt, Mom, and I'm sorry you are, but…this one is on you. Not Gilly."

Silence. My skin tingled, and a knot formed in my throat with regret. Had I gone too far? Would Gilly be pissed at me? I made a fist and hit my forehead twice before saying, "You should talk to her, really. You've given very little indication that you're interested in the process."

"She's my daughter! Of course I'm interested!"

"Wouldn't hurt to say that or back the sentiment up with action."

What was wrong with me? I was spewing out truth bombs like there weren't repercussions, and the irony wasn't lost on me. Sure, I was keeping something major from Nora, but at least I was unfiltered with my mom. "What about Nora Atwood?"

"Right."

She sniffed, but I refused to feel bad for sticking up for Gilly. Grace and I did our best to have as much fun as we could, but I could see the little bit of sadness in her eyes about our mom. She'd never admit it though.

"Well?" Impatience had me tapping my foot. I wanted to end this call and get back to Nora, but at the mention of her name, I needed to know what my mom had to say.

"She reached out to me *again* about contacting you. I don't understand why you're avoiding her and not answering her emails. I gave her your work number. I expect you to answer. She's my goddaughter and from what I hear, she's doing well at the foundation."

Why is she asking for my number?

Didn't she just say she was having a great time here? Was that a lie and she still wanted the sham marriage? My expression hardened, and my pulse raced as I placated my mother. "Yeah, I'll answer."

"Great. Now, I'm going to move things around. Tell your sister I'll be back soon."

"Soon? What is soon?"

If my mom came back, hiding this dumb ruse would be more difficult. Nora could hear her call me Anthony and…yeah, not good. "What's the rush?"

"After the guilt trip you sent me on, I figured I'd better come back to be with your sister," she said, making me roll my eyes. Ever so dramatic, my dear mother.

"Okay, stop." This conversation made me want a drink despite my hangover.

"I'll talk to your father and see if we can handle things from home. Now I need to go. I love you."

"You too, Mom." I hung up and waited a beat before moving.

It seemed all the parts of my life were about ready to crash-land together. My mom's return meant I had to come clean to Nora, but that could burst the bubble we were in. That fun, wonderful bubble, where money didn't matter at all. I pinched the bridge of my nose and let myself pout for five seconds.

I was a grown man and could handle this. I didn't have a choice.

Without a real plan, I went into the kitchen and found Nora soaked. My T-shirt on her was plastered to her skin, showcasing every curve and her pebbled nipples. My body tightened with need, and she looked up at me with her lips curved. "Everything okay?"

No.

"Are you trying to be sexy?" I asked, my voice gruff and low. The way her gaze focused on me and didn't see dollar signs. The slope of her neck that always smelled so damn good. I walked over to her and turned off the water and spun her around.

"N-No." Her chest heaved, and with each breath, her breasts strained against the wet cotton. I brought my hands up to her breasts and tweaked the outline of her nipples, making her buck against me. "Fritz," she said, tipping her head back and giving me access to her neck.

I teased the sensitive skin with my teeth and lips until she was a withering mess. "You're so beautiful, Nora. It drives me crazy."

She hummed into me, and by the time my mouth was on hers, she kissed me hard. While using our chemistry as a way to distract myself from the lies wasn't my best moment, it also wasn't my worst because despite our differences, we fit together.

Now I had to figure out how to tell her the truth and hope nothing changed.

Chapter Twenty-Two

A FEW DAYS LATER, PETER DUBOWSKI SAT WITH HIS HEAD IN HIS hands and bounced his knee up and down so many times the chair shook. My gut twisted with guilt. My finance guy didn't come through for him like he did with Carla. The details blurred together, but the main point was that he didn't think *the business had a solid enough plan to invest in.*

He had layouts, a menu, a financial sheet to track all purchases, yet…not solid enough. The coffee Carla provided tasted like acid in my mouth. It was a good brew, but watching this guy's dreams be crushed in front of me ruined the flavor. And to think I gave him a moment of hope before it was crushed.

"Peter," Carla said in a calm voice. "There are other investors, other banks. I'd be happy to look over your plan and help you with it."

"There's no one else. I've tried all of them, Carla." Peter looked up at the sky, and the slump of his shoulders reminded me of me. How I felt at work. Hopeless. Without direction. At a crossroads of wanting to make a change, but without a single clue how to do it.

"Do you know anyone else, Fritz? I know this is asking a lot, but maybe there's someone…?" Peter asked, trailing off and his face hardening into defeat.

My mind whirled with a spark of an idea.

It was *insane* and not even fully formed, like ten percent of an idea that I had no business thinking about. What if...I...fronted the money? My mind buzzed with excitement at the fact I could invest money in this proposal without taking a hit. The risk wasn't my livelihood, but there was a chance I could fail. That this could blow up.

"Wait," I said, my throat dry and my hands shaking with adrenaline. "Let me see your plan."

He handed over the packet—color coded and organized to perfection, and I scanned the mission statement.

Green products to promote healthier living.

All organic ingredients and vegan recipes.

Plans to collaborate with other local businesses, like Carla's and the vegan dessert place Nora told me about.

They could partner with Nora once she starts her business.

All the air left my lungs as I knew, in my gut, this was what I was searching for. This moment *right here*. I'd heard about silent partners, but never thought about *being* one.

"I'll do it," I said, not letting myself count the reasons this was risky. "I'll invest in your business, Peter. I want to be a silent partner."

Peter frowned and shared a look with Carla. "I appreciate the gesture, I really do. Carla said you're a great guy, but Fritz...we need one hundred thousand dollars to get the location, insurance, inventory."

"I understand. That's no problem." I already had my phone up, researching contracts. "I need to have my lawyer help me write up some contracts that protect us both during this, but I'm interested. I want to invest in businesses that help our community *and* the earth."

Peter blinked a few times before he tilted his head to the side. "You're serious."

"Yes, man." I held out my hand. "I want to do this. I think I need to. It's hard to explain. Once we figure out details, I want to help launch Creative Café."

With a wild grin on his face, Peter pulled me in for a hug. Carla bounced in her seat. I felt high, like that time I ate too many shrooms abroad when I was in my teens. My soul seemed to separate from my body, and I buzzed everywhere. If this worked, I could get an income from it. A certain percentage.

What if I do this for a couple businesses and quit my job? God, the pipe dream was closer than it'd been in years, and I slapped my knee. "I'm going to set up a meeting with my lawyer, and we'll reach out to you once we have the contracts. Can I take a copy of this?" I pointed to the plan, and he nodded so fast his glasses slid down his nose.

"Yes, take all of it. Any of it. I can't believe…is this really happening?"

"I'll be real with you." I wiped a hand over my face. "This is terrifying as hell for me, but it's the right move. We'll have a lot of kinks to work out as we navigate this, but I'm excited. I want this."

"That's more passion than I've had with other potential investors, so I'm in. Send me the details, and I'll be there."

With a new spring in my step, I walked from the table toward my car. I loosened my tie, and my cheeks actually hurt from smiling. This was crazy. Investing one hundred grand. The café could totally bust too—not have enough offerings for people to want to go there, for them to not make enough profit to even out. Hell, they could choose a terrible location. There were so many reasons it could fail, yet I was stoked to try.

As I got into my car and started the drive home, my mind kept thinking about how Peter reminded me of Nora. A little odd, quirky, passionate. He had a dream and did all the things, but it was still out of reach. Nora was *almost* like that.

She was given a choice to prove to her parents she could do it, and she wanted the easy way out, but that was before. She was different now. Enjoying her time being normal. God, I couldn't wait to tell her about Peter. I just had to figure out how to mask it without the full truth of who I was.

I parked the Beemer in the same spot and headed inside without a sign of Nora. Her typical audiobooks blared from her door, making me smile. It caused me to water and check out my own plants to make sure they were doing well. I couldn't have her plant babies die on my watch. She'd never forgive me.

Six weeks into this crazy ride, Nora had charmed me. She'd only have six weeks left, and while that caused a dull ache in my chest, it motivated me too. The selfish part of me wanted to find all the ways to keep her here, near me, while the competitive part wanted to show her that life without all the mansions and staff was just as good. After I *misted* two plants, watered another, clipped two of the larger ones, and scattered the hair Nora left for me—yes, she left me a baggie of hair. I didn't know if it was hers or not. Didn't ask—I plopped onto the couch and got out my phone. Call me love-sick or cheesy, but I wanted to see her.

Fritz: Hey Doc, you got plans tonight?

Nora: Yes. I'm sorry! I'm working on a big presentation I need to nail. I'll be here all night.

All night? Would she eat? Could I steal her for a quick dinner?

It wasn't like I could head into the office. I'd risk someone calling me Anthony. I sighed, weighed my options, and tapped my fingers against my thigh. But knowing her, she'd work through dinner and not eat because she'd be so into the work.

I could bring her food. Just a quick meal, and I'd be in and out.

Fritz: Did you bring something to eat for dinner?

Nora: No, but I'll find something here.

Fritz: I'll bring you food.

I already was up and throwing on a pair of jeans and an old base-ball tee from a charity game in college. Tossing on a Cubs hat and grabbing my wallet, I headed out and got into my car. I'd shown her pizza, Chinese, milkshakes and fries, but had she tried the best steak-burgers in all the land? Doubtful.

After stopping at the drive-through, I headed toward my parent's foundation and relaxed at the very few cars in the parking lot. Fewer cars meant fewer people who'd recognize me, and I grinned as I walked in and headed left down the hallway. Nora sat in one of the conference rooms, her laptop a few inches from her face and papers everywhere.

"This looks fun," I said, my pulse quickening when she glanced up at me and beamed. A full-face, too many teeth showing type of smile that I wanted to see over and over. No one had ever looked at me with that much joy.

"Oh, I don't know if I'm happier to see you or the food you have. I forgot lunch." She got up from the table, and as she neared, I had a total freak out.

Did I kiss her? Hug her in greeting? Or did we act cool, chill, friendly here? This was her work and my family's place, but she thought I was a chauffeur, and sweat pooled on my brow as she stepped toward me. She reached for the bag and leaned closer, her chin tilted up, and she pressed her lips against mine once, then again.

"Mm, I wish I could spend more time kissing you right now, but this table is a mess." She bit down on her lip and gave me a shy look. I still was frozen to my spot. She had *kissed* me. It wasn't a big deal in the grand scheme of things, but it felt big. Huge, even.

"Fritz? You okay?" Her lips curved down, and I snapped out of my weird mental state. It had to be the fact I was here, with her.

"Absolutely. Let's eat, and then you can tell me all about this project."

We ate fast and shared anecdotes about our day—she discovered how easy it was to burn a bag of microwave popcorn, and I explained all about Peter's new place.

"I'm thinking," I said, wiping my mouth with a napkin, "all these small, local businesses would be great to partner with when you have your place."

Her eyes lit up, and she looked out the window, almost as if she were lost in thought. "The older man with his jewelry, Carla's coffee, Peter's pastries. They all add an extra element to the plan, don't they?"

"You want plant therapy, right? I imagine you'd also have a greenhouse for people to buy plants, but I've been thinking about the therapy angle. If you have classes there, you could also host support groups and provide coffee and pastries. It's obviously your idea and vision, but these partnerships could really help the community and ensure your success."

"You've given this some thought," she said, putting her takeout wrapper into the trash and sitting back down across the table from me. "Do you think they would want a partnership if my business were up north? I worry about that. The jewelry angle is easier because he can ship stock once a month or so, and when I run low, I'd order more to sell. But perishables, I'm not sure."

The weight in my chest doubled. *Up north.* It was foolish to assume or imagine that she'd stay here, but in every scenario, I saw her here. In our college town. I should've known better. No matter how much I enjoyed our time together, she'd be gone. Either at the end of the twelve weeks or when she learned who I really was.

"Right, good point," I said, clearing my throat and needing to change the subject. I didn't have a single reason to explain why I was grumpy. She hadn't changed course at all. Not once. This misunderstanding was on me. "Now, talk to me about this presentation."

"Okay." She picked up some papers and pointed at charts. "Since they are letting me actually do things now, they wanted me to do a full-scale analyzation of all social medias. Honestly, I think they were hoping to give me something silly to keep me busy, but either way, I'm happy to showcase the numbers. They have a horrible social media presence and do nothing to track clicks, ROI, or engagement. Nothing. They don't preplan posts or make an effort to have a consistent brand."

"Wow." I scanned the sheet with charts and graphs. "This is a ton of information."

"Yes. And I'm comparing it to my parent's charity, which is significantly smaller scale. Yet their numbers are three times as good. Our donations double yours, purely from our online presence and awareness campaigns. If the goal is to raise more money to donate it and be actionable, then there is a lot of work to do."

"This suits you, Nora." I smiled at her as pride filled my soul. "This is amazing work. I can't wait to see what you do when you have your own business."

"Thank you." She blushed, but it didn't last long. The fact she took the compliment and *owned* it was sexy as hell.

My nerdy little plant girl was gaining confidence, and it was hot.

She pointed to her laptop and groaned. "The problem is putting it together to make it easy to read with clear next steps. I get carried away with details, and I know I can lose my audience."

"Big pictures, big images, big impact." I pointed at the two charts that showed online engagement and donations comparison between her parents' and my parents' foundation. "Start with that."

"Okay, okay." She clicked on her laptop and ran her tongue over her lips. She connected her laptop to the large screen and adjusted her slides. "I think I got it."

Nora moved a bunch of slides around and worked in silence as I watched. She hummed to herself, made facial expressions as she talked to herself, and it was so dang goofy. I forgot where I was and to keep on the lookout for anyone who could blow my cover, because Nora was so mesmerizing, that when someone knocked on the glass, I sucked in a breath and made myself choke.

I hit my chest and coughed as Nora looked at whoever entered.

"Ah, getting it all ready, huh?"

Angelica.

Shit.

Nora nodded, but the light faded from her eyes.

I gritted my teeth. Angelica had *better* have been treating her right.

"I'm confident it'll get us on the right track here," Nora said, forcing a tight smile.

Angelica walked farther into the room, and I knew the second she saw me. Her mouth parted, and she raised her brows in question. "Trying to go over my head here, Nora?"

"Can I talk to you about an errand outside for a moment?" I said, bolting up and seconds away from panic. My voice came out stronger than I wanted, but Angelica seemed to get the idea. She frowned and followed me outside the doors.

The glass walls were a pain, so I led us farther into the building, where Nora couldn't see us.

"Fritz, what in the hell?"

"Look," I said, pinching the bridge of my nose as my lie was including more and more people. "She doesn't...she thinks I'm just Fritz. Not Anthony. I'd like to keep it that way."

"Um, why?" Angelica frowned, and a combination of disappointment and curiosity oozed off her with her furrowed brows and tight lines around her mouth.

"It's hard to explain."

No, it's not.

"Try me."

"We all know why she was sent here, and at first, she insisted on meeting *Anthony* to call in a favor. That favor was a sham marriage so she could get her money. I just…panicked. She didn't recognize me, and it felt nice to not have someone want me for money."

She sighed and reached over to squeeze my forearm. "I heard tidbits about what happened with Samantha, and I'm sorry you've gone through this. But, Fritz, this will not end well if you don't tell her the truth."

"I know that. I really do. I just need to find the right time." My stomach twisted in horrible knots, knowing the timer was getting closer to zero.

"I won't say anything, I swear, but…" She trailed off, her tone tightening. "You're playing her."

"What? I'm not…I'm not doing this to hurt her or anything. Actually, I really—"

"Um, hey, guys," Nora said, making me clutch my chest.

She stood right behind us. A few feet.

Fuck. How much did she hear?

My pulse rushed to my ears, and I could barely make out her question as my body thumped with worry.

"Could one of you help me?" she asked, tilting her head to the side as she fidgeted with her fingers.

Angelica brushed past me, and I followed, numb and freaking out. If she heard any part of that conversation without context, she could *hate me.*

And I'd deserve it.

I had to figure out what she'd heard and fix it. Immediately. My feet weighed a million pounds as I followed the two of them back into the room, and each breath felt like knives stabbing my throat. "What's going on?" My voice cracked. I studied Nora's every move. If she overheard my conversation, then she'd be upset. Or glare at me. Or throw something at me, at least.

She looked up with the warmth in her eyes I'd become accustomed to, and my body sagged in relief. "I can't connect to the printer, and it keeps asking me to search for one?"

"Oh, I can help with that." Angelica moved closer to her and typed on her device. When she was done, she gave me a hard look. "I'll see myself out. Fritz, have a good night."

"You too, Angelica." I smiled, but it was too forced and awkward.

Nora didn't notice, and for that, I was thankful. I sat in the chair next to her and made a vow to be more careful. With her huge presentation in two weeks, it'd be cruel to upset her before then, so until that was done...I had to make sure she didn't find out the truth. Because if she learned I wasn't who she thought I was, it could ruin everything.

Chapter Twenty-Three

A week later, I had all the paper work necessary to set up another meeting with Peter. But I hesitated on making the call. So much rode on this, and without even thinking, I made the short walk toward Nora's apartment and knocked.

Her world had shifted, and if anyone would have advice on doing something crazy, it'd be her. No audiobooks or music drifted from her place, and the quiet threw me off. Nora was never quiet. A prickle of worry had me cracking my knuckles as I waited for her to answer.

I knocked again. "Nora, you there?"

The door swung open. "Hi, hey. Yes. Here I am," she said, rather breathless, and like that, the tension eased off my muscles. Her face and smile brought me a joy I hadn't felt in a long time.

Best not to think about that too much.

"Can I talk to you about something?" I asked, still fidgeting with my fingers. I really didn't think this through—how could I talk to her about this risk with Peter without actually telling her details? I squeezed the back of my neck as a line appeared between her brows.

"Talk? Um, yes." She chewed the side of her mouth and ushered me in, and her movements were stiff. She walked toward the kitchen table and paused. "Uh, is this a kitchen table conversation or a couch one? I've never had *the talk* with someone before and I'm actually nervous and don't know where to sit. If we're on the couch, it could be weird sitting close and honestly, the plants don't need any negativity."

"Nora," I said, laughing and putting my hands on her shoulders. She froze, her body becoming like concrete, and I kissed her neck. "I'm sorry that wasn't clear. *We* don't need to talk, if that's what you thought."

"Ah," she said, sighing and spinning around in my arms so we were chest to chest. A slight blush painted her cheeks. "Well, I feel like you have enough experience to know never to tell a lady *you need to talk*. Especially, before kissing her."

"Oh, that's what I did wrong, then." I bent lower and lower, taking my time bringing my mouth to hers, and she let out a little groan when I finally pressed my lips against hers. She tasted like mint and smelled like flowers. She hummed against me and dug her fingers into my shoulders and kissed me hard. It started out as sweet, but it turned hot really fast. She ran her hands over my pecs and shoulders and nipped at my bottom lip before pulling back.

"So what did you need to talk about then?"

"You tease." I narrowed my eyes and tried to yank her back to me, but she escaped my grasp. "Was that payback? Get me hot and bothered for fun?"

"Perhaps." She wiggled her brows and went into the living room. She changed from work attire and wore an extralarge pink shirt and those tight little shorts underneath, and I joined her on the couch, moving her legs over so they rested on my lap.

It felt cozy. Warm. Nice.

She studied me with slightly parted lips and nudged me with her foot. "Go on then. You look nervous."

"I haven't really planned this out in my head," I said, leaning my neck back onto the edge of the couch to stare at her ceiling. "So this might not make sense, but you're the first person I wanted to talk to about this."

She smiled and nudged me again. "I have conversations with plants, Fritz. I can handle whatever you throw my way."

I laughed. "Fair point."

"No pressure either, okay? I don't think I've seen you this worked up before. Take your time. I just like being with you. Do you want the TV on? Sports? YouTube of a greenhouse in the rain?"

"No, no," I said, looking at her and my chest feeling lighter. "When you're able to open your place...what if you get stage fright?"

"Why would I when I've been dreaming about it my whole life? Stage fright? No. I might have nerves and not sleep for a year, but stage fright is just anxiety about not doing well. I've done so much research and planning. I'll be in the best position possible. Sure, things could go wrong, but I've planned for that."

"So you're saying, enough preparation should help with...taking a huge chance on something knowing it could easily fail?" I rubbed my hand up and down her calf muscle, kneading the soft skin and grounding myself in the moment. My heart raced, but it wasn't out of only fear. There was excitement and the possibility of *what if* this thing with Peter worked.

"I think there is always a chance of something to not work. You adjust. You alter. Those aren't necessarily failures. I take it you're at a crossroads of doing something big?"

"Sort of." I sighed, hating the fact I couldn't be honest with her yet. After the conversation with Angelica the week before, I came to the conclusion that once I knew for sure Nora wasn't going to ask for the fake marriage for money, I'd tell her.

I needed that assurance that money wasn't a motivator, a solution to her problem. Yes, it meant I continued a semi-lie to her, and Gilly disagreed at my urge to double down, but Samantha had poked a huge hole in my soul doing what she did.

I had to protect myself from feeling that hurt again. So either I told Nora right at the conclusion of her time in Normalville and hoped she decided to stay here, or...if she told me she didn't need Anthony Carter for any reason, then I'd tell her.

But neither were options right now, and I continued talking. "I have a chance to do something that gives me a feeling that I've been searching for—for a long time, actually. It makes me feel like I'm doing the right thing and excites me. But doing it is a real risk and could end up hurting someone else too."

"Hm, that's tough." She pursed her lips and moved her attention to her plants. "If this is something you want, this feeling you said, then I think you need to follow through with it. From what I know about you, Fritz, you do the right thing. You're patient. You're incredibly quick-witted and smart. You'll figure out all the things you need to do to make it the best you can. I have no doubt there. If I've learned anything from being here, away from my parents and endless credit, is the things that scare us the most tend to be worth it."

"What do you mean?" I slid my gaze to her and counted her bright-orange earrings today. Her faded pink hair had grown out a little bit, and her smooth creamy neck had one freckle on it. She was so fucking pretty, my breathing hitched.

"It's silly to someone like you," she said, blushing and looking down for a second. "But I was terrified of learning how to get food on my own. Clothes. Basic houseware items. I had no idea what to do, and it was mortifying to be my age and not know. Going to a job that was handed to me with people who thought I was ridiculous? Horrifying. Going on those dates you insisted to *get experience* was exhilarating and scary."

"I hope there's a *but* coming because now I feel bad."

"But," she said, grinning at me, "every one of those experiences has been worth it. I now can *adult* pretty okay, and all those moments led me to you." She narrowed her eyes as a soft, warm expression relaxed her fast. "I don't know what this thing is for you, but I promise you, you'll regret *not* trying it rather than going for it."

"God, you're right." I nodded to myself, to her, and let the feeling settle over me. I had to go for this because I'd regret it if I didn't. I had the contract, and my lawyers looked it over. Both myself and Peter were protected.

The only harm would be losing one hundred thousand dollars if Peter went belly-up with the business. I'd be a silent partner and meet with him once every week for an update, but that was it. I could offer guidance, but he'd handle the rest.

I had to trust the contract was solid and that Peter wanted this enough to not fail.

"I'm going to do it." I stared at my pixie neighbor. "I'm going to take a risk."

Her answering smile was filled with tenderness and pride. She reached over and squeezed my forearm. "I knew you would."

I watched her fingers move over my skin and adjusted our positions so my hips aligned with hers. "One day, I'll tell you about it."

"I can't wait." Her breathing picked up, and I flirted with the edge of her shirt. Her eyes darkened, and I wanted to make sure Nora continued to take risks and learn and experience all the things she could before…this ended.

"Tomorrow," I said, nuzzling her neck and teasing her sensitive skin. I was obsessed with her collarbone and how she let out a deep groan when I licked a line to her ear. "I'm taking you somewhere."

"Like a date?"

"Like a date." I nibbled on her earlobe, not hard, but just a tease, and she arched her back underneath me. "But it's not a typical date. You haven't been on one like this." I kissed down toward her chest, sliding the shirt up and over her head so I could see all of her. She wore a lacy purple bra that hid *nothing*, and I bit down on her pebbled nipple, over the fabric.

"Mm," she said, groaning and running her hands through my hair. "I like atypical things. Have you seen my life?"

I laughed before biting her other nipple, taking the pointed nub between my teeth and teasing it until she thrashed beneath me. She was so sensitive and reactionary. I could spend months exploring all the way she moved, moaned, or lost control around me. "That is true, Nora," I said, licking down the center of her stomach.

Her rib cage expanded as her breathing quickened.

"So what do you say? Will you go on an atypical date with me tomorrow?"

"Mm," she said.

"Full sentence, baby," I said, sliding my fingers into her shorts and waiting. She tried shimmying her shorts off, but I needed her words first.

"Yes, yes, date tomorrow, but right now I need—"

"Need what?"

"You."

That one syllable word sent a flurry of emotions throughout my body, but the dominant one was lust. I could give her that part of me over and over. The part I was afraid of giving her was my heart.

Chapter Twenty-Four

WE'D BEEN ON DINNER DATES, SPENT PLENTY OF TIME NAKED IN bed, on the couch, in the shower, yet standing outside her door with the dumb plant in my hands felt more intimate than any of those things. Nothing had changed, yet it *felt* different.

I wore jeans, a white button-down shirt and brown shoes. I rolled the sleeves up and trimmed my beard. I looked good. I was careful not to let the Edelweiss plant spill over onto my shirt or the ground. I still couldn't believe I'd found one or that I was doing this. It was by far the cheesiest thing I had ever done.

"Fritz, hi," Nora said, opening her door and stepping out into the foyer.

My mouth literally dropped open. She wore some one-piece outfit that was all pinks and purples and yellows, and it hugged her curves in every way.

It had tiny straps on her shoulders and ended on her upper thighs, and I *loved* it. My tongue swelled eighteen sizes too large, and it took a second for me to speak. "Nora, fuck."

"Do you like it? I bought it for tonight!" She spun around, giving me a great view of her bare back and ample ass.

"What is this material? It's like it's painted on you." I reached out to touch it, and the silky-smooth fabric felt like heaven. Without ruining it, I gripped a bit of it and yanked her toward me. "Kiss me, woman, or I might die."

She giggled against my mouth, and I probed until she let me slide my tongue in. God, she was perfectly weird and gorgeous. With restraint that showed how much of a saint I was, I pulled back. If we kept kissing, I'd rip off her pretty new outfit and leave her naked for the entire weekend. I was sure of it.

"Quite a kiss, Fritz," she said, running her fingers over her swollen lips.

"Quite an outfit," I said back.

She blushed, and her gaze moved toward the plant in my hand. "Oh, do you need me to take a look at this for you? I am the plant doctor if you didn't know." She winked at me.

Oh, I *loved* flirty winking Nora.

"Actually, I got this for you. Instead of a bouquet of flowers, I figured this was better for a couple of reasons."

"You bought me a plant?" she asked, her voice getting all high, and she blinked a few times.

"Yes, but not *any* plant either. This is an Edelweiss. The story of it signifies strength and courage, and you, Doc, are filled with strength and have tons of courage." I held the plant out to her, sweat forming on my brow at her reaction.

She took it, stared at it, and didn't say anything.

Shit.

"I didn't buy a bouquet because I figured they would die, and while they are pretty, they don't last. This plant is not only pretty, but also represents courage and bravery. It's perfect for you." I cleared my throat, and my entire body tensed from her lack of reaction. I thought it'd be a good idea and unique to who she was, but the longer the silence went on, regret swept in.

"Look, I can take it back. I researched what plants had meanings and even joined this social media group to learn about it. If you don't like it, I can it find a new home." I grabbed for the pot, and that seemed to snap her back to the present.

"Don't you dare." She moved it out of reach, her eyes shining with...tears?

Did I make her cry? Damn it. "Nora, why are you...I'm sorry."

"Sorry? You're sorry?" she asked, her voice rising as she shook her head. "This is the best gift I've ever gotten in my life. The *absolute* best. It is so kind and thoughtful that I'm having a moment, so you shut your mouth and stand there and let me take this in, okay?"

"Yes, ma'am," I said, smiling so large my face hurt. She *loved* it. I let her stare at the plant as she blinked a lot and chewed on her lip. "I'm really glad you like it."

"I'm obsessed. Like doesn't begin to cover it, and I don't know what to do. My heart is racing, and I want to jump on you, make out with you, and go take care of the plant and make sure she settles in. I'm going to call her Fritzy."

"Fritzy?" My brows disappeared into my hairline. "Really?"

"Yes. I think it's fitting," she said, her lip curving into a smile as the water in her eyes fell down her cheeks. "I can't even begin to describe what this means to me. All the dates I've been set up on, all the rich boys my parents tried to get me to be into...all those gifts have *nothing* on this. I need you to know this means a lot to me, okay?"

"I understand," I said, somehow knowing that the panic in her voice matched the panic growing around my heart. They were the same. I cupped her face and kissed her once more, slowly. "We have some time before our date. You could go get her settled if you want, but not the whole welcoming committee, okay? Just a quick intro."

"God, I like you so much." She plastered a wet, messy kiss on me before she ran back into her apartment, and I leaned against the wall grinning like an idiot.

"Wow, what did I just watch?" Gilly, my goddamn sister, stood at the entrance to the complex. She had wide eyes and a half smile, but her tone wasn't lost on me. She might've assumed Nora and I were... close, but I hadn't told her the full of it. "Fritz, is this for real?"

I pushed off the wall and made sure the door was shut. "Not the time, Gil, please."

"I texted you I was on my way," she said, frowning as she stared at Nora's door. "Dude, does she know the truth now?"

"No, not yet." I winced as my sister's gaze cooled. "Look, I'm taking her on a date and——"

"You need to tell her. This is fucked up. Especially after our pasts." Gilly shook her head and pinched the bridge of her nose. "Tomorrow, we're talking."

"Fine, tomorrow though. You need to go, *now*." I pointed at the glass doors, my heart hammering against my rib cage over and over as the weight in my stomach grew. Nothing she said was wrong, but how did she not get that I needed this to *not* be about marriage for money?

"If you care for her...she deserves to know. It shouldn't change anything if you explain it start to finish." She reached for me and squeezed my arm. It was then I noticed the sadness in her eyes.

"Wait, why did you come over? Is everything okay?" My goddamn mind could only be stretched so thin, and with the upcoming meeting with Peter, the date and lies with Nora, I wasn't sure I could handle it if Christopher did something to my sister.

I'd kill him.

"Did he do something?" I asked, feeling my blood pressure spike.

"No, not Christopher." She smiled. "He's been...no, it's not him. It's about Mom. That's all. Nothing major and I'll get over it."

A knob turned, a squeaky sound filling the room, and I froze. *Nora.* Fuck!

"Oh, sorry!" she said, her singsong voice filled with so much joy. "Did the Carters have something urgent come up?"

"Yes, but it'll be taken care of *tomorrow*," my sister said, her intention crystal clear to me. "Bye, Nora!"

My sister waved and narrowed her eyes at me before leaving. I took a shaky breath at how close that was. *What if Nora heard?*

"You sure it's all okay? We can always reschedule if you need to do your job."

My jaw tightened, and my molars hurt. "No, no, come on. Let's go."

I held out my hand and waited for her to take it. She did, and I focused on making tonight enjoyable for her. No thoughts of Gilly, our mom, the mistaken identity issue, or what would happen when she went back home.

It was just us.

"THIS IS *AMAZING!*" NORA SCANNED THE ANIMAL SHELTER WITH HER wide eyes. She spun in a circle and kept repeating it over and over how great this was.

And we hadn't started yet. "Doc, hold on. You don't even know what we're doing. It could be gross. What if we get assigned to do litter cleanup?"

She scrunched her nose and shrugged. "If it helps them, then it'll be amazing."

She walked to a cage with the name *LEAFY* under it, and a tiny gray cat sat curled up in the small kennel. "They look so sweet and scared."

"I imagine so. At least they are safe here, fed, warm. It could be worse if this place didn't take them in." I kept a hand on her lower back, but she reached up and intertwined our fingers. Small gesture, huge impact. She held my hand tight, like she could only convey her thoughts and excitement through squeezes.

Just another cute layer of my neighbor.

"Fritz, Nora, thank you both for your time." The volunteer coordinator entered the room. She eyed our outfits and frowned. "You might get dirty."

"I prefer it that way," Nora said, beaming at her. "He surprised me with this date night, so I promise I didn't choose to wear this here, but I'll do anything. It can be washed."

The woman smiled and picked up a clipboard. "Appreciate the can-do attitude. Tonight, I need you to clean cages and water bowls first. Then, if you want, just play with them. The dogs get all the attention for playtime, but cats need human connection too."

Nora nodded as she eyed Leafy again. "Of course, yes, we'll do it all."

"Agreed. We're here to help," I said, already planning my next move. The date was intended to show Nora how getting your hands dirty was better than writing a check *sometimes*, but I had an ulterior motive.

One I was pretty sure she was going to think of on her own.

"I heard this place does an educational program where they pair up with schools to show kids how to care for animals." There, I lobbed the idea at her.

"How wonderful. This is such a humbling experience." She put on gloves and went to the first empty kennel. "It makes me feel foolish that I thought a social media campaign would be enough to help."

"Not foolish. Misdirected. And those do help sometimes. Your heart was always in the right place. Now, you have more experience getting your hands dirty." I followed her and put on gloves and got the cleaning materials.

There were at least thirty kennels to clean from the coordinator's list, and that would definitely take more than an hour. I'd planned on doing an hour here and then a fun dinner, but Nora's face was set in determination. "What are you thinking about?"

"This is amazing, Fritz. This date. Really. It's right up my alley, but I'm struggling with the fact I don't *do* enough to help. I'm privileged and…" She trailed off, her shoulders slumping as she lost a bit of her mojo.

"Hey, hey, look at me."

She did.

"Strong and courageous. That's you. This isn't a failure. You need to readjust your plans. Your words, babe, not mine."

She grinned and leaned over for a quick kiss. "I might keep you around, Fritz."

"I might let you."

After that, we got to work cleaning all the items on the list. They broke it down to do half the kennels for our shift, and someone else would do the others the next day. I sweated a lot, and Nora had a smudge of something brown on her forehead, but it was so cute, I didn't tell her. We replaced water bowls and put all the cleaning supplies away before she looked at me with a crazed expression.

"Playtime," she said, moving toward the narrow hallway to poke her head into the office there. "I think we're ready to spend some time with them now."

"Excellent. I'll unlock one at a time, and when you're done, just let me know."

"Do they get excited when they're let out?" Nora asked, her voice small again.

"Yes," the woman said, smiling as she let out the first cat. Sir Greg was the name. He was thin and a dark gray with bright-blue eyes. "Greg acts like he hates people, but secretly loves them."

"Oh." Nora reached in her hand, letting Greg sniff her. He warmed up really fast, and soon enough, Nora was playing with the older guy and laughing her face off.

Seeing her smile did weird things to my chest, and the more she played with the cat, the stranger that feeling got. Dressed in her beautiful, sexy outfit, she sat crisscross on the floor with the cat, covered in dirt and evidence of sweat all over her, yet...she was so fucking gorgeous. She caught me staring at her. "Best. Date. Ever."

"Good." I bent down to pet Greg and found the pang in my chest grow. How could we put him back in the cage? What if he liked us? What if he thought we were going to take him home? Shit.

A pressure grew behind my eyes, and I stepped away.

"You know..." Nora said, picking Greg up and speaking in a soft, low voice. "Greg reminds me of you, actually."

"Are you saying I'm getting old and think myself a royal?"

"No," she said, laughing. "He just has this thing about him. Makes you feel at ease. Taking care of a cat isn't that much work, you know."

"Nora," I warned, already thinking along the same lines. I couldn't stand to put Greg back in the small kennel when he could've gotten his hopes up. She handed him to me, and the cat purred when I scratched his head. Purred.

Fuck.

"Take him away, please," I said, my throat getting tight. This plan had backfired. This was supposed to be about her, and now I was thinking of adopting a cat because he could be sad? Who the hell was I anymore?

I was staring at the other end of the room when I felt a hand on my shoulder. Then, she moved and wrapped her arms around me from behind so her head rested against my back. I never cared for being the little spoon, but with her tiny arms holding me, it felt right. "Nora."

"I know why you brought us here, and I can't thank you enough for everything. I can see myself involving shelter cats at the greenhouse. Maybe I could let some live there or have a class for kids? Maybe I have adoptathons there or bring awareness to the shelter. I know exactly why you brought me here, but, Fritz? I think you needed to come here for a reason too. Life has a weird way of working out and I know you're fighting it, but Greg is yours."

The tightness grew in my throat, and I cleared it a few times before nodding. Life did have a weird way of working out, and Greg wasn't the only one who felt like mine.

Chapter Twenty-Five

GRACE AND GILLY EACH HELD A MIMOSA THE NEXT MORNING AS SIR Greg moved from the couch to the carpet, eyeing them like he couldn't decide if they were enemies or allies. I had to agree. I didn't need a guilt trip from them. I *knew* I had to tell the truth.

With her huge presentation coming up…it felt rude to distract her from it. Once that was done, then I'd come clean. Tell her everything.

Gilly took a large swig and set her glass down, but Grace held hers with her knowing eyes pinching at the sides. "G, I don't wanna hear it." I held up my hand. "I will tell her, eventually. When the timing is right."

"This is worse than what your sister did. She was still herself, just hid the fact she had a trust fund. This is pretending to be someone you're not," Grace said, a little pink to her cheeks. "This isn't you. You're not that guy."

"When I saw her at the airport, and she assumed I was the chauffeur, I took the easy way out. I didn't think she'd make it a week before giving up and going back to her palace, and then I'd be off the hook. If I'd known that we—that I'd feel—" I paced the living room, and Sir Greg tracked me with his shrewd gaze. "She has me feeling all sorts of ways when we're together. Different. Like…I don't know. She bought me plants. I own plants *and* a cat now. I look for ways she could add things to her dream plant business idea and just…" I pulled on the ends of my hair. "I like her. A lot."

"So you're scared," Grace said, smiling a bit. "This is for real then."

"I know I need to tell her. And I will, but yes, I think you're right. I am scared, but I didn't invite both of you over here to lecture me. We have shit to talk about." I cleared my throat.

Grace's face paled, and she set the mimosa on the table, untouched.

Gilly sighed and reached for Sir Greg and put him in her lap. The traitor decided she was a friend and curled next to her. "I love him."

I smiled. "Yeah, it's been a weird couple of weeks for me. Learning all sorts of things about myself."

"Like the fact you're a cat person."

"That." I ran a hand over my jaw and felt the pressure in my chest build. It got so heavy that it overflowed, like someone forgot to turn the faucet off in the sink. I *had* to tell them. "I'm doing something crazy this week."

"More than…what we've already discussed?" Grace said, furrowing her dark eyebrows. She had a twinge of an accusation in her tone, and I narrowed my eyes, looking at the mimosa and then to her stomach.

I wasn't the only one with secrets, but I wouldn't *dare* guess why she wasn't drinking. Not my business or surprise. But I enjoyed how she sat up straighter after my pointed look. I winked, trying to tell her without words that I wouldn't just blurt it out. If she and Brock were *really* having a kid, I couldn't wait to spoil that baby rotten. And get them clothes because Grace and Brock wore too much athletic gear. They needed someone to teach their baby style. Even Nora had her own style that was unique and fun, but she'd probably dress a kid to match her flowers.

Whoa. Nora and a baby. Hmm.

"Fritz, what is it?" Grace asked, her voice pleading.

I got lost in the thought of babies, and my face heated. "Ah, sorry." I blinked a few times and stared at the plants in the corner of my room, curving my lips up remembering how Nora broke into my place to put them there. Courage. She was all courage, and I could show some too. "I'm meeting with a man this week to help launch his business. It'll focus on being green and providing jobs to the community."

"Okay, that sounds cool," Gilly said, playing with the end of her skirt.

"I'm going to be a silent partner. I'm fronting all the money for it. If he fails, then I don't get it back. I just…I feel *hopeless* at my job and don't feel like I do enough for the community, the world. I don't know. This is terrifying to try a new venture, but I think…I gotta try it."

There, I'd said it. I told them the truth, and now they'd tell me I was a fool. An idiot. I tensed, waiting for the questions and accusations, but none came. I glanced at them, and they both wore smiles. Wait. "Why are you smiling?"

"I think that's fantastic." Gilly nodded and elbowed Grace in the side. "You've been in a rut since the whole Samantha fiasco, and if you're excited about this, then I'm so glad."

"You don't think I'm being dumb?"

"For wanting to help bring business to our community? For following something that makes you happy? No, I don't." Gilly stood up with Greg in her arms. "I trust that you had the right people look over any contracts."

"Yeah." The pressure loosened a bit in my throat. "G, what do you think?"

"I agree with Gilly. You've always been passionate about life. You've had this zest that borders on annoying where you found joy and mischief in everything. I want to see that Fritz again. Maybe it's your job, or the fact we're getting older, or the Samantha thing…but find that zest again."

"I fucking love you guys," I said, moving to hug Gilly and pulling her toward the couch to hug Grace at the same time. Their support flowed through me, motivating me even more to try this thing with Peter. It could work, or it wouldn't, and then I'd know.

"We haven't had a group hug in months!" Gilly wiggled out from the embrace, and Sir Greg exited the room fast. Group cuddles were probably not a cat thing. "Well, to update you both, Mom has been giving me shit about missing all the wedding plans and saying I'm not flexible enough for her. I just…I've moved three different things for her."

Grace started reminding her of how the wedding was about the couple getting married, not anyone else, and I nodded. But my phone buzzed on the table. I reached for it immediately, thinking it could be Peter, but an email from Nora Atwood popped up.

My gut tightened. Did she find out the truth and was emailing me good-bye? A fuck-you email? The subject said *meeting*.

I sank onto the chair as every bone in my body seemed to double in weight. She wanted to meet *Anthony*, again? Was she back on her marriage nonsense? The favor I owed her? I pinched the bridge of my nose as disappointed rooted me to the spot. I thought she was happy hanging out with me, experiencing life away from the mansion. She was becoming independent and growing, so for her to think she needed a marriage…it stung.

Plus, what reason would she want a fake marriage to get the funds when she only had a month left?

I clicked the email as my ears rang. It was a hard pill to swallow knowing that she didn't feel the same way about me as I did her. She was a breath of fresh air right after it rained, where the earth smelled cleaner, different. I was just a what…distraction? A way to pass the time until she got back to her life?

Dear Anthony,

I've heard a lot about your contributions to the foundation and would like to set up a meeting to discuss a partnership with you. A deal, even. From what I've learned about you, this would be beneficial to both of us. I hope you're well. Your mom set us up an appointment in two weeks, but if you're free before then, please reach out. Looking forward to it.

Nora

I exhaled slowly as the words blurred together, the sinking feeling in my chest getting worse the more I read it. My contributions. Did that mean…money? A partnership meant marriage, right? And it would benefit the both of us? God. I blew out a frustrated breath, and the uneasy knot in my gut grew.

Maybe it wasn't *marriage*, and I was projecting that?

No. That was a hard sell.

That had to be it. I swallowed and put my phone in my pocket, content to ignore the email until I figured out what to do. Grace and Gilly were midconversation about teacher shit—that happened every time they were together more than thirty minutes, and I focused on them. It wasn't until there was a break of silence that Grace stood up from the couch and put her arms behind her back.

I frowned at how awkward she seemed. "G, what are you doing?"

"I had a plan or something on how to do this. But it's all out the window." She blinked a few times, and her breathing picked up.

My body tensed, and I had a feeling about what she was going to say. My lips curved up, and I crossed one leg over the other. "Do it, Grace. I promise you, it'll be fine."

Gilly tilted her head. "What are you talking about?"

Grace exhaled for a full minute before she stared at my sister. "I love you, Gilly, you know that, and I'm sorry the timing isn't ideal for your wedding or shenanigans but..." She paused and gave a small smile. "I'm pregnant."

"Holy shit!" Gilly flew off the couch and wrapped Grace in a hug. "Oh my God, oh my God. Little Grace or Little Brock will be here? How far are you? How do you feel? What did Brock do?"

I couldn't stand to watch them hug and not join, so I did. I wrapped my arms around my two closest friends in the world as Grace cried and Gilly sniffed. My face warmed at all the feelings I had in the moment, all good ones. Grace would be the best mom in the world, and Brock...he'd be a grumpy, protective dad. That's for sure.

"I just want the record to state that I figured this out on my own."

"Shut up, Fritz," Grace said, resting her head on my chest as Gilly's rested on hers.

We were a pretzel of arms and embraces, and despite the drama with our mom, with my indecision about my life, and the issue with Nora...life was good. Better than good. Things would be okay. I just had a feeling.

THREE DAYS LATER, I WALKED INTO THE APARTMENT UNIT DRESSED in the same thing I always wore—fitted black pants, a button-down gray shirt, and a black tie. My hair was styled the same, and my shoes were scuff-free. The only difference was the exhilarating way my heart beat in my chest. It was official.

I fronted Peter one hundred thousand dollars to start a business. We signed the papers, and we'd meet again in two weeks. It'd work, or it wouldn't, but my skin seemed to buzz with a new feeling. Anticipation. Without even thinking, I knocked on Nora's door, and the familiar sounds of her audiobooks filtered through.

What a beautiful nut.

"Oh, hey," she said, opening the door and dragging her gaze up and down my body. "Wowza. You in a tie is a good look." She reached out and trailed her finger up the tie and pulled on it, bringing me closer.

She grinned up at me, the light hitting the purple gems in her ear today, and just seeing the warmth and trust in her eyes evaporated the negative feeling I'd carried around since getting that email. I hadn't avoided her the past three days, I'd just…kept my distance. She was working on her presentation, and I'd met with Peter.

"I missed you," she said, blushing a bit as she leaned closer to me. She hesitated before pressing her warm lips against mine, and the second they touched, my body roared to life. I gripped the back of her head and kissed her back. A slow tangle of tongues and teeth, soft moans, and hungry touches.

"Me too," I said against her mouth, pushing us inside her place. She clawed at my chest and shoulders, arching her body against mine and flooding me with her heat. Part of me wanted to strip this baggy T-shirt and shorts right off her and lose myself in her body. The other part needed to know *why* she was still emailing Anthony.

A small third part wanted to call my mom and yell at her for setting up a meeting, but I pushed all thoughts of my *mom* out of my mind. Nora was right here in front of me with wet lips. I dragged my lips from her mouth to her neck, nibbling the skin there and inhaling her floral, earthy scent. I'd definitely miss the way she smelled when this ended. Like nature at its finest, a campsite after a rain shower.

"You want some food? I learned how to make a mean macaroni." She winked, and I was done for. A winking, *confident* Nora was my own catered-to-me version of Kryptonite. Even in her *save the whales* T-shirt and with hundreds of plants around us.

"Look at you go. Yes, feed me, woman." I reluctantly sat at her kitchen table and stared at the plants in the living room. They were slightly larger than when she first got them, and a large poster hung uneven on the wall with the watering and trimming schedule. Would her kids take turns watering plants? Our chores were sweeping the stable or cleaning the china. Nora's would definitely have to plant.

Why the *hell* was I thinking about kids? It had to be Grace's recent news.

I pulled on the collar of my dress shirt and loosened my tie. The summer heat must be getting to me. "Work going well?"

"Yes. I'm almost ready to present to the board about a new direction they could all go. I have nine days to get ready. It's…hm." She chewed on her bottom lip as she stared at me for a beat. "I feel like I could do real work here, and I know my parents had a role in getting this position—"

"Had a role? That's why you got it," I said, clarifying while hoping I didn't sound like a dick.

"True," she said, smiling and tapping her fingers on the counter as she leaned against it. "I just feel like I'm *finally* earning a little respect. I'm learning a lot from them."

"The foundation has some great people to learn from."

Nora got out a box of noodles and a block of cheese. Wait, was she going to make it with real cheese and not from the box? Whoa. Settle down, Chef. With her back to me, her shirt rode up a hair when she reached for a grater, and after checking out her ass, I had to ask about the grater.

"Nora, you literally microwaved foil a month ago. How in the hell did you get a grater? That's like level three and you're on two."

She pursed her lips and pointed the device at me like a weapon. "I researched, thank you very much. I'm a quick learner. In fact, I have a question for you since you've been around the Carters for so long."

Shit. My throat tightened, and I eyed her thermostat. It had to be ninety degrees in her unit. Maybe I should get it fixed or looked at. "What's your question?" I croaked out.

"How long have you worked for them? Do you do more than just chauffeur? I feel like you do." Her tone wasn't suspicious or accusatory. I tried searching for a hidden meaning or a trick in her words.

Did she find out who I was and wanted to play a game? No, that wasn't Nora. I cleared my throat. "I've been around a while to know a lot about how things work."

"Do you always want to work for them?"

"No," I said, one million percent truthful. "I think it'll be nice to always help out or be available, but I don't want the foundation to be my career."

"Yes, but if it's worth anything, I think you could do more for them. You're kind and intelligent and witty as hell. They talk warmly about you when I bring up your name." Nora smiled, not having a single clue that I was dying inside.

This was too close. Way too close to the truth. My stomach soured, and my palms sweat buckets. Literal buckets. I wiped them on my pants and took off my tie. If she was talking about me to other people there, they could totally spill everything. Ruin it all before I had a chance to explain. Which I would. Tuesday night. After the presentation. When I hoped she'd understand and forgive me because this *thing* between us wasn't temporary for me.

"Fritz?" she said, her voice softer than before. She frowned and walked up to me, running her dirt-stained fingers through my hair. "Hey, you got all quiet on me."

"Sorry, lost in thought." I gripped her hips and dug my fingers into her curves. I wanted more time with her, away from all this. The lies, the foundation, my family, my bank account. It might've been selfish of me, but if I only had a limited amount of time with her, I wanted her to myself. I knew just the thing.

"Nora, will you come camping with me this weekend?"

"Camping?" Her eyebrows disappeared into her pink hairline. "Like...sleep outside?"

"We'll have a tent." I smiled at the panic on her face. Her eyes widened, and she scrunched her nose. "You play in dirt every day, yet the thought of being in a tent is too much for you?"

She blinked a few times and tilted her head to the side, looking at me through her lashes. "You've done this before, yes?"

"A ton. It's one of my favorite getaways."

"So you know how to prevent bears and tigers from eating us?"

I snorted. "Correct."

"Do I have to?"

I fisted the end of her shirt and pulled her so she straddled my lap. Pink tinged her cheeks, and I ran my hands under her shirt, holding onto her waist as she sucked in a breath. Yeah, we'd be removing all clothing after the food was done. "Don't you want to experience everything you can while you're here?" I licked my bottom lip, and she trailed the movement, her breaths coming out in little puffs.

"Maybe?"

"You're not sure?" I slowly moved my hands up to tease her breasts and kept going until I traced her collarbone. She sighed against me, and I pressed a kiss on her forehead. "I'll protect you from any and all animals. We'll have a fire, eat s'mores, explore nature, and I'll show you a really good time in the tent."

She stared at me for a second and then looked at her plants, and I snorted. "We'll only be gone forty-eight hours max. Your plant babies will be fine."

"If they die, it's your conscience. I'll tell them to haunt you for life. And that'll be weird to have a little flower ghost following you."

"I expect nothing less," I said, grinning as she rolled her eyes. "It's settled. We leave Friday afternoon."

Chapter Twenty-Six

I WAS IN MY HAPPY PLACE.

Shitty cell service, weathered jeans and a ball cap, all the gear we'd need in the back of the truck, and Nora in the passenger seat in her *camping* gear. It seemed my dear neighbor looked up the most stereotypical camping outfit she could find and bought it. Jeans, large brown boots, a blue plaid shirt, and a green vest four sizes too large for her.

She white-knuckled the handlebar as I pulled onto the campground I'd reserved for the weekend. Sir Greg was all taken care of and content in his new home. I could enjoy the weekend with Nora before potentially unraveling everything with the truth.

"This will be fun, I promise you," I said, even though she looked like I was dragging her to a funeral. "Doc, it's nature."

"I understand, yes, but this is...totally new. Like no realm of my life has been close to this."

"False," I said, putting the truck in park and undoing my seat belt to free myself. I leaned over and cupped her face. "You like mud. This is just a lot of it. Think of all the trees you could adopt."

She narrowed her eyes and leaned forward to kiss me. "You're lucky you're cute."

"I know. I get it all the time," I said, making her smile. We got out of the truck, and Nora put her hands on her hips, sighing as she glanced around the barren land. There were trees in every direction, the sky hardly visible, and the smell of woods lingering in the air. "Where should we put up the tent?"

"Preferably in a hotel somewhere down the road."

"Stop. You have to at least try to enjoy it." I walked up to her and put my hands on her shoulders, giving them a squeeze. She melted against me, flooding me with her floral scent. "Just think of all the stories you'll have after this."

"If I get eaten by a bear, there won't be any stories. Only a funeral. I don't want my obituary to say mauled by a wild animal. I prefer a more graceful exit from earth."

"And what would you consider graceful, Doc?" I asked, biting her earlobe solely to get a reaction out of her. She trembled, and I wrapped one arm around her middle and picked her up with one swift motion. She yelped, and I carried her toward the fire pit. "You sit and look pretty. I'll be manly and get the tent ready. Unless you want to sleep on the dirt and admire the stars?"

"I'd rather give up all my plant children than do that."

I snorted. I set her down and took my time letting my fingers linger on her body, my muscles tightening with an ache I couldn't decipher. This was more than lust. More than protecting or being her friend. It was deeper.

But out in the woods, the fresh air and elements…I didn't overanalyze it like I would've back in town. I just let it flow without questioning it. She ran her tongue over her bottom lip and played with the hem of her shirt, her cheeks bright pink and her eyes wide. A rush of *possessiveness* went through me, the urge to block out all the bad shit in her life stronger than I'd realized. Strange that only months ago, I couldn't stand the sight of her. Not the sight—because she was always pretty—but what she stood for. I was so damn wrong.

She shifted her weight on the log and caught me staring at her. "What? Do I look weird? Does this outfit not work? I researched camping gear and chose accordingly."

"You look beautiful."

She grinned and bit down on her bottom lip, and it was like all the tension in her body disappeared. "Have you always been such a charmer, Fritz? I bet you were. Were you a sports guy in high school or the class president?"

"Ah, wrong on both accounts. I was the overly obnoxious newspaper kid who got along with everyone."

"You were homecoming king though, weren't you?" she asked, her eyes twinkling with mischief. "You're way too charismatic for your own good. The Carters must adore you."

"They do," I said, thankful my tone came off natural. Light. "They really do."

She laughed and raised her arms over her head. "So this is your thing. Camping. Outside. Without power or air conditioning. Why do you like it so much?"

"I imagine the same reasons you like your greenhouse and plants. It's relaxing. I disconnect from life and just…exist." I got the tent out of the back of the truck and took out the poles after laying down the tarp. I'd gone through it so many times, I knew what piles to sort them into to make it seamless. My muscles stretched as I bent, and I pushed the sleeves of my Henley up. Sweat formed on my brow, but with the sun setting soon, the temperature would drop soon.

"This part isn't bad." Nora wiggled her brows at me and brought her knees up to her chest. She rested her chin on her hands and grinned so wide I could see every one of her teeth. "If camping is watching you bend over and show off those meaty forearms, then I like it."

"You tease." I narrowed my eyes at her for a moment before pointing at her. "Come here."

"What? Why? I'm perfectly content on this log here."

"You're doing this." I spoke more directly. "Get your cute pink-haired ass over here. You're no princess here. It's us versus the wild."

She didn't move, and I took a step toward her, making her bolt up. She eyed the tent and scrunched her nose. "I just…what? Connect the sticks?"

"The poles, yes. You connect them and place them into the right holes."

"That sounds sexual," she said, elbowing me before approaching half the tent I had pitched. She bent and yanked on one of the poles, making it snap. She yelped and jumped back like a bear charged at us. "Ugh."

"Try again or we're sleeping outside. I've done it before. Right under the stars with bugs and bears having free rein to eat us."

"Shut up," she said, setting her face into determination before she bent again.

"Ah, I see what you mean about enjoying the view. I'm liking this so far. Could you remove your shirt and keep going?"

"Fritz…Fritz," she said, her tone changing. "I'm sleeping with you, and I don't know your last name. How is that possible?"

My ears burned like I'd roasted my head over the campfire. "Must not have come up."

"Well, Fritz, *what?*" she asked, her lips already curving into a smile, like my answer was simple and easy.

Panic.

Nothing.

No words, sounds, thoughts entered my mind. Just *nothing.*

"Unless," she said, her voice going all low.

That deep timbre sent a DEFCON 1 warning inside me, autofilling that sentence with worst-case scenarios.

Unless you've been lying this whole time.

Unless you're an asshole.

Unless you're a Carter, and you've been pretending to be someone else the entire time.

"Unless," she said again, tapping her finger against her lip, "you're like Cher. Madonna. Bono. Sting. I mean, no offense, but Fritz is a bit odd, so it adds up."

"Anthony," I said, about ready to throw myself into the lake. Why, of all the names in the world, did I have to say *that* one? My birth name. The hidden identity I'd been protecting. I pulled at the collar of my green plaid shirt and focused on an ant hill on the ground. It was about the size of my fist, a little uneven. There weren't too many ants running around it, and *oh my God*, I was such a moron.

"Fritz Anthony. Nice name. Leanora is a real mouthful and makes me sound a million years old."

"A mouthful, sure, but it's a nice name. Fritz is an old nickname from the name Frederick, which…I don't even know a Frederick," I said, sighing in relief that the last name debacle came and went. Tuesday. After Tuesday, I'd tell her everything.

She just had to get through that presentation first.

"Okay, Freddie, let's get this tent up."

I showed her how to assemble the poles and stakes, and after fifteen minutes and only one other freak-out—where a rustle sound came from the trees—we had our tent ready to go. Nora crouched down and went in.

"Whoa, this is roomy." She plopped onto the ground and sat crisscross. "I'm camping. Quick, take a photo of me."

"Great idea. No one would ever believe you." I got my phone out and snapped a photo of her sitting there with a huge smile. "There. I should post it with a crazy hashtag, right? Hashtag save the poor trees or hashtag save the firewood."

"You." She narrowed her eyes, reached out to grip my shirt, and yanked me into the tent so I fell onto her. Her eyes lit up as I lay on top of her, her lips inches from mine. "You're trouble."

I pressed my mouth against hers, just because it felt good, right, and peaceful. She dug her fingers into the back of my head and pulled me closer so she held all my weight, and when I went to push off, she held me tighter.

"I like this," she said, a new vulnerability in her voice. It lacked the usual luster she carried around like an accessory, and instead, there was a hesitancy.

The pang in my chest swelled up in a painful way, and I nodded. I knew *exactly* what she meant. She traced a finger over my eyebrow, and her gaze flicked between my eyes and my mouth. "You push me to try things, and no one has really done that. My parents tried, but it took them freezing my funds. How pathetic is that?"

"Pathetic isn't the word." I chewed on it for a second, trying to say the right thing. Because she wasn't pathetic at all. "We all go through things that make us change, grow, learn. Yours is no different than that. You grew up."

She chewed her lip and played with the end of my hair. "I think I can do this. On my own, for real."

"Like stay here and start your business?" I asked, my chest expanding with hope, and an unfamiliar warm sensation spread through my limbs. It had nothing to do with her body pressed underneath me and everything to do with the feelings I couldn't seem to *stop* from happening.

"Yeah."

"I think you can too. I *want* you to."

"There are a few things I need to solidify, hash out, then…I can't wait to share it with you," she said, swallowing loudly. "You're the first person I want to tell about what I've been working on, just not yet." Her earrings twinkled on her ears and her lashes fanned over her cheeks when she blinked, and fuck, Nora sneaked her way into my heart so much, I wasn't sure how to get her out.

She wanted me to be the first? What an exhilarating feeling.

"I can't wait to hear about them," I said, kissing her again. "Okay, I want to spend hours with your body, but we need to get some things set up before dark. So let's tackle that and then return to this very position?"

She grinned. "You got it."

"Great. I need you to find wood for the fire while I unload the truck." I reluctantly got off her and held out a hand. She gripped it and I pulled her up, but the previous joy left, and a scowl replaced it.

"Wood? I need to get wood?"

"God, the amount of that's what she said jokes you just set up," I said, laughing. She didn't though. She glanced at the trees while she picked at a nail, and it hit me. She was nervous. "Okay, we'll be buddies. Unload together, then get the wood?"

"So I won't be a lone target for a panther?"

"Correct. Plus, I read that panthers don't attack people who aren't alone," I said, teasing her.

She swatted my arm, and God, I loved camping, but it had never been *this* fun. It was all Nora's fault.

Chapter Twenty-Seven

NORA PROPPED HER FEET UP ON A LOG AS SHE STARED UP AT THE midnight sky. The flames from the fire danced perfectly to capture her cheekbones and pointed nose, and for the millionth time, her innate beauty hit me right in the heart. I took a sip of the beer and nudged her foot with mine. "What are you thinking about?"

"Everything all at once." She sighed and lowered her gaze from the sky to my face, pursing her lips to the side. "How can I have such big dreams about starting a business, yet my first trip to a superstore was last month? Makes me question myself. Plus, I hate that I didn't understand the joys of campfires until right now. S'mores! S'mores, Fritz. I'm twenty-two and having my first s'more. That should be a crime."

"Wow, lots to unpack there."

She snorted and lifted her leg so it rested on top of mine. The position reminded me of Grace and Brock, so comfortable with each other that it seemed natural. I liked it.

"You asked what was in my brain, and I told you."

I reached over with my free hand and intertwined our fingers. Again, it was so *natural* and easy. "Easiest one to unpack is the s'mores. Why would you experience it if you've never had a campfire or bonfire? Give yourself a break on that. I've never ridden a horse, and I'm not going to beat myself up over it."

"S'mores are not like riding a horse."

"It's just an experience. There's not a set time or age one needs to experience certain things. Which leads me to my second point. You're going to succeed. I don't care if you've never even pruned a plant before—you have grit, a strong mind, and dare I refer to my cheesy gift, but you're courageous. If you're close, then finish it. Don't stop because it *might* not work out."

God, saying the words to her validated what I was doing with Peter.

She didn't respond, and I wondered if I'd upset her. I glanced at her, and she stared at me with a fierce look, one that made my heart stumble. She got up from her chair and took the two steps to get to mine. She lowered her onto me, straddling my lap.

"Thank you," she said, her soft lips grazing my neck.

Damn. My blood pumped hot as she ground her hips against mine. I cupped her ass over her jeans and breathed her in.

"You are...amazing," she whispered, those sweet full lips moving from my neck to my jawline. Goose bumps spread across my flesh in ripples. She lifted her head up and stared at me with so much tenderness in her eyes, my throat tightened.

I cupped her face with my hand and thumbed her bottom lip, loving how she gasped. She jutted her chin toward the tent, her meaning very clear.

"I can't seem to get close enough to you, could we...go in the tent?"

"We will, but," I said, groaning and leaning back into the chair, "camping rule number one is never leave a fire unattended. We need to wait for it to die down."

"Wow." She tensed and looked over her shoulder at the fire. "My first real attempt at seduction, stifled by flames."

"Not stifled," I said, moving my hand from her face to her neck. She leaned into my grip, and I gently turned her around so she sat on my lap facing away from me. "Not at all stifled. Doesn't take much for you to seduce me anyway."

Her back rested against my chest, and I brought one hand to her neck, the other to her waist. I tilted her head back and pressed a kiss right where her shoulder met her neck, and she let out the longest, deepest sigh. That pleasant, satisfied sound rooted itself right in my soul. After kissing her smooth skin, I nipped it.

She jumped. "How long until the fire dies?"

"Thirty minutes or so," I said against her neck, moving my hand under her shirt and up her stomach. She sucked in a breath, and I continued tracing her rib cage. My fingers met a lacy bra, and I slid right under that to cup one of her breasts. Her nipple hardened against the palm of my hand, and I pinched it. "Think of how much I can tease you until then."

"I might die." She squirmed in my lap, rubbing against my cock, and my body tensed with an aggressive need. I plucked her pebbled tip again and brought my other hand to repeat the process on her other breast. She moaned and leaned farther back into me, resting her head on my shoulder.

"Relax, Nora," I said, caressing her and taking my time. My body hummed with lust, but knowing we had to watch the fire provided mandatory patience. My dick throbbed, but there wasn't anything I could do about it, except enjoy my time with her against me. So that's what I did.

I ran my hands up her legs, over her arms, along her neck, and chest. I massaged her gently, and every time she gasped or let out a little whimper, my blood pumped harder. I'd been with women who liked foreplay, some who didn't, but this type of seduction was the *best*. She joked about her seducing me not working, but she had to realize every sound she made got me hotter. Made me want her more.

My pulse pounded in my body as I leaned us both up to look at the fire. It was just embers now, and I stood and set her on the ground. "Be right back. Getting a bucket of water."

I filled one from a spigot a few yards away and tossed it on the rest of the ash. Doing so sent a darkness all around us, the lights from the stars barely escaping through. I could only see Nora's outline, and my heart lodged in my throat as I reached for her.

Her fingers shook as we made our way to the tent. I unzipped it, looking for the flashlight, but she stopped me. "No."

"No flashlight?"

"I just want to feel you. All of you," she said, her voice soft and tender. She reached for my waist, and she pulled me closer to her before I ducked inside the tent. Then she kissed me.

It was a slow, passionate kiss as she slid her tongue inside my mouth, taking charge of the embrace. She groaned into my mouth and arched her back, her sounds and tastes and smells driving me insane. She started undoing the buttons of my shirt, and I covered her hand with mine. "Inside," was all I could say, my words becoming more difficult as lust fueled my brain.

"Okay."

We went in, and I let her take the lead. It was a new experience to hear her movements, feel her weight, but not *see* her. Every whisper of her finger over my body, every rush of her breath just wound me tighter. We undressed fast, and Nora crawled onto my lap.

"Fritz," she said, kissing down my neck as she traced my pecs. "I just..." she said, trailing off when I traced my fingers down her spine.

Her skin was so smooth and smelled like lavender.

"I know," I whispered.

She kissed me again, taking her time and grinding her hips against me. Her movements weren't smooth or perfect—but they were sexy as hell because they were hers. Natural. Pure Nora.

She pushed me back onto the sleeping bag so our chests were squished together, our skin sticky with sweat, and she tensed right as my cock nudged her entrance. "I'm on the pill."

"I'm clean," I said against her mouth. In a bout of paranoia after the Samantha situation, I got tested every month to ease my mind. Anticipation fluttered through me at the thought of entering her bare —something I'd never done.

She lowered herself onto me, my dick easing into her, and she huffed out a breath. "You feel good."

"Come here," I commanded, my thoughts, emotions, and lust all combining into an exhilarating feeling. I kissed her, trying to tell her all the things I was feeling. The sounds of the trees around us provided the perfect background noise, and every touch was amplified.

The way she kissed me back and nipped my lip. The way she oh so slowly rocked her hips on me, taking me deeper. The way her hardened nipples grazed my chest. The way her grip on my shoulder tightened. I reached around and took her ass in my hands, squeezing, and wanting more of her.

She never quickened her pace as my muscles tensed with the need to release. She felt so good, warm, and mine. Her body. Bringing her pleasure. She was so tight and perfect, I needed to adjust to last. "Baby, I need to flip you over," I said against her lips.

"Do it."

I did.

I had her on her back, and I sucked one pert nipple into my mouth, swirling my tongue around it until she squirmed. She dug her nails into my back, and I licked her sweaty skin on my way to her other breast, biting the nipple before taking it into my mouth. I loved her tits and how she responded to my touch.

I also loved her noises and confidence. I kissed right over her heart and slid back inside her, groaning at how right she felt. This wasn't just fucking. It was more. Being with her, like this, was the same feeling I got when I came home, but also the same excitement I had going on a vacation. She was joy and comfort.

"Fritz, *please*," she begged, jutting her hips forward and taking me deeper.

I wrapped her legs around my waist and quickened my strokes. Electricity tingled on my spine as she tightened around me. She clenched her thighs as I went faster, and I lifted her lower back a bit, and that did the trick. She trembled, gripped her thighs around me harder, and moaned out my name with the sexiest, throatiest sound. "*Fritz, oh God.*"

I wanted that sound on replay, forever. Her hands flew everywhere, and she tightened around my cock as she fell apart. Her orgasm fueled mine, and I couldn't hold out anymore. I thrusted harder, gripping her hip with one hand, and when she slammed her mouth against mine in a hungry kiss, white-hot pleasure overtook me.

Fuck. I kissed her back as I came, my ears ringing from the strength of the orgasm. My muscles burned, and the smell of sweat and sex filled the tent, but it was *incredible.* I let out a long breath and kissed her quickly. "Wow."

Nora didn't answer. She arched her neck and pressed her lips on my forehead, thanking me. "Top five night of my life, Fritz."

My voice stopped working then and there. She took it. She took all my power with that sweet little forehead kiss and confession. Had I ever been anyone's top five night? Had anyone ever kissed *my forehead* like I mattered to them? Even if I'd convinced myself I wasn't in love with her before now, that gesture did it.

Sweet, weird, compassionate Nora had my heart, and I couldn't wait to tell her Tuesday night. I'd lay it all on the table and try to convince her to stay with me here, for...ever.

Chapter Twenty-Eight

"Peter, good to see you," I said, holding out my hand Monday afternoon as we met at a bar. It was nearly five o'clock, so a beer was in order. We had to celebrate. "Please, get what you want."

Peter smiled and adjusted his glasses before ordering a Sam Adams. "Anthony...uh, Fritz, right? Sorry. After reading through that contract with Anthony written everywhere, I wasn't sure what to call you."

"Only my mom calls me Anthony. Makes me feel like I'm in trouble," I said, laughing and pointing to his binder. "So let's get to it."

"Right." He sighed and opened the black folder and pulled out a thick stack of papers. "Here are all the plans so far. I have a location and went to tour it, but I wasn't sure what the process should be with you. Do you need to approve it?"

I studied him as he fidgeted in his seat. The hunger in his eyes reminded me of Nora—he *wanted* to start this business, and it would be weird if he had to answer to someone. The paper work we signed left some things open for discussion, but it came down to trust and passion. I trusted Peter to do this, and he had the passion to make sure it worked. "No, this is your choice. Any decision is yours. I just want to be informed and updated on it. If there's something major I see, I'll speak up, but this is your dream, man."

His muscles relaxed just as the beers arrived. We clinked our glasses together and continued looking over the plans. "Once I put a down payment on the location, and budgeted for rent, utilities, licenses for one year, that gives me enough to start with designing it."

"Branding will be huge too—social media, getting the word out, partnerships with other places around town. Being a college city, you should think about offering discounts to college students or a rewards card type of thing."

"Oh, excellent idea!" Peter said, jotting down notes. "And yes, Carla mentioned you had a contact who was great with social media? Said they've already gained a large following in the few weeks she's been helping them. Nila? Nelly?"

"Nora." My face warmed, and my heart skipped a beat. God, the woman was something else. Goofy outfits, weird hair, but the best soul in the world. "Nora Atwood is phenomenal at social media and getting your name out there. I can give you her contact information if you'd like? I'm not sure if she has room to help out just yet, but I know she'd be flattered to be asked."

"Please. Maybe she can direct me to the right person to help or something."

"Of course." I wrote it on the corner of his page and gave him a tight smile.

"I think my biggest question for you is how much do you want to be involved? I know you said you want updates, but this is new for both of us, and I want to get this right. Do you want to see the place when I put an offer? Do you want to be part of the design process? I've heard horror stories about investors threatening to pull funds if they don't like something, and I'm not saying you're like that, I just… want to make sure I don't piss you off." He tugged at his collar again.

I tried to look approachable. Palms open on my knees, leaning into the chair, easy smile. He had no real reason to know I would *never* do that. "I think we agree to meet once a week and go over anything new. Or maybe we just do a phone call if nothing changed. I assure you, I won't pull funding because I don't like the wallpaper. The money is yours to sink or swim. We'll need to build trust with each other, and I think we will, but until then, we do this. Have a beer and talk shop."

"Okay then. Should we go over the mock-up of the inside I did earlier today?"

"Please."

The next hour flew by with pictures and sketches of his Green Café. The list of vendors he wanted to get stock from, the local places he wanted to purchase pastries, and the organic farm that sold coffee beans. It didn't have the flash and bang of *instant* money, but it'd be good. It'd be consistent, and the location he chose was right near campus. Students would visit, and business would be steady. My lawyer thought it was too low to only include ten percent earnings for me even though I fronted the entire start-up money, but it was fine by me.

I wasn't going to quit being a lawyer, and I'd have that steady income. This side project just kept my soul alive.

We parted ways with an agreement to meet at Carla's shop the next Monday, and my brain shifted from Peter to Nora. Her presentation was tomorrow, the big day, and so much depended on it. Her general sense of pride, her proving herself to the foundation in a big way, but most of all, the truth. I owed her the real truth, and then we could *be* together.

My plan was to get a clover plant for good luck, but the first place didn't have any. Neither did the second. I was standing in line at a nursery three miles out of town when she called. "Hey."

"I can't decide on a background. White seems too boring, but it's clean, and gray washes out the graphics, and black is way too much, and yellow could work, but I'm not sure. What's your favorite color?"

I grinned so hard the cashier gave me a weird look. I immediately him showed the phone so the poor guy didn't think I was staring at him like that. "Wow, hello to you too. A forest green?"

"Oh, yes, that could work. Duh! I love green. Did you know that? I feel like the guy I'm sleeping with should know my favorite color is ivy green."

I snorted and moved up in line. "I feel like I knew that even without you telling me. But by your rapid-fire speech, I can tell you're nervous."

"Um, maybe." She clicked her tongue. "I know I said don't come over tonight, because well, you're distracting in a very sexy sort of way, but what if you did? Let me go through the presentation with you? Would you be up for it, please?"

I would've said yes, no matter what, but the *please* had my heart clenching. "You got it. You haven't eaten anything yet, have you?"

"Nope. Just two pickles."

What a beautiful weirdo. "I'll get some burritos and head over. I'd love to hear your presentation, and I promise to try my best to not distract you. I just can't help you're attracted to me so much."

"Ugh. I want you to tear my presentation apart. Tear me apart."

"Mm, that sounds fun," I said, setting the plant on the counter and handing the cashier my card. He swiped it, and I signed the receipt all before Nora sighed through the phone. "What? You're the one who said *tear you apart.*"

"My presentation. Not me, well, maybe me. Tomorrow. I don't know. My mom called to wish me luck, and my dad's doing better, and they said they're proud of me. Tomorrow, if I mess up, it'll all be for nothing."

"Hey," I said, my voice firmer. "Knock that shit off. You're courageous as hell, and I love—that about you." I hesitated and mouthed *what the fuck* to myself. Was I really about to declare my love for her on the phone when she was mid-freak-out? Not my best moment. "You're not going to mess up. Not on the important parts. You might stumble on words or spill coffee on your boob to make it look like you're lactating coffee, but your content will kick ass. Your research. Your plan."

"Can you just follow me around to give me pep talks forever?"

"Sure thing. I'll quit the firm now and start tomorrow."

She laughed, the wonderful sound making me smile even more, and I got into the car with the good-luck clovers safe in the front seat. I put the seat belt on them. I took a picture to show her because her weirdness definitely rubbed off on me.

"I'll be there soon. Try to relax, would you?"

"I'll google *how to relax* to see if that helps."

I rolled my eyes even though she couldn't see me and hung up. For someone who didn't think love would be worth it again, it was a terrifying feeling. Like I was on the drop of a roller coaster and I realized my seat belt wasn't fastened all the way. I was midair, trying to grab onto something to hold me down, and I just hoped Nora would be that something after I told her the truth. Everything. The thing about Samantha, my reservations about the marriage, and how despite all of it, I fell for her.

I turned on my *feeling good* playlist and tapped my fingers against the wheel as I drove to our place, thinking about what life could be like with her. Crazy adventures of things she hadn't done before, lots of plants and podcasts, happy hours and volunteering. God, she could have some of Gilly's students visit her greenhouse, or she could bring them plants for the classroom. She would fit in so easily with Grace and Gilly once everything was out in the open.

I parked my car in the drive and sucked in a breath at the BMW in the street. The black car with the license plate CARTER4. The eerie sensation of someone cracking an egg on my skull and letting it drip down rooted me to the spot.

My mom was here.

Why?

A million thoughts raced through my mind, each fighting for dominance. Did she have a key? Was she in my place or Nora's? Why did she stop by? Did I miss a call? I forced myself to breathe and darted inside with the damn plant shaking in my arms. If she was at Nora's, she could ruin everything before I had a chance to explain. Worry clawed down my spine as I unlocked my door and found her sitting on my couch. "Mom."

"Anthony," she said, her face splitting into a grin. "Oh, I missed you."

She got up and pulled me into a hug before I could set the plant down. "What's this? A plant? Why? Don't you have enough already?"

"Why are you here?"

"I've been gone for weeks, and this is the hello I get? Did I miss something?" Her brows came together, and worry lines appeared all on her face.

"No, it's not that. I just..." I stepped back and rubbed the back of my neck, like that motion would provide an answer that would make sense to her. "I have plans. That's all. With Nora."

Her eyes lit up. "Oh, so she finally met with you. Good. I figured it would be easy with her right across the hall. Have you heard about how she's doing? Angelica said she's coming along. Really surprising everyone so far."

"She's kicking ass," I said, my voice firm. It irritated me to hear a sliver of disbelief in her voice. "Honestly, our foundation would be lucky to hire her full time."

She blinked and her shoulders tensed. "Her parents will be so pleased."

"Yes, I imagine they will." I felt like a jerk and pointed to the plant, like that would explain the rush of protectiveness I had toward my neighbor. Telling her about my feelings for Nora would need to be strategic, not a bomb dropped the second she got back. "I'm really glad to see you and that you and Dad are back. I'm in a hurry now, but let's get lunch or dinner and catch up. You look great."

She smiled and patted my face. "I'll let you get to your plans. Please, let's get lunch soon."

"Love you," I said, giving her a half hug before guiding her to the door. I opened it, and she was four steps into the hallway before Nora's door opened.

It was a clash of titans, the war of my worlds. The two lives I kept, and they were going to collide and destroy everything.

"Mrs. Carter! Hi, wow! It's so good to see you!" Nora rushed out with a gigantic smile, and my mom returned it.

"Nora! Look at you!" My mom pulled her into a huge hug and stared down at her like a proud parent. "You look wonderful. Your hair! What a fun color!"

"Thanks. Yeah, it's short." Nora twirled with the end of a piece that was out of place.

"I was just dropping in to say hello to this one, but it seems he has plans." My mom jutted her thumb at me, and I couldn't fucking breathe.

This one.

She could say Anthony. She could ruin this before I explained. My mouth tasted like cotton that sat out in the desert sun for six hours, and I waited, helpless, as both the women looked at me.

Nora's gaze softened, and she chewed on the corner of her lip with a hint of a smile. "Yeah, he has plans with me. If I recall, you were bringing me food? Which I'm not sure if you could hear, but my stomach is making whale sounds."

I nodded, my throat deciding not to work anymore. It seemed that I *could* be stressed enough to not talk. Gilly would be thrilled.

"Interesting," my mom said, her nostrils flaring as she stared back and forth between Nora and me. I hated that knowing gaze, the questions on the tip of her tongue, or the tension clogging the air around me, making it harder to breathe. "Well, I'll be off. Have a good night."

"You too, Mrs. Carter!" Nora waved, completely unaware of the hurricane raging inside me.

My palms sweated. My feet adhered to the ground. That was *so close.*

"She is so elegant, don't you think?" she asked, walking up to me. She tilted her head to look up at me, and her smiled faded. "Are you all right?"

Shit. She was the one worrying about the presentation, not me, and I needed to *get it together.* "Yeah. Yes." I cleared my throat. "Let me get the food, and we can go practice to your heart's delight."

"Foooood," she said, wiggling her brows as she followed me into my apartment. My mom's expensive perfume still lingered in the air, and a part of me was afraid she'd pop back in and say my name.

I grabbed the bag of burritos and the clover plant. "Okay, let's go."

"What's that?" Nora asked, already walking closer to me with her gaze locked on the pot. It was about ten inches wide and nothing wild, but she tilted her head like it was something fancy. "Are those clovers?"

"It's a good-luck-tomorrow gift," I said to her, focusing on the way she sucked part of her bottom lip into her mouth. "Even though you don't need luck, I wanted to get you something."

"Fritz," she said, closing her eyes and taking the plant and food, setting them on the counter. She cupped my face and stared at me in silence for a full thirty seconds. "Whoever you thought about giving that ring to didn't deserve you. You are the sweetest man."

She pressed her soft lips to mine, the sensation sending a shiver through my body. It was new to think about Samantha and *not* recoil or immediately get angry. It was like Nora took that memory and changed my mind. I smiled against her mouth, letting go of all the worry and stress my mom brought with her. *Tomorrow.* All that would be fixed tomorrow.

"This isn't too sexy or too distracting, right?" I teased, making her laugh and shove me away. I pulled her back and kissed her again and again. Her cherry lips were my favorite flavor, and her floral scent my favorite smell. "Are you thinking about me *tearing* you apart?"

She flicked my nose and picked up her plant and the bag and walked right out of my place without a word. I laughed. "Very distracting view."

"You are the worst."

Her tone didn't match her wide smile, and I locked up, followed her into her place, and swore to myself that by this time tomorrow, she'd know everything.

And then, I could tell her I loved her.

Chapter Twenty-Nine

THE LANDSCAPING OUTSIDE THE FOUNDATION BUILDING COULD USE a little work. We hired out for it, but it seemed whoever was supposed to come hadn't in weeks. There were weeds everywhere, and I bent down and picked a few right near the front door. My mom would be pissed. Appearance was important to her. Always had been. It was how first impressions were made and part of the reason Gilly and I were vain. We knew it, accepted it, and acknowledged it.

"Anthony, what are you doing?" My mom's voice pierced the momentary peace.

I took the day off work to stop here to not only encourage Nora, but also to check in. They retained me as their lawyer when needed, but it wasn't enough to warrant more than two monthly visits. Why not do both at the same time?

"Wondering why the landscaping is horrible."

"Hm. It is." I could almost hear her purse her lips and lift her nose in the air with disappointment. I pushed myself up and adjusted my tie. She eyed me from head to toe and smiled. "You look handsome even with that animal on your face."

"Beard. I like it." I scratched it, eyeing the door just in case Nora burst out of there. Unlikely, but I couldn't risk it. She was already so nervous. She woke me up at four am to practice, one last time.

I could almost rehearse the presentation myself at this point. It was good. Damn good. I sensed her inquisition, and I diverted. "Have you talked to Gilly yet?"

She sighed and dropped her gaze to the weeds. "We're going to grab dinner tonight."

"Good. I'm glad. You two need to talk this out, but Mom, don't guilt her. This is about her and Christopher, who is the best dude for her. If you want to make up with her, get to know him."

She nodded, and her gaze softened. "The thing I'm most proud of in my entire life is how close you and your sister are. There aren't words to express how much I love that you two get along and are there for each other."

"We fight, but yeah, she's my best friend." I made a mental note to call Gilly after the dinner with our mom to check in, but to also tell her that I told Nora the truth. I hated knowing I'd disappointed my sister and Grace. It was a horrible feeling, but nothing compared to the how upset Nora could be. I had to get through that, and that meant telling my mom an abbreviated truth.

"I have a favor to ask."

"Is this about my goddaughter?" she fired right back, all the softness gone. "Because I'm not sure what I saw, but I have questions."

"She knows me as Fritz. It's a long story, but can you *not* call me Anthony inside?"

Her brows nearly touched her hairline, and she gave me the *mom* look. Even though she and my dad weren't around a lot growing up, that *look* was still ingrained in my mind. "Fine. But I want every detail."

I nodded and relaxed, content that she wouldn't blow it for me. I opened the front door and ushered her in first, and I followed. The glass walls showed a bunch of people at work, and Nora stood at the front of a conference room in a bright-red shirt and black skirt. She seemed way too tidy, but she looked professional. Good. Perfect. I tapped on the glass, and she glanced up from her papers and grinned.

She pushed the door open, and I went in, smiling at her and *almost* kissing her. I wasn't ready for the gossip and questions until I told her the truth. So I settled on putting my hands in my pocket. "All ready to go?"

"What are you doing here?"

"To support you and help out." There, that was true.

"Mrs. Carter will be in on the meeting, which I didn't realize. I'm thinking…that opener when I talked about values and finding your north star? I should adjust it to sound less preachy, right?"

"Nora, you're overthinking it." I reached over and squeezed her forearm. With all the glass walls, that didn't seem too scandalous. She wore her nerves like an accessory, and I could almost feel them myself. "I've seen your presentation so many times, I *know* it's good. Try to have fun with it. You have nothing to lose."

She took a deep breath and paced the front of the room again. More people entered the hall, each holding a coffee cup and a clipboard as they neared the conference room. My heart pounded in my chest. I wanted to do more to comfort her, to reassure her, but I did nothing.

"Nora," Angelica said, walking into the room with four others behind her. She smiled, but it was tight and quick. "Are you all set up?"

"Yes, I am." Nora straightened and put on her game face. The same face she used when I showed her how to cook or how to create a budget. She was dialed in. "Please, everyone have a seat."

She swallowed and connected her laptop to the large screen, sliding her gaze to me. "Are you staying? Is that allowed?"

I frowned. "Do you want me to go?"

"I didn't know if this would be weird if you watched this? I assumed…is this part of your job?" she asked, fidgeting with the wires and pink lining her cheeks.

"Oh, right." My own face heated. "I'll go then."

She looked up at me, her brown eyes swirling with anxiety. I gave a half smile and winked. "You'll be great. Just think of how we can celebrate tonight."

She nodded, and I tapped my knuckles on the table twice before walking toward the door. More people came in from other departments, which I thought was weird. How big was this damn presentation?

My mom approached the door as I was about to leave, and she clapped as she walked in. "Nora, dear, I just called your parents to tell them how wonderful you've been to the foundation. They are thrilled."

Nora beamed. Seeing her smile eased the growing tension I had that this wouldn't work out.

"So, Fritz, are you glad your mom's back?" Frank, a finance guy, asked, sending a rush of *oh shit* through me. Buzzing formed in my ears. I clenched my fists at my sides, wishing on every piece of karma I had left that Nora didn't hear that question.

"Yeah," I said, my face flaming in the lie.

"You Carters are always on the move," he said, laughing like he'd told a joke.

I wanted to punch him. I could almost feel Nora's intense stare probing me as I looked toward her. She stood still, parting her lips as she glanced at Frank, to my mom, and then me. She blinked a few times, and I said, "Nora, wait."

"Anthony," she said, my birth name sounding like the worst of all cusswords. Her entire face flushed, and she deflated. Her shoulders slumped, and she covered her mouth with one hand, the other wrapping around her waist as her eyes watered.

Fuck.

I was such an asshole. "Hey, I promise it makes sense," I said, drawing the attention of the people sitting closest to me. This was the worst thing that could happen. The literal worse. My skin felt too tight for my body, and the sinking feeling in my stomach grew by the second.

"Right," she said, sniffing and looking at the ceiling.

My soul hurt for her. For her to find this out minutes before a presentation she worked her ass off for, this was my own version of hell. I glared at Frank, who had no idea what he'd done, but it didn't matter. The damage was done. By my lie.

"Fritz, are you staying or going? I'd like to get this started." Angelia arched a brow.

"He should stay, right? He is a Carter after all," Frank said, again making me want to throttle him.

"No, it's okay," I said, my voice scratchy and hollow. It reflected how I felt—torn up inside and wanting to whisk Nora away to explain everything to her. "I'll go."

I rushed out the glass door, turned right, and went into my mom's office to have a full-fledged mental freak-out. Nora had to think the worst. I would too. I was conned by Samantha, and it fucked me up for over a year. But this was different. It wasn't a plot to steal money from her. I had money. It was to get out of getting married.

To not have another woman use me for her own selfish reasons.

But was I that selfish, too? God. I pulled on the ends of my hair until they hurt. I knew there was a chance she'd be upset when I told her the truth. The full truth. It had been years, maybe decades, since I had such a physical reaction to something. My jaw tensed every few seconds, a migraine forming. My stomach soured with guilt, and my mind raced with the fact that Nora might not forgive me.

The look of betrayal on her face. The hurt shining in her eyes— eyes that gazed so warmly at me that morning. I pinched the bridge of my nose and stepped out of my mom's office, watching her from a distance where she wouldn't see me.

She paced the front of the room and pointed to the screen, her cheeks bright. But that was the only sign something was off. That she was upset. The rest of her looked professional, put together, and beautiful.

What had I done?

It was a special form of hell waiting for her to finish. I tried to read the faces of everyone in the room, seeing if they liked it or not. There were half smiles from most, but it was my mom who wore a huge grin. Relief eased some of my tension, but I would never forgive myself if Nora fucked this up because of my mistake.

I bounced my leg on the floor as I waited and waited. It took twenty minutes before they started standing up, and I wiped my sweaty palms on my pants, ready to walk in. My mom raved about how impressed she was and squeezed my arm as she left. That was a good sign? Probably. Frank and Angelica stood around talking, but once they saw me, they bowed out with a quiet good-bye.

"Nora," I said, my voice breaking on the second syllable. I cleared my throat and rocked back on my heels. She hadn't looked at me yet.

"You let me believe you were someone different this entire time," she said, an icy tone I hadn't heard before. She unplugged the laptop and met my gaze, zero warmth in her brown eyes. Disgust. Hurt. Anger. "You're Anthony Carter. Not *Fritz Anthony*. God, I'm such an idiot."

"Hey, no. There's an explanation for this, I swear. I was going to tell you tonight, after the presentation. I didn't want to upset you or distract you from this," I said, pleading with her. She only had a stack of papers left to clean up, and I had a feeling she wasn't going to wait around to hear me talk.

"Worked out well, didn't it? Seconds before it started, bam, I find out you're an asshole."

There was a countdown, a time limit, before the bomb went off ending whatever we had. I could hear the ticking. "Please, I just...I want to explain."

"Explain. Tell me why you let me believe you were someone else. A chauffeur for Christ's sake." She put her hands on her hips. "Tell me in the simplest terms you can, why you lied to me for weeks while we were...together." Her voice cracked, and I stepped toward her. She held up a hand. "No, do *not* touch me. I don't even know you."

"That's not true. I'm the same person, just with a different name. Only my mom calls me Anthony—everyone else uses Fritz. You do know me, Nora, more than anyone." This was bad. Really bad. The ice in her eyes seemed to double, and I ran a hand over my chest, hysteria latching onto me. *What if she won't forgive me?*

"I feel *humiliated*. Your mom told me to *go easy on you*. So not only did you fuck me, you told others about the lie?"

"Wait, no. I mean yes, but not like you're thinking."

"Then tell me what I'm thinking. Please." She cleaned everything up and had her stuff in a bag. She crossed her arms and glared at me with nothing but hurt shining through. I had to bare it all if I even had a shot at fixing this.

And it looked like now was the moment.

"Someone pretended to be in love with me for a year. She lied and conned me because she wanted my bank account. She blackmailed my sister for thousands of dollars and—"

"So you're telling me you went through this…and decided to do the same thing to me?"

"No, wait! No! That's not…Nora, you started talking about marriage that first day I picked you up, and you stared right through me like I was the help!" Great, I was yelling now. Really helping my case.

"Instead of telling me, then and there, you let the lie start. It's been weeks, Frit—Anthony—whatever. You should've told me before we got involved." Her cheeks reddened, and her eyes filled with tears.

"I'm so fucking sorry."

"Yeah, I am too. I thought this…well, it doesn't matter what I thought we were." She sniffed, and tears fell down her face.

She might as well have stabbed me in the chest with how much it hurt to see her cry. "It matters to me, Nora. I *love* you. I want to fix this. I'll do anything. I need…you've become a part of me. I can't—" My own voice broke, and I pinched the bridge of my nose, desperate and not giving a shit that people watched us from the hallway.

"If you love someone, truly, you don't lie to them." She jutted her nose into the air and gripped the handle of her bag tight. "This isn't fixable. Good-bye."

She walked out of the conference room and instead of going right, and farther into the office, she went left and walked out the door. I couldn't move. The words *"this isn't fixable"* cemented themselves into my chest, slicing my heart into pieces one at a time.

If I learned anything about Nora, it was that she meant what she said. If she really thought this wasn't fixable, then we were done. Over. No more camping trips or plant talk, or volunteering, or sharing our dreams. The woman to show me love *was* possible had walked out of my life for good, and it was my own damn fault.

Chapter Thirty

SHE HADN'T RETURNED ONE CALL OR TEXT, HADN'T ANSWERED HER door, and now that I thought about it, I wasn't sure she even came back to the apartment. I listened for any sign she was there—a clinking of keys, a door opening, the main lobby door squeaking, but two days later, it'd been dead quiet. It was safe to assume she wasn't coming back to the apartment, and that killed the little flicker of hope I'd had. If I could get more time with her to explain, I could fix this thing. Two days without knowing she was okay. Two days of my mom and sister telling me I deserved this.

Two days of regret turning into heartbreak—something I wasn't sure I'd survive a second time. I took a long swig of beer at my counter and made up my mind. I *had* to make sure she was okay. The growing unease in my gut was to the point I couldn't go thirty seconds without worrying. She had nowhere else to go. Did she stay at a hotel? Take a rideshare two hours north? I grabbed the extra set of keys on the counter and marched across the foyer. I knocked, waited, and opened the door. "Nora? You in there? I just need to know you're okay."

No answer.

I'd been in this unit countless times since buying the building the year before, but there was never such an empty feeling like hers had now. Her plants were all here—except the clover and the Edelweiss. My heart skipped a beat that maybe she'd taken them with her. If she did, that meant they had value to her, that I mattered.

Even though she'd been in here Tuesday, two days ago, everything felt different. Her perfume wasn't lingering in the air, and the lack of audiobooks made the silence more profound. I scanned my phone at all the unanswered texts…all delivered and read, but no response.

Fritz: Can I please see you? Even for just a minute.

Nothing.

Fritz: Are you coming back to your place?

Three dots popped up, and my body zinged to life. She was responding! Finally! Breathing became difficult as the dots appeared, disappeared, and then showed up again. It was a special form of torture. Fuck it.

I called her. The ringing went on for almost a full minute before she answered. "Nora!" I shouted, cursing at myself for being too aggressive. "Thank you for answering."

"I'm not planning on talking to you, *Anthony*, besides telling you that whatever we had, is over. Leading me to believe you were someone else, despite your past…I just…I can't trust you."

"What does this mean? Where are you going to live? What about your stuff?"

"I'm back home."

"But what about the money? What about your business? Don't you need to stick it out another month?"

"No. I don't want to."

"But Nora, this is your—"

"Fritz, please, this is hard for me too. Just…let me go."

My eyes prickled as the weight of everything hit me. In her silence, her absence, I'd let myself believe that with enough time, she'd forgive me. She'd realize that this wasn't to hurt her and that every single thing I shared, felt, experienced with her was real. But how could I ignore her request? I'd be an asshole to continue pestering her.

With a broken heart, I asked the final question. "There's nothing I can do? I love you, Nora. I need you to know that."

She sucked in a breath and sniffed, the sound of her sadness gutting me. "I don't think there is. Good luck with everything."

"Yeah, you too." I waited for her to hang up, the finality of the conversation causing a horrible shred in my soul. If she was back home, what did that mean for all her things? I could have my mom ship them back, or I could do it but sign my mom's name. Probably better that way.

Fuck. My head pounded, and I wanted to sink into the carpet and disappear for a minute. Just shut off the emotions. Her plants would die if she didn't ship them, and without thinking, I filled up a pitcher of water and followed her chart. I misted, poured, and sprinkled hair on the soil. I scanned the place one more time for the two plants I gave her and found them in her bedroom, right next to her bed.

God. That did me in. She had the gifts I gave her *right* next to her bed, like they mattered to her. I sat on the edge of her mattress and texted the two people who had been there for me through it all. Grace and Gilly.

Fritz: I fucked it all up. Can we meet?

Grace: come on over.

That's all it took. I locked up Nora's place and walked outside to call an Uber. There would be alcohol tonight, and I wouldn't be driving.

As I waited for my rideshare, I typed a list of all the things my mom should ship to Nora's family. All her clothes, bedding. All the things she bought as she experienced life on her own. I gave instructions on how to ship the plants and hit send.

Maybe it'd be easier to start getting over her if I got rid of all traces of her. The hard part would be the way she worked herself into my heart. That would take a while to survive.

The front door of Grace and Brock's house opened the second I got out of the car, and Grace stood there with a beer. "You look like shit."

"Feel like it too."

"You should."

"I know. That's what makes it worse. I did this. I fucked it up." I took the bottle and downed half of it. "It's cool I'm drinking this near you?"

"I appreciate you asking, but yes." She gave a tight smile and pulled me into a hug. "I'm sorry you're going through this."

"Again."

That was the kicker. The real shot to the groin. Two years, two heartbreaks, two women who wanted my last name for very different reasons, but the bottom line was money. Grace led me inside, and I fell onto their couch, filled with a self-loathing and anger.

Oh, anger was a stage of grief, right? Was I moving on that fast? This was promising. "It was just my fucking name. That's what I don't get. Everything else…it was me. All me."

"I know, but Fritz…you had the chance to tell her. You should've before you *slept* with her."

"I get it. I do." I squeezed my eyes shut. "I told her I loved her, and she said it was too late. I feel this hole inside my chest, and it hurts." My throat got tight.

Grace reached over and wrapped her arm around my shoulder. "Would it cheer you up to know you're the godfather?"

"Hey, we didn't agree on that," Brock said, coming out of the kitchen with his blue eyes zeroing in on me.

"It's a given, dude. Of course, I am. Who else would it be?" I asked, sharing a look with Grace. I *loved* getting a rise out of Brock. Always had. It was my favorite thing to do when we got together.

Brock sighed. "Fair point."

"Then I accept. And yes, that does make me feel better." I snorted, and Grace hit me in the side. "How are you handling potential parenthood, Brock? Well, I take it?"

"Oh, he's read every single book he can and babyproofed the house even though I'm not due for eight months. It's been wonderful," Grace said, standing up and moving to sit on Brock's knee. He wrapped his arms around her and kissed the top of her head.

It always pleased me to see that grumpy-ass man fawn over Grace. Same with Christopher and Gilly. They'd found their matches.

I thought I'd found mine.

And back to mopey miserable mode. I grabbed a pillow and

propped it up behind my head and groaned. "Could you knock it off with your cute shit? I'm heartbroken."

"You'll bounce back," Brock said, in a rare moment of kinship. I opened one eye and found Grace with the same puzzled expression. "What? I actually care about the guy."

"Wow, today has been a real roller coaster."

"He's right, though. You'll be okay."

A fierce anger had me sit up straighter. "That's the thing though. I don't want to just *move on*. I fucking love her. That woman is my perfect match. It's unexpected and random, and God, there are so many weird things about her, but I *love* them. She had the same zest for life as me, the same humor. She put audiobooks on for her plants. How strange is that?" I said, my throat closing up again. "She asked me to let her go."

"Are you?"

"I don't have a choice, do I? I can't ignore her wishes without making her hate me more." I finished the beer and rubbed my palms over my eyes. "What do I do?"

Grace sighed, that hopeless sound proving that it was over. There was no hope. "Give it time. I'm not saying give up on her, or *not* try again, but I think some distance is needed."

"Okay, like a few days? A week? A month?"

"I don't know…that's something you'll need to figure out on your own. I think you screwed up, horribly, but I also understand why you did it. Everyone has their own threshold of what's forgivable and what's not. If this crossed her line, then I'm not sure what you can do. But give her time and space."

I nodded and hated that she was right. This wouldn't be solved today, or tomorrow, or next week. It might never be solved. I'd have to live with it either way.

FOURTEEN DAYS HAD PASSED SINCE NORA'S PRESENTATION. TWELVE days since hearing her voice and her asking me to leave her alone. Twelve days of watering all her plants and lying on her living room floor listening to plant-themed songs. The playlist started as a joke before she left, but now I wallowed in my sadness with it. All the songs I wanted to play and make her laugh.

The pain hadn't gone away. I still thought about her every day, every night, and wondered if her hair was longer. Did she change her earrings into a rainbow or buy a new outfit that hugged her curves? Was she watching baseball or trying new foods?

Was she happy?

I stared at her ceiling fan and thought about if I was even happy. Working with Peter had been the highlight of my week, and I was set to meet with him at Carla's place in an hour. I wished I would've agreed to be more hands-on with him, just to keep busy. My evenings sucked. I sat at a job all day that didn't inspire me and came home to an apartment without Nora across the hall.

Grace's words kept repeating in my head about time. Distance. What was the right amount of time? My mom stopped glaring at me once I told her the full extent of it, and Gilly stopped by every other day. She, too, stopped making me feel worse and let me mope. I didn't need anyone to tell me it was my fault. I knew.

I sighed and pushed myself up off the ground, the unsent text sitting in my messages. It was just a *how are you* text. I wanted to send it so badly but refrained. Not yet.

I needed to start thinking about moving the stuff out and getting a new tenant—Mom did reach out about sending Nora all her stuff and she'd said no. The fact she didn't want a single part of her life here wasn't a good sign. I picked one of the plants, a bright-yellow flowery thing. *Heather* was her name. It'd be a good gesture to bring a plant to Carla, and honestly, I was just a person who bought others plants now. They were better than flowers or gift cards. They had meaning. I let myself out. The hollow, Nora-size hole in my heart remained there as I drove to meet up with Carla and Peter. I drove in silence and ran a hand through my hair a million times, like that would ease the tension.

I'd even shaved my beard. I looked like me again. The old me. The lawyer me who helped out at his parents' foundation. I didn't *feel* like me, but it was a start. I parked my car after an uneventful drive where I got lost in my depressing thoughts and made my way toward Carla's new property. Glass windows covered the front, and there were boxes everywhere inside. I pushed opened the door, and two faces popped up from behind the counter.

"Hey, guys."

"Fritz, hey!" Carla grinned and shoved a box of napkins onto the bar top. "What ya got there?"

"A 'congratulations on your new business' plant." I set it next to her, and her grin doubled.

"That's *perfect.*" She picked it up and studied it and placed it where I imagined the register would go. Peter came up and shook my hand, like he had the past three times we met, and his brows came together.

"Things going okay for you, Fritz?"

"Yeah, sure." I shoved my hands in my pockets and eyed the empty venue. It had that feeling of potential, just brimming under the surface. Carla chose a perfectly small location that wouldn't cost too much. She'd have room for a few tables, but the goal was coffee. Situated right in the heart of downtown businesses, there were at least seven buildings within easy walking distance. "You chose well, Carla."

"Thank you." She moved toward the wall opposite me, and a cute leafy-coffee mug logo was printed onto a poster. It was clean, elegant, and underneath it had the word FAB 'BREW' LESS on it. I snorted.

"I see what you did there."

"Nora came up with it."

Ah, a punch to the chest. "That's…great."

"She was an amazing recommendation, Fritz. Seriously. I heard she's opening up a greenhouse and is looking for some partners to collaborate with. I loved her energy," Carla said, my brain slowly catching up to digest her words.

"She didn't get the money?" I asked, my spine stiffening at the possibility she wouldn't achieve her dream. *And it'd be my fault since I drove her away.*

Peter's frown deepened as his phone rang. He apologized and answered, but I paid him no attention. I wanted to ask Carla a million questions. "When did you talk to her? Was she okay? Happy?"

She didn't miss a beat. She opened her mouth as Peter greeted the caller. "Hey, Nora. I've been doing what you asked and posting those videos as I make progress. I've already gained two hundred followers in a week!"

Nora! Nora was on the phone. I spun around and stared. He gave me a weird look, nodding at whatever she said. My heart thumped and twisted, and a swoosh of excitement passed through me. This could be good. Maybe. Hopefully.

"No, I'm with Carla now, about to meet with my silent partner. Yeah, he's been great to work with. I could pass his information along to you if you want?" He smiled at me, not having a clue of the storm inside me. "Yeah, sure."

Peter moved the phone from his ear and held it up...like he was taking a photo. The familiar dings of a video call starting filled the room, and I froze in my spot. Nora would be able to *see* me.

"The logo you did for Carla is incredible. Look at it!"

"The colors pop against the brick wall, don't they?" Nora said, her familiar voice wrapping around my soul like a warm hug. I squeezed my eyes shut and took a step back, out of view. This was wonderful and horrible at the same time.

It was so good to hear her, but the pain of missing her had doubled.

"Wait, turn around, Peter." Nora's tone changed. Peter spun, the camera going over me for one second, before she said, "What is that on the counter?"

Heather. Her plant.

Carla laughed. "Fritz brought me a plant."

"Fritz," she said, the magic gone from her voice, and instead, a deep, sad tone echoed through the phone. "Fritz Carter brought you that plant."

"Uh, yeah. He's right here."

Yes! No! Maybe? I had no idea what I wanted. But Peter pointed the camera at me, and I awkwardly lifted my hand. Maybe it was better that I couldn't see her. It'd hurt too much. "Hey, Nora."

"Is that from my place?"

"You mean, the unit across from mine? Yes."

"It's still alive?" There wasn't anger in her tone now, just curiosity.

"Uh," I said, my face flaming red. "I've been taking care of the plants. I rehomed *Heather* to Carla here, thinking it would be really great for her coffee shop."

Silence.

Great. Cool. Not awkward at all. I rocked back on my heels and hoped she couldn't tell I sweated.

"You shaved."

"Yup." I scratched my chin, self-conscious as hell. Did she hate it? Like it? The woman who spoke too much was too damn quiet, and I hated it. My insides hurt. I needed fresh air.

Peter and Carla looked back and forth between each other and me, and it was too much. I pointed over my shoulder. "Peter, I'll catch up with you later if you need to have a meeting."

"No, no, sorry. I know you gotta go. I'll call you back later, Nora. Can't wait to talk about strategies later." Peter hung up the phone and eyed me.

It would be easier to come clean. "We had a thing. It recently ended, and that was the first time we've talked since. I'm sure you felt the awkwardness."

"Oh baby, did we." Carla shook her head. "Woo. That was secondhand embarrassment over here."

"Thanks," I deadpanned.

"What did you do?" Carla asked, her intelligent eyes assessing me with a new light. "You have guilt written *all* over your face."

"Kept something from her thinking it protected me." My jaw tightened. I just wanted time to explain, to show her it all was real, to get her to trust me again. With all the time that had passed, there wasn't *that* moment where I could form a plan. But something about their comment intrigued me.

If she was looking for partners…that meant she didn't have her money? Did she not fulfill her parents wish of working here for twelve weeks? God, did the thought of being near me mean she'd lost the shot at her dream? "Did you say she's…uh…looking for a partner? Did she say why?"

Peter frowned and scratched his forearm. "Wants to open up a therapy greenhouse and wants to partner with a cause in the community to help. She didn't get too into the details, but it sounds like she has funds to start it but wants to do more to connect with people."

An idea hit. A wonderful, probably terrible idea. Nora was all about campaign awareness. Her stupid bracelets, hashtags, flyers. She loved bringing attention to causes that were special and important to her. She wanted to do things that mattered to the world. Helping her from behind the scenes to make her greenhouse into a nonprofit...yes. That I could do.

I tapped my chin, ignoring both Peter and Carla, and paced the café. Social media was where she shone, but if I could help bring awareness to *her* dream, her project—helping those who needed therapy and could use plants as that escape. I could get donations, help spread the word...but how? I was off social media for good reason, but I'd break my hiatus for her.

"Peter," I said, loudly, making him jump. "What can you tell me about gaining followers?"

"What?" he asked, frowning and sharing a look with Carla.

"Nora might not forgive me and I understand that, but I want to help her. Can you show me what you did?"

Chapter Thirty-One

MY FIRST VIDEO POSTED WITH MY #BIGPLANTENERGY #greenhousegoals #atwoodoutreach #plantdad hashtags, and I showed a stream of all her plants with their names and mentioned her mission. It didn't do as well as I'd wanted, and I'd spent the entire weekend brainstorming.

My kitchen counter was covered with sheets of papers with possible videos, each one sounding more stupid than the last, but I wasn't deterred.

There was a comment that asked where someone could donate to and bam! I searched Nora's social media and found her donation link if someone wanted to get involved. Copy and pasted that baby over to my page and went back to the research stage.

Engagement. That's what I wanted.

I scrolled through hundreds of videos, searching hashtags and what did well, and was faced with a hard choice. If I wanted to gain traction, I'd have to show my face. Those were far more popular than the ones without people in them. It was worth a shot. Sighing, I eyed the plants she gave me and tested out some angles to make sure the light hit my face right. I wore a white T-shirt with the words #plantlife I'd I found online. It was tight, and with my recently trimmed beard, I looked good. This couldn't hurt the situation.

"I have a confession to make. I'm a plant dad." I paused, made sure I was in view as well as the plants she gave me. "I didn't want to be. My neighbor sneaked into my apartment to gift me these plants. She showed me how nature can heal a person. I might've been uptight, but these babies changed my whole attitude. This is Jonathon and Ernie. They prefer rock music and crime podcasts. Jonathon is a pilea and needs indirect sunlight, and Ernie is a fern. Ernie is a tough one. I have to evenly moisten the soil for him, and he likes humidity. Which, come on. It's hot AF outside."

I made eye contact with the camera, winked, and stopped it. My entire body flushed, and I felt like I was going to hurl. This was so out of my comfort zone, but it felt right. My own way of telling my love story with Nora, and if I could help bring awareness to her cause, then I'd be able to forgive myself. I added my hashtags and added #NeighborNora and made sure my profile's bio said JUST A PLANT DAD WANTING TO HELP NORA CHANGE THE WORLD. GET INVOLVED HERE with the link to her campaign.

My heart raced, and I posted the video. And now I waited. Trying not to freak out or second-guess myself. I didn't have to wait long. I took a swig of beer and clicked on the notifications.

Comments started coming in.

YOU CAN BE MY PLANT DADDY.
  I'll donate if you take off your shirt.
  Can you water me?
  Shirtless with succulents, please. You can tend my garden.

I SPIT OUT MY DRINK. THIS SHIT WAS TOO MUCH. IF NORA WERE here, she'd cackle at how ridiculous this was. This was good, though. More comments and likes and shares meant exposure.

I could do that. I could use my face and objectify myself if it got people watching my videos. Yeah. Okay. I took a deep breath and finished the beer. If I was going to do this *fully*, then I was going to need liquid courage.

Leaving my place, I went into Nora's and set the phone up at an angle so they could see my whole body. My face burned, but I ignored it. This was for Nora. Plain and simple. I picked up one of her plants, Jones. "Hey all, I want to talk about Jones here. He's a real quirky plant. He prefers audiobooks about gardening and is really moody when it comes to direct sunlight." I paused, repositioned myself, and got closer to the camera. "If I get to a thousand likes and reshares, my next post will be given shirtless. Let's see what you can do, plant world."

I stopped recording and posted it.

My blood hummed with adrenaline, and it was hard not to check my phone every five seconds. Notifications came in, but there had to be a way to post consistently without having it take over my life. Three a day. That was my goal. Three videos a day, some shirtless, some not, and then I'd adjust from there. It was a long shot, but I was a desperate man.

TWENTY-ONE VIDEOS LATER, I HAD SIX THOUSAND FOLLOWERS AND so many notifications about other people using my videos to make their own, I ignored them. People were making videos with mine, and I couldn't believe it. Others were using *my* hashtags for Nora, and I got a rush every time I got a like. Each one of mine and Nora's plants had a video story talking about them, and like I promised each morning in a video, if they donated to the link, I'd post a shirtless video.

Things were getting weird.

I was officially pimping my body out for Nora. I had fans messaging me and wanting to meet, and it was surreal. Social media life was not for me, but I had to continue on. Today's post was all about Nora. The reason to start this entire thing.

"My nightmare of a neighbor turned out to be my best friend and just look at her." The video went to a picture I had of her smiling wide at the animal shelter. "This pink-haired beauty believes in the power of plant therapy, and you should too. She taught me how gestures and helping out come in different sizes. Have you donated to a cause that helps others?" I had the camera come back to my face.

I sat on Nora's couch with her plants in the background. "I'm new to being a plant dad, but *not* to living on this planet. We need to take care of her. Drop a comment if you donated to the link in my bio, and I'll share a video of me watering my plant children, in my underwear, later. I need at least five hundred donations."

I stopped recording, made sure it stitched together well, and posted. I leaned onto her couch, wondering if Nora saw any of these and hoped she did. In the three weeks since she left, I'd come to terms that I might've broken what we had for good. The longer time went on, the more I missed her. Even now, I craved her laugh, her floral scent, and way she looked at me.

Like she loved me for me and nothing less.

My phone went off, and for a second, I thought it'd be Nora. But it was Grace and Gilly.

Grace: HOLY SHIT FRITZ YOU HAVE FANS

Gilly: This is INCREDIBLE. Have you made #bigplantenergy swag yet? You could totally sell it!

Grace: I'd buy ten things with that on it. Seriously. I am loving your grovel for Nora.

Grace: #plantdaddy

Gilly: #shirtlesssucculents

Fritz: I hate you both.

Fritz: This is surreal and weird, and I hate it.

Grace: You can't stop, Fritz. Nora's social numbers are growing every time you post a video.

I read Grace's text twice with my breath in my throat. Really? Could this actually help Nora?

I wished there was a way to see if she saw this happening, just so she knew how much I loved her. How much I believed in her, her dream, and the way she lived her life. I ran my hands over my eyes and pressed in and took a deep breath. I wasn't sure when the end of this campaign was, but these posts were what kept me going each day.

Work was the same, boring and soul-crushing, but these posts were how I stayed connected to Nora. I tended to *not* read through comments or all the notifications of who mentioned me, but I wanted to see if people were talking about it. In my search of my hashtags, I found videos of people talking about me and Nora.

ONE USER, @PLANTSAREMYLIFE844, POSTED A VIDEO AN hour ago.

"SO FOR ALL OF US THIRSTING OVER FRITZ, CAN I JUST STAY something? He talks about his neighbor to help spread word of her cause but let's be real. He's into her. They had a thing. They had to. I mean, if he was taking applications for plant mamas, I'd be first in line and knock anyone out who got in my way but...discuss." #FritzandNora #Flora #TeamFlora

SHE HAD HUNDREDS OF LIKES AND COMMENTS AND—*HOLY SHIT.*

@NoraAtwood followed you. Say hi!

I bounced from the couch, desperate for action. Did I message her? Call her? DM her? What did I do? Fuck! I paced her living room, my insides flip-flopping like an Olympic gymnastics routine, and settled on the only choice.

I wouldn't message her. I didn't need to. My posts told her how I felt about her, and if she saw those and didn't care...then there was nothing left to say. I checked her website daily to see progress on the greenhouse, but she hadn't posted in two weeks.

I waited like a desperate fool when she posted short clips, only her voice coming through and not her face. Just a glimpse of her would be great, but for now, I had to be okay with knowing she would at least see my videos. That follow from her put a spring into my step and invigorated me to keep going.

My Saturday consisted of cleaning my entire apartment, watching the Cubs, and checking my phone. Constantly checking the notifications was a dangerous addiction, but this was my life now. A nervous energy went through me as I clicked my last video. Thousands of views. Hundreds of comments...most of them stating they donated to Nora's website. There was no way to confirm that it was true, but judging by her growing numbers and her following me...things had to be going well.

@lonelygirl19082308 commented: *wow this is a great idea? A plant therapy greenhouse? Sign me up.*

@plantbabygirl3989 commented: *seriously, like where can I find this place?*

@aloeveranerd09877 commented: *nature has a way of healing us, Nora is a genius.*

I chewed the side of my lip as I read the comments, solidifying why Nora had to follow her dream. I knew. Despite her weirdness, her heart was in the right place from day one.

I stalked a few of my most active followers' profiles to see what other videos they liked. There were videos where someone started the video innocently and when the beat dropped, bam! They were shirtless, or doing something sexy, were apparently a huge trend.

I made a sour face at the thought of making a post like that, even as I'd already accepted the fact that I was going to make one. Whatever it took.

The combination of the filters, lighting, and the music that I'd need to make this post the sexiest I could was going to take some preparation.

An hour and a half later, I posted my first thirst trap. There was no going back. I was in this for the win. The video started with a fully-clothed me in Nora's apartment, innocent music dubbed in. Upbeat pop. Then, the music got louder and the beat dropped. My shirt came off, and I moved my hips a bit as I watered her plants. Did I take time between takes to do push-ups to make my muscles stand out more? Yes. It was a great tip and made my chest look better with the light.

As I filmed myself, sweaty and bare-chested, I hoped Nora knew this was for her. It was all for her.

THE HASHTAGS #BIGPLANTENERGY #FLORA #TEAMFLORA WERE everywhere, and right before I exited out of the app and headed to work, a greenhouse sent me a message. I followed fifty accounts that were focused on plants and therapy and, of course, Nora's personal account.

I had hundreds of notifications I didn't check because they were all various forms of fan mail—which still felt weird as fuck—but the greenhouse message caught my attention. Was it Nora's? I clicked so fast I had to try three times because my thumb wasn't hitting the right spot.

@GABLEGREENHOUSE HEY FRITZ! LOVE YOUR POSTS ABOUT PLANT awareness and how much joy they bring to the world. Would love to have you visit and help us out. If interested, let us know. Happy to contribute to a charity of your choice. Also, we want to talk about selling some merch with #bigplantenergy. Have a lot of ideas if you're open to discussion.

CHARITY OF MY CHOICE? NORA'S DREAM. I LOOKED UP THEIR location, and they were only an hour north. They had a huge following online. Thousands of followers and likes. Their website said they partnered with local churches in their area, so they definitely gave back to their community. I started typing a response but hesitated. Was this Nora's competition? Did I want to head there? I let the message sit unanswered and wouldn't make any decisions yet, especially if it would hurt Nora.

Merch though…that could make a profit. They had a huge reach, and I could raise funds for Nora to make it a nonprofit. Hmm. With the following I gained, people could buy shirts with the dumb sayings. I could even include a slogan or a logo from Nora's greenhouse. Yes— I could help sell stuff to promote her brand. I nodded to myself and messaged back. Talking to them wouldn't hurt.

@Fritz When you thinking?

@GableGreenHouse Tomorrow afternoon would be best for us.

We have some killer ideas that would help spread awareness to Nora's greenhouse idea.

@Fritz I'll be there.

Wow. Despite the heartbreak, I was having…fun. It was unlike my typical areas of interest, but fuck it. I was a real plant dad now and owning it. Now, I just had to see what their ideas were and hope it didn't conflict with my plan to support Nora.

The next day, I pulled up to Gable Greenhouse and parked my BMW. While I was glad to have my car back permanently, I did miss the truck. It had more room. There weren't a lot of cars in the parking lot, but it was still hot as balls outside. I made my way inside, the scent reminding me so much of Nora, I swore I could feel her there.

The earthy scent of dirt and flowers. I closed my eyes and took a deep breath.

"Fritz?"

What the fuck. I snapped my head to the right and about fell over. Nora stood right there. In front of me. Her pink hair had faded and grown out a little bit, but she was still her. The earrings, the baggy shirt, the goofy backpack, and large eyes. My heart about beat out of my chest wanting to be closer to her, to be home again. Her saying my name stole all the oxygen from of my lungs.

Because she was fucking beautiful, and distance did nothing to lessen my feelings for her. I opened my mouth to say hi, to say something, but nothing came out. Not a word.

She chewed on the side of her lips as she furrowed her brows. "By your expression, I take it you didn't plan this."

I shook my head and wiped a hand over my face. "You look beautiful," I said, my voice scratchy as my feelings threatened to overflow in choppy half sentences.

She swallowed hard and squeezed the straps of her backpack so hard her knuckles turned white. Her eyes glistened as we stared at each other. I had no idea what was going on in her head, but she hadn't run. She didn't slap me. Those were good signs.

"Why are you here?" she asked, wetting her lip with her tongue.

The pull to her was so strong, I forced myself to take a step back.

"They wanted to talk about selling merchandise with some of my hashtags. I was going to do it and donate everything to you. Shit." I ran a hand through my hair. "They messaged me saying they could help spread awareness for your business. They loved the idea of the greenhouse for therapy," I said, way too fast.

She took a step back. "They messaged me the same thing." She looked back toward the parking lot, her jaw set in determination. "We were set up."

If I can get Nora back, I'll owe them forever. "Looks like we were. Hey," I said, my stomach dropping as she took a step away from me. "Don't...don't go. I miss you."

She sucked in a breath and closed her eyes, a tear streaming down her cheek, and stopped at her chin. "Why did you...your videos. Fritz, I..."

"Look," I said, emotion clogging my voice in a painful way. I walked toward her so the tips of my shoes touched hers. That was the only part of her I allowed myself to touch. "I love you. I might've fucked this up, me and you, but that doesn't mean I won't do everything I can to support you and your dream. That's what you do when someone lives in your soul. You help them even if it kills you."

Her jaw trembled, and she blinked a lot. "You said I taught you about life."

"You did," I said, laughing and taking a chance and cupping one side of her face. "That being yourself is the best you can be. That following your passion and helping others is a way of life. That new experiences aren't predetermined by age. That plants really fucking matter. God, I never thought I'd care so much about plants, but now I think about them every day—"

Nora *kissed* me. She slammed her mouth against mine and threw her entire body against me. She felt the same, warm and curvy and *mine,* but there was no lie between us this time, and that made all the difference.

"Nora, Nora," I said, stopping the kiss as she dug her fingers into my chest. "I love this, *you.* But I have to know if you forgive me. I want us to be together."

"Yes. Yes." She laughed and wiped tears from her eyes. "I've missed you so much and saw your videos, and Fritz, how could you not know how much I love you, too?"

"Thank Christ." I kissed her again, tilting her all the way back into a dip.

"I can't believe you made all those videos. Shirtless," she said, laughing against my mouth. My skin heated, but I didn't care. She was in my arms, kissing me, and every second of those videos was worth it.

"I got you back. So mission complete." Then I kissed her again and spun her around.

She grinned, the light hitting her earrings just right, and this was the happiest moment I'd experienced. Nora was back, we both were chasing our dreams, and we were doing it *together*.

Epilogue

SIX MONTHS LATER...

I WAS LATE...ISH. NOT BY THE VERY DETAILED AGENDA FOR wedding day, but by the *Gilly will freak out if everyone wasn't there an hour early* type of way.

It wasn't intentional—I just wanted to see my girlfriend at the greenhouse to make sure she ate. Nora was doing all the flowers for the wedding, and when she focused, she forgot how to human. The extra trip cost me twenty minutes, but when she looked up from the arrangements with stars in her eyes—for me—it was worth it.

That warmth hadn't left her gaze since I got her back, and I never wanted it to go away. I made sure to overcommunicate with her, show her every day how much I loved her, and soon...she would be Mrs. Anthony Carter. If she wanted. If she wasn't ready for that, that was fine too. I'd be faithful and committed to her in any form because being in love—the all-encompassing, soul-consuming love—was my jam.

There were a lot of emotions going through my chest as Gilly's wedding day finally arrived, but they weren't plagued with the salty bitterness Samantha instilled in me.

Nora shifted my entire mind when it came to love, and I found myself excited to see Gilly marry the one guy who understood her. I parked my car in the church parking lot, got my tux from the back seat, and locked the doors. It was a cold day in central Illinois for a February wedding, but the sun was out.

"Hey, Fritz!" Grace yelled, her large pregnant belly popping in the tight dress she wore. Her jacket hung unzipped, and Brock jumped out of the car to help her walk. "Brock, chill. There's no ice."

"You need to pay attention."

"Oh my God, I'm fine." Grace rolled her eyes, and I grinned. "I put the coffeepot in the bathroom closet yesterday, and suddenly I'm not able to walk?"

Brock grumbled, and I joined them, giving Grace a quick hug. "Pregnancy brain a real thing, huh? Putting coffee in a bathroom closet isn't normal," I said.

Brock's face hardened.

The day I got tired of annoying Brock was the day I wasn't well.

"Here and there," Grace said, sighing at the two large floral arrangements on either side of the doors. "Wow. Nora did…these are beautiful." Her voice clogged, and I knew how she felt.

They weren't typical, wedding-like floral arrangements. They had Nora's flair all over them. There were at least ten different flowers in there, not all the colors matching, kind of like her earrings, and there were pieces of student artwork paired in them. My own eyes stung a bit, and Grace reached over to squeeze my hand.

This was happening. Gilly would become a Callahan.

Grace sniffed, and Brock immediately handed her a tissue and wrapped his arm around her. "Are your feet feeling okay? Do you want me to carry you?"

"Brock, I swear to God, I'm fine."

I snorted, earning a death glare from Brock. Ah, I was so glad we were all sharing a table the whole night. Just think of all the ways I could annoy him.

We made our way toward the bridal suite where Gilly and our mom fidgeted with her dress. Seeing my sister stand on the pedestal in her dress, my breath lodged in my throat, and fuck, my eyes stung even more.

"Today is the day!" Gilly said, doing a weird wiggle. She spun around and held out her arms. "How do I look? Fabulous, right?"

"Honey, you're *gorgeous*." Mom beamed at her.

Grace started crying, Gilly frowned, and Brock groaned. It was all too much, and I burst out laughing. "It feels like a sitcom right now."

"It's just…Gilly, I love you so much, and you look amazing, and I'm so happy for you," Grace said between hiccups. She waddled up to Gilly, and they hugged. Not one to be left out, I joined their hug and glanced at Brock over my shoulder.

"Care to join, big guy?"

"I'm good."

"Brock! Get over here now and hug us, goddamn it!" Grace said, the tension and emotions easing around us.

Brock took his sweet time joining the hug, and my mom snapped a million photos on her phone. It felt like the end of a really good era.

That was how Nora found us when she walked in with two bouquets and one small arrangement for me. "Oh, oh my," she said, the laughter evident in her voice. "This cuddle puddle looks fun."

"Feel free to join and touch my ass if you want," I said, winking at her.

She grinned right back and did just that. Nora joining the group hug was the final piece of the puzzle to my heart and soul.

The wedding planner snapped her fingers from the hallway, not at all moved by our very open displays of affection, and told us to get a move on.

I had a tux to put on. "Can I steal you away for five minutes?" I asked Nora, letting my gaze run from head to toe. She'd changed since the greenhouse. I was so used to seeing her in baggy shirts and either her weird shorts or jeans and boots. But this dress…shit. It was a soft pink with purples and yellows blended into it, and it hugged *every* curve. Her collarbones peeked out at the top, and I trailed a finger over one, enjoying how goose bumps broke out down her arm. "Please?"

She sucked in a breath. "You know I can't say no to when you use that tone."

"Hope that never changes."

I took her hand and grabbed the bag with my tux as we went into a small changing room. She unzipped the bag as I undressed. "What did you think of the arrangements out front? Do you think she'll like them? I had some of her and Christopher's students make artwork for them."

"They are amazing. My eyes got watery when I saw them." I took off my shirt and undershirt, my belt, and my pants. Nora's eyes flared. "Oh, you admiring the view?"

"I missed you last night, and this morning." She licked her bottom lip and ran her hands over my bare chest. "You don't have any unforeseen best bride man duties, right? I get you all to myself tonight?"

"Sure do," I said, cupping her chin and pulling her toward me. I kissed her. Soft then hard, but slowly. I was in no hurry and just wanted to feel her lips on mine, taste the sweetness of her mouth, and enjoy her. "Hey, I love you," I whispered, watching her open her eyes and sigh.

"I love you, too," she said back, the blush on her cheeks matching her dress. We stared at each other for a beat, her hands on my chest, mine on her face, and she took a shaky breath. "Would you ever want to get married in a church?"

"Are you proposing to me, Nora Atwood?" I asked, my heart tumbling down a mountain in my chest. "I'm not emotionally prepared for this and would feel better with clothes on."

"No, I'm not," she said, swatting my chest and handing me the first part of the tux to put on. We had the same routine of getting dressed in the morning. We did need to figure out if we wanted to rent one of the units or not since we lived together, but those were small details.

"Then why do you ask?"

"I love your family, your friends, *you*, and I know you said it didn't matter if we ever got married, as long as we were together...I wondered how you saw it going if we ever were to." She glanced at the ground, her face even redder than before.

I finished putting on the pants before I cupped her face, forcing her to look at me. "Your greenhouse. So many tea lights. Ten people, max. Local musician, just a solo artist. Late at night, for sure."

She blinked fast, and if I weren't mistaken, her eyes got a little misty. "You've thought about this."

"A lot."

"God, I love you, Fritz." She jumped onto me, full-bodied, making me take a few steps back to hit the wall. It knocked a picture frame onto the floor, causing a loud bang. Nora didn't stop kissing me though, and I kissed her right back.

That was until someone banged on the door with a loud fist. "Pictures start in five minutes, with or without you," Gilly said, laughing at the end. "I mean it. Nora, get your ass ready. You're in them too."

Nora's eyes widened, and she looked down. "Wait? I'm in the pictures? I didn't know that. This isn't…I shouldn't be."

"One, you look amazing. You always do, but baby, you're in. You're part of the family now, so yeah, you're going to be in the pictures." I kissed her forehead and set her down, my body humming with a happiness I hadn't experienced before.

Grace, Gilly, and I had all found our perfect partner, and our trio had doubled in size. "You going to stare at my amazing chest all morning or help me get ready for the photos you're definitely in?"

That snapped Nora into action, and she flicked my nipple. "You're lucky I love you."

"Oh, I know."

I really, *really* did.

After a few minutes, we were both ready, and we left the dressing room hand in hand to go take photos for my sister's wedding. It was a top five moment for me for sure, and I couldn't wait to make even more memories with Nora. It would never be boring with her, that was for damn sure.

***

Thank you for reading! Did you enjoy?

Please Add Your Review! You can sign up for the City Owl Press newsletter to receive notice of all book releases!

And don't miss more romance like RESCUE ME by City Owl Author, Lauren Connolly. Turn the page for a sneak peek!

Sneak Peek of Rescue Me

BY LAUREN CONNOLLY

One of these houses is mine. I'm just not exactly sure *which* one.

A sigh pushes out, weighty and exhausted, from deep in my chest. The sun set hours ago, back when I was still on the highway. Trying to read the tiny print on each of these mailboxes isn't easy after staring out the windshield for the past two days. My eyes practically crackle, begging me to close them.

Sleep. Just go to sleep.

"That one! I…I think."

I pull up alongside the curb, letting the heavy engine rumble on as I flip through photos on my phone. Martin sent me a picture two weeks ago, a selfie of him with a large tan house behind him that looks like the one I've stopped in front of. Unfortunately, the homes on either side of it are mirror reflections.

Normally, Martin's preference for uniformity doesn't bother be. Tonight, though, I wish he had picked a weird bungalow with daisies painted on the siding and a turquoise front door. Just so I know, without a hint of a doubt, that I am parking in front of *my* house.

And I am definitely parking because I need to pick one of these clone homes before I drive myself mad puttering around this neighborhood all night.

As I shut down the engine, the whole car settles as if she's ready to sleep for the night.

"Enjoy your rest, Penelope," I mutter to the steering wheel.

I need a bed bad. A pounding started in my temples way before I even crossed the Louisiana/Mississippi border. The headache comes courtesy of long hours in the car paired with my hair being pulled up into a high, messy bun. I'd let the heavy mass down if I wasn't terrified of its condition. Two days' worth of greasiness has built up. I doubt removing my hairband would even do anything. The hair would likely continue sitting on top of my head, permanently reshaped.

My priorities have changed: before a bed, I need a shower. The vision of scrubbing a thick lather of shampoo into my scalp plays in my brain like a porno. I can imagine the transformation of the knotted mess into its normal smooth cascade.

"Butter on bread," my mom always says when she affectionately tugs on a strand.

Not sure I approve of being compared to a boring slice of white bread, but I take comfort in the fact that she's simply referring to my complexion and hair color rather than my personality.

When I push the car door open, the heavy New Orleans air embraces me. It is almost as warm and wet as an actual shower but nowhere near as refreshing. The humidity sits on my skin, weighing me down as I trudge up the front walk of a house that I hope is mine.

The easy solution would've been to just call Martin on Friday night when I decided to change my travel plans. That way my fiancé would be waiting out on the porch, ready to wave me down.

Instead, I chose the surprise method. I'd like to convince myself that this is a romantic gesture.

I just couldn't stay away from you for two more weeks!

In reality, my silence arises from shame. Whenever I let my thumb hover over his number, I couldn't even imagine how the conversation would go.

"Hey, honey! Guess what? I lost my job!" I whisper under my breath and pause with my foot on the bottom step leading up to the elevated porch.

Well, I guess I *could* say that.

Now that I'm here, potentially a few steps away from Martin, the words don't seem so inadequate. Depressing? Yeah sure. But I can clearly envision his face, how his blond brows will dip in the middle as he scowls. Not *at* me but *with* me. I can taste the glass of red wine he'll pour me as he rages over the unfair treatment.

That's when I realize why the need for surprise. I don't actually want to *talk* about how I got fired from my dream job. All I want is to see my anger reflected in the face of my partner. To feel connected to him in a way I haven't in a while.

With the moving plans, and Martin preparing to start his residency down here, and me trying to finish up all my large projects before going remote, we've barely talked. I can't even remember the last time I looked him in the eyes during a conversation. We usually just shout to each other from opposite rooms.

And sex? Well…it's been some time.

As I knock on the mystery door I hope is mine, I make a resolution. Whether I find Martin in this clone house or the one next door or the next street over, when I finally locate my fiancé, the first thing I'm going to do is stare deep into his eyes. I'll hold his gaze until our connection is firmly reestablished. Then—after a shower—I'm going to jump his bones.

Light spills into the dark night from around the edges of the curtains. At least that means whoever lives here, hopefully Martin, is still awake. After the polite taps of my knock ring out, the steady pad of footsteps sound behind the door. I brace myself, ready to stare my fiancé down.

Only, Martin doesn't open the door.

A small slim woman dressed in a robe stands before me. She is adorably petite. I could practically fit her in my pocket. Her bare feet peek out from under the floor-length robe, and her long brown hair lays in a damp mass over her shoulders.

Envy spikes hard through me. Clearly, this woman has just taken a shower. My greasy strands weep in envy.

Also, her appearance makes it clear my navigation skills have failed me. I am no closer to my own glorious shower, having no idea which one of these houses Martin bought for the two of us to live in.

"Sorry. I thought this might be my house. Do you know a blond man? About so tall?" I hold my hand a few inches above my head like the sleep drunk idiot I am.

I'm ready to continue describing my fiancé out of pure desperation when I notice the woman's face. With a stranger knocking on her door at midnight, I would expect confusion or annoyance. But if I had to guess, her slack-jawed, wide-eyed stare is closer to horror.

Apparently, my need for a shower is even direr than I knew.

"I told you I'd get it..." The familiar rusty voice drifts from behind the stranger as my fiancé trots down a set of stairs visible just over her shoulder.

The showered girl shuffles back, so I have a clear view of Martin, clad in only a pair of gym shorts, his hair just as gloriously damp from a recent cleaning as the woman in front of me.

Our eyes meet. His top half stops, but his bottom half doesn't get the memo. Instead, one of his bare feet slips on the wooden step, and he lands hard on his ass, shocked gaze never leaving mine.

So, this *is* the right house.

It's just everything else in the world that is wrong.

Whatever way I might want to interpret this situation is made impossible when I flick my eyes back to the stranger, who I now realize is wearing *my* green, cotton robe. Red splotches scorch along the tops of her cheekbones, and guilty tears pool on her lashes.

Something dark and sickening rolls in my stomach, but I flash freeze it. After one last look at the boy I've loved since my senior year of high school, I turn to the girl he chose to hurt me for.

"You can keep the robe." Reaching out, I clasp the doorknob. "And the man." I wrench the door closed on the most devastating scene of my life and sprint back to my sleeping car.

Penelope revs to life, more dependable than any man could ever be.

I shift into first gear and tear down the street, not caring who I wake up. With the roar of my sweet girl's engine, I can't hear Martin shouting.

But I can see him. In my rearview mirror, he sprints down the street after me. I skid around a corner and lose sight of him.

And he loses me.

I drive in an emotional fog, unable to dislodge the frozen ball of grief in my chest. The devastation sticks to the inside of my skull, blocking my ability to think.

It's only when I almost run a red light that I realize I shouldn't be driving.

Pulling into the next parking lot, I somehow end up in the drive-through lane of a fast-food joint. Functioning on autopilot, I roll down my window when I reach the speaker.

"What do you want?" The woman asks with the complete disinterest that can only be achieved by someone employed for the night shift at a drive-through.

The question hits me hard. Acting as a chisel, it splits the ice in my chest apart.

Grief flows free.

"What do I want?" I laugh, high-pitched and manic. "Oh, I don't know. How about a job? Or a home? Maybe my dignity?"

And now I'm crying.

"Um…we serve chicken."

I've gone insane. Martin's betrayal has turned me into a raving loon who drives around New Orleans in the middle of the night scaring fast-food workers.

This isn't me. I'm not this *type of weird.*

"Oh. Right. Of course." Swiping away the tears blurring my vision and pulling in a few choking breaths, I attempt to read the glowing menu. "I guess a family meal then."

"Eight, twelve, or sixteen pieces?"

The cracked ice in my chest has given way to a massive aching hole.

"Better make it sixteen."

"You want it with sides?"

I'm not going to be able to manage many more of these questions without the crazy laughing/crying returning.

"Yeah, whatever sides are popular. And biscuits, please. I'm gonna need a whole lot of biscuits." A sob makes the last word come out choked.

She rattles off the total, and I pull around to the window to pay. A short woman wearing a goofy chicken hat gives me a kinder smile than I was expecting after my breakdown.

"I slipped an extra biscuit in there," she whispers while passing me the armload of fried comfort.

"Thank you," I mutter, keeping my eyes to myself and hoping I never run into this lovely woman again.

For a moment, I park and consider consuming the entire order myself.

The idea is tempting.

But I still need a shower and a bed.

Penelope's engine purrs like a comforting embrace, as I pull back out on the road. The headlights point toward my childhood home.

My parents are about to get a late-night visitor, bearing fried chicken and a broken heart.

Don't stop now. Keep reading with your copy of RESCUE ME by City Owl Author, Lauren Connolly.

And find more from Jaqueline Snowe at www.jaquelinesnowe.com

Want even more romance? Try RESCUE ME by City Owl Author, Lauren Connolly, and find more from Jaqueline Snowe at www.jaquelinesnowe.com

When the universe screws you over, adopt a dog.

Paige Herbert doesn't know how she lost control of her life. Friday morning, she had her future planned. Sunday night, she's jobless and staring at her half-naked fiancé and a woman wearing her green robe.

Taking refuge in her childhood home, Paige decides this time around her life partner will have four legs instead of two. But her newly rescued pit bull is in bad need of obedience training…and the perfect guy for the job has Paige forgetting the past.

Dash Lamont doesn't want to go back to jail. Out on parole and working at an animal shelter, he's focused on living life by the rules. And number one on the list: avoid temptation. And then, in walks Paige.

The woman parks in the middle of Dash's well-ordered life, demanding his attention with her offbeat conversation, sinful curves, and dream of a refurbished classic Chevy. Despite his decision to keep his distance, he somehow finds himself agreeing to her plea for help.

As the two spend more time together, awkward attempts at flirting, late-night dancing to jazz music, and a chance taken at a Halloween party lure the hesitant pair down a sensual road.

But when sins of the past work against the newly budding romance, Dash will need to decide whether to take his chance on love or stay in his safe lane, watching as Paige drives off without him.

Please sign up for the City Owl Press newsletter for chances to win special subscriber-only contests and giveaways as well as receiving information on upcoming releases and special excerpts.

All reviews are **welcome** and **appreciated**. Please consider leaving one on your favorite social media and book buying sites.

Escape Your World. Get Lost in Ours! Romance and speculative fiction from City Owl Press at www.cityowlpress.com.

Acknowledgments

Writing a book is never easy or solitary. This story couldn't have been done without my editor, Mary. Fritz's story always jumped out the most to me, but all the brainstorm sessions and check-ins made all the difference. Fritz and plant-lady Nora wouldn't be nearly as polished or fun without Mary's input. Also, this entire series was all because Mary took a chance on me out of a slush pile. I'm forever grateful.

Another huge thanks to the whole City Owl Team. These covers are absolutely some of my favorites, and I still get all gooey-eyed when I see them on my shelf. I'm so thankful that Grace, Gilly, and Fritz found a home at City Owl Press!

About the Author

Jaqueline Snowe lives in Arizona where the "dry heat" really isn't that bad. She identifies as a full-blown Gryffindor and prefers drinking coffee all hours of the day. She is the mother to two fur-babies who don't realize they aren't humans and a new mom to the sweetest baby boy. She is an avid reader and writer of romances and tends to write about athletes. She is usually watching sports with her baseball-obsessed husband when she isn't writing.

www.jaquelinesnowe.com

facebook.com/jaquelinesnowe

twitter.com/jaquelinesnowe

instagram.com/jaquelinesnowe

bookbub.com/profile/jaqueline-snowe

About the Publisher

City Owl Press is a cutting edge indie publishing company, bringing the world of romance and speculative fiction to discerning readers.

Escape Your World. Get Lost in Ours!

www.cityowlpress.com

facebook.com/YourCityOwlPress

twitter.com/cityowlpress

instagram.com/cityowlbooks

pinterest.com/cityowlpress